The fabulous Snobby Cats of Heavenly Hills

The fabulous Snobby Cats of Heavenly Hills

Lynne Westwood

Cover design by Leah LeFlore
Interior design by Melissa M. Griggs

ISBN: 978-1-6024734-8-5

08.01.23

Dedication

This tale is dedicated to God and to animal lovers everywhere. Also, to my beautiful daughter who inspires me, and to my wonderful sister and friends who encourage me. And, of course, to our cats ~ Dutchess and Diamond.

Preface

This story is a tale of true and loyal friendships that survive through thick and thin. So, curl up with a warm bowl of creamed fish stew or a slice of mousey mint pie and come see how the wealthy felines celebrate in the elite and posh city of Heavenly Hills. Oh, and bring your imaginations! You may decide you want to be a Snobby Cat, too!

Introduction

Important Note to Reader: These cats are so special; they have unique names that refer to them by age:

Newborn–7 years
    girls are called fluffettes
    boys are called tommy-toms

Age 7–15 years
    girls are called fluff-fluffs
    boys are called tom-toms

Age 15–Adult
    girls are called fluffs or lady-fluffs
    boys are called toms

Grandparent age
    girls are called Grandfluffs
    boys are called Grandtoms

1

"*G*raduation is tomorrow and I refuse to be called *tom-tom* one more time," snarled Diamond.

"I am so sick of that *tom-tom* name," spat Kool.

"We're older now and being called *tom-tom*s is so immature," complained Jett.

"We've been branded with that goofy name for fourteen years," continued Diamond.

"*Tommy-toms, tom-tom*s, it's gettin' real old," agreed Kool.

"That settles it then," decided Jett. "Those names have got to go!"

The tom-toms snarled and shook their heads in disgust.

Diamond Castleberry III is a gray and white fourteen-year-old Maine Coon. His fur is long and he has a thick lion-like ruff around his neck. On one side of his white fur coat is a gray heart, and on the other side, a gray bat. He has a gray diamond on the back of his head and a fluffy gray tail. As well as having a cute face, he has mesmerizing turquoise eyes. He's a popular cat and is well liked by both tom-toms and fluff-fluffs, *especially* the fluff-fluffs. He's co-captain of the undefeated soccer team at Paw Valley Middle School.

Kool Katt is a beefy fourteen-year-old rare Calico tom. He has long white fur with brown, black, rust, and tan designs. He has dark brown eyes, huge feet, long whiskers, and a thick ruff. He's a real sweetie underneath all that tom-tom. He is very popular as well, and co-captain with Diamond of Paw Valley's soccer team that has enjoyed victory after victory for the past three years.

Jett Stone is also fourteen-years-old. His fur is solid black and he's tall and buff. His piercing eyes are gold and he resembles a panther. He is a skilled athlete and has won numerous trophies as captain of the tennis team at Paw Valley Middle School.

Diamond boldly declared, "We're full-on *Toms* now, certainly after Graduation tomorrow night!"

Kool snarled, "No one, and I mean no one calls us *tom-toms* again and gets away with it!"

"That's right, buds," agreed Jett, "I'm done with it!"

The three good lookin' tom-toms clinked their bowls of tuna juice in agreement of the dismissal of those silly tom-tom and tommy-tom names.

Diamond, Kool, and Jett have been best friends ever since they were little tommy-toms. They are distinct, wealthy cats, all born with silver rings around their tails. Tomorrow night they are graduating from the eighth grade with honors in academic and athletic achievements. Right now, they are lazily sipping tuna juice at their favorite after school hangout, The Shooting Star, owned and operated by Diamond's Auntie Belle.

Auntie Belle is a beautiful white and gray Maine Coon. She is quite fluffy, as the Castleberry family tends to be. She also has stunning turquoise eyes. Her seaside café, The Shooting Star, is hip and trendy. Cats, big and small, stop in regularly for a meal and a bowl of tuna juice or a seafood squeeze-freeze. The teenaged cats stop in practically everyday to meet their friends and relax after a hard day at school.

Every wall in Auntie Belle's seaside café boasts pictures of movie stars and famous felines. To name a few, there's a dated black and white photo of *Kit Meow*, there's foxy *Foxx Deezel*, the fun and only *Dory D. Generous*, beautiful *Catrah*, *Rické Delicious*, *Lance Lot*, and the cast of *Distressed House-fluffs of Hissteria Lane*. By the kitchen door is an old picture of handsome *Tabby Hunter*, the hot Country Western howler. Many years ago, before Tabby became a star, he and Belle were high school sweethearts. They were even engaged to be married, but the road and fame eventually took him away. Auntie Belle doesn't talk about him much, but will always keep his picture on the wall. There's also a photo of the hilarious hosts of the morning show, *Alive with Super Pops and Witty Kitty*. Near the entrance of the restaurant hangs an autographed picture of *Shakatra*. She is the hottest *Cat*ino Pop Star in the world! Her new album "Kisses and

Claws," climbed quickly to number one on the charts the first week it was released. She has a hot salsa style that makes all felines want to forget about everything and start dancing. On the wall by the panoramic window is a photo of the mega-famous moviemaker, *Sven Steelbird,* smiling whisker to whisker with Auntie Belle. Hanging on the back wall is a very large portrait of the beloved *Professor and Mrs. Felinestein.* Many decades ago, the genius and her husband invented an annual vaccination that dramatically slows down the aging process of felines to that of lengthy human years.

Auntie Belle padded over to the tom-toms table. "Need refills?"

The tom-toms snarled and pushed their bowls to the edge of the table. They were not in good moods the day before Graduation.

As she poured the juice, she commented, "You young, handsome cats make an old fluff like me wish I were young again!"

"Sit down, Auntie, and chat with us," said Diamond. He slid over so she sat down and scratched his chin with her razor sharp claws. He stretched out his neck and urged, "Just a little behind the ears, Auntie." Power purr.

"You're spoiled," complained scowling Kool.

Auntie Belle continued scratching Diamond and asked, "So, what are you serious cats snarling about over here?"

Jett explained, "Well, after tomorrow, we won't be branded with that sissy *tom-tom* name any longer."

Auntie Belle laughed, "So... for one more day... I can call you *tom-toms?*"

"No!" growled the tom-toms.

Kool hissed, "If those *fluff-fluffs* call us those names one more time... " He hissed again, longer and louder than ever.

Diamond cut in, "Auntie Belle, you just don't understand. Those names are so degrading, now that we're older and more mature."

"Oh, yes," she laughed. "You're all over the hill! To the geriatric ward with all three of you!"

They were laughing at each other when a commotion over at the back table grabbed their attention. The noise was unbelievable. A group of fluff-fluffs were giggling and hissing and growling and whoa, the perfume!

Kool announced, "The *fluff-fluffs* are here."

"We should have known," replied Diamond. "There's always so

much fanfare when they're around." He twitched his nose, licked his paw, and smoothed his whiskers.

Jett put his ears back and exclaimed, "Dude! Can they be any louder?"

2

"*I* so totally dislike that *fluff-fluff* name," Dutchess snarled to her fluff-friends.

"Oh puh-leez!" agreed Lashes. "And *fluffette*. Those names are so insulting now that we're older. I don't like it one little bit when the *tommy-toms* call us those names."

Dutchess agreed, "I don't either. It's completely irritating."

Dutchess, her best friend, Lashes, and the cheerleading squad just arrived by the side door and squeezed into the back corner booth. Their fluff-friends are Jolene, Clairese, Coco, and Blanche, who are all in agreement about those annoying fluffette and fluff-fluff names. There was plenty of hissing and growling coming from the back corner booth.

"After tomorrow, no more of that!" spit Lashes.

"That's right!" spat Dutchess.

Blanche and Jolene hissed and Clairese and Coco growled.

Dutchess Woo is the cutest Siamese cat in town. She is tall and slinky, smooth and tan, with chocolate brown legs, ears, and tail. She has gorgeous blue eyes that match the sky. She is fourteen-years-old and co-captain with Lashes of Paw Valley's cheerleading squad. She is very popular.

Lashes Holcomb is a purrty Persian kitty. She has soft and fluffy caramel-colored fur, light brown legs, ears, and tail. She is quite cute with her curly whiskers, bright blue eyes, and big smile. She is also fourteen-years-old and lots of fun to hang around.

The members of the cheerleading squad include Jolene, who has gray and white stripes, Clairese is a red tabby, Coco, who is decorated with a tan and white marble coat, and Blanche is a pure white fluffy Persian with green eyes.

Dutchey was hissing with her fluff-friends when she felt a pair of intense turquoise eyes piercing her from behind. She turned around and glanced around the room. She spotted Diamond staring at her, appearing to be in some sort of trance. She stared back at him and a new thought crossed her mind, "He sure has gotten cute lately. Grrrrr…"

Lashes turned to her friend, "Growling, fluff-friend?"

Dutchess found herself sinking deep into Diamond's trance. She thought, "He's gotten so big and handsome lately. What happened to that scrawny, long-furred *tom-tom* I used to hang with?" She didn't even hear Lashes.

"*Dutchess!*" yelled Lashes.

Dutchess jumped. "Huh?" She looked at Lashes with a blank stare and then motioned toward the tom-toms table. "There's the *tom-toms.*" She turned around and stared back at Diamond. The fluff-fluffs looked over at the tom-toms and burst out laughing.

"They are cute *tom-toms!*" exploded Jolene.

Kool sighed, "More commotion from the back table. They just can't get enough of us."

Still stuck in their trance, Diamond nodded at Dutchey and she nodded back. He secretly dreamed, "She's gotten so beautiful lately. Well, she's always been cute, but maybe her eyes have turned a deeper shade of blue, or maybe it's her Siamese legs, they grew longer or something." He couldn't quite put his paw on it.

Without thinking, Dutchess said her good-byes to the squad and jumped off the bench. She grabbed Lashes, yanked her off the bench, and pulled her by her tail backwards across the freshly waxed floor.

"Bye, fluffs. Okay, okay, I'm coming," Lashes said, sliding across the slippery floor backwards. They both fluffed out their fur and padded over to the tom-toms table.

3

"*Hey, tom-toms!*" the fluff-fluffs burst out as they approached the table.

Auntie Belle laughed, "Don't be too hard on them. They're having a bad day." She jumped off the bench and went back to work.

The tom-toms growled low. Their ears went back and they glared at the fluff-fluffs.

Diamond decided to make the first statement. "You know, after tomorrow, you can't call us *tom-toms* anymore." He was staring straight at Dutchess. Still scowling, Kool and Jett maintained their glare.

Both fluff-fluffs broke out into hysterical laughter.

"We couldn't resist!" teased Dutchey, laughing so hard she could barely stand up.

"It's fun to tease you! Right up to the last minute!" laughed Lashes.

"Would you *fluff-fluffs* care to join us?" Kool teased, yet still being polite, even after their little outburst. He and Diamond jumped off the bench and waited for them to jump up.

"Talk to the paw," Lashes said sarcastically, putting up her paw. A few seconds passed as they glared at each other. Dutchey hissed at Diamond and Lashes stuck her paw in Kool's face. The tom-toms stood strong and looked them straight in the eyes, staring holes through them. Jett looked on and growled from his spot on the bench.

Finally, Dutchey laughed, "Okay, I guess we deserved that." She and Lashes jumped up on the bench and squeezed in on either side of Jett. Diamond and Kool jumped up and sat down and all five cats looked fiercely at each other with their ears back, then they all burst out laughing. "You know," Dutchess said with her nose in the air, "after tomorrow you can't call us *fluff-fluffs* anymore, either." They looked at each other and busted up laughing again.

Auntie Belle returned with three bowls of tuna juice and passed them to the fluffs and kept one for herself. She announced, "I want to make a toast! To the best lookin' and smartest cats I know who are steppin' out of Paw Valley Middle School and going into the unknown world of Heavenly Hills High School."

Everyone cheered, "Here, here!" They clinked their bowls, drank, and purred.

Diamond added, "Here's to us—The Fabulous Snobby Cats of Heavenly Hills!" They clinked bowls again and happily lapped up their tuna juice.

Auntie Belle smiled at the young ones and chugged her juice. "I'm so proud of you kittens," she said as she picked up her bowl and went back to the kitchen.

"Thank you, Auntie," the cats sang.

Diamond continued staring at Dutchess, smelling her perfume. He was so captivated; he didn't even hear Lashes ask about the after-graduation party at the Heavenly Hills Country Club.

"Diamond... *Diamond!*" yelled Lashes. "Can't I get anyone's attention today?"

"Huh?" mumbled Diamond, still staring at Dutchey.

"You're not obvious, bud," said Jett.

"No, not at all," agreed Kool. Both toms laughed at their friend. Diamond looked away from Dutchey with a goofy grin.

Lashes repeated, "Diamond, how are the plans coming along for tomorrow night's party at the club?"

Diamond snapped back to reality. "Oh yeah, the party. It is going to be so awesome! Great food! Great music! Great company!" He puffed out his chest and pointed to himself as the great company part. "You are all going to love it! I want you to be surprised, so I'm not saying another word!"

"Oh, come on, handsome. You can tell me," purred Dutchey, leaning closer and whispering in his ear, "Purrrtty please. Tell me, Diamond."

"It's confidential information." He looked the other way.

"Oh come on, tell me. Purrtty please, tell me."

Dutchey was leaning so close to Diamond, she was practically on top of him. Then, *"reow"*—he fell right off the bench. The fluff-fluffs laughed hysterically, in fact, all the cats in the café were looking over and laughing, especially those fluff-fluffs in the back corner booth.

"Hey Grace, how's charm school?" teased Kool.

"Ha-ha," said Diamond, shaking out his fur.

Jett said to his buds, "Come on, *toms.* Let's go to the gym at the club. I need to work out."

"These *fluff-fluffs* are just too much," commented Kool.

"But you gotta love èm," agreed Diamond, shaking out again. "They sure do smell good."

"They smell good and look good," added Kool, winking at Lashes.

Jett got around the fluff-fluffs by jumping clear over the table and landing on the floor.

"See you later, *tom-toms,*" waved Dutchey. The tom-toms shook their heads and hissed.

"Bye, *fluff-fluffs,*" snarled Kool.

"Bye, *toms,*" Lashes said with a big smile.

The tom-toms stopped to say good-bye to Auntie Belle with whisker kisses. Then, out the front door, they went.

Dutchey and Lashes sat at the table a moment longer and finished their drinks. Dutchey looked up at the clock and remembered, "Oh, no! It's almost noon and I forgot to set the timer for *All My Kittens* and *Nine Lives to Live.*"

"Oh, no!" gasped Lashes.

With that, the two fluff-fluffs were off to Dutchey's mansion.

"Bye, Auntie Belle. Bye, fluff-friends," they sang as they slipped and slid out the front door.

4

It was a warm, blue-sky day as Dutchey and Lashes raced to Dutchey's mansion. They ran as fast as they could through the streets of Heavenly Hills, a very beautiful city indeed.

Heavenly Hills is located beside the ocean and is adorned with hundreds of trees and colorful flowers blooming on this late spring day in June. There's also the boardwalk and the marina where all kinds of boats and luxury yachts are docked. The fluff-fluffs ran past the fashion boutiques and jewelry stores, the bakeries and the bistros. They ran even faster past the art gallery and specialty stores, around the tuna cannery, over the bridge, and up the hill to Castleberry Grove, the elite Northwest side of town.

Lashes and Dutchey are both excited about graduating from the eighth grade tomorrow night, but they are a little sad, too. Change is always hard on a cat. Adjustment is a big issue. New school, strange new cats, new competition, but their best friends, Diamond, Kool, and Jett will be there, so maybe they won't be such scardey cats. After all, they will have all summer to have fun. They will have time for hiking, bird watching, and tree climbing during their annual summer get-away to Whisker Pines. There's also cheerleading practice and then tryouts. But, most of all, sleeping. Felines do need their beauty sleep. They have no idea that at this very moment, Diamond is talking to his parents and grandparents about he and his friends "helping out" at the country club this summer.

Dutchey's mansion is magnificent. The front yard is grassy with tall trees that have been climbed more times than there are fish in the ocean. Along the driveway are beautiful flowers in bloom and swaying palm trees. Her backyard has a breathtaking view of the ocean.

Lashes and her family live a few streets over, by the cliffs. Their families have been friends as far back as anyone can remember.

Out of breath and laughing, the fluff-fluffs rested on the front steps of Dutchey's mansion.

"Let's go up the maple tree," gasped Dutchey.

"Okay," breathless Lashes panted.

There is a big old maple tree outside Dutchey's upstairs bedroom window. They ran around to the side of the house, jumped over the fence, climbed the trunk, jumped the branches, and dove onto the window seat inside her bay window. They sat and stared at each other, panting. After a few moments, they both took deep breaths.

"I love a good race," panted Lashes. "It's so exhilarating, but now I'm hungry." She jumped down and turned on the television and Dutchey scampered downstairs to grab a bag of crunchy treats and coconut splash drinks. When she returned to her bedroom, Lashes commented, "Purrfect timing, Dutch. You just missed seeing that icky furrball medicine commercial."

"Don't you just hate it when that cat hurls up that nasty furrball?" exclaimed Dutchey in disgust. "Eeewww!"

Lashes snarled, "I am so grossed out!"

"Ick! Me too!"

Lashes reminded Dutchey, "Set the timer for tonight's *Fluffy, the Rodent Slayer.*"

"Okay." Dutchey fiddled around with the remote control.

All My Kittens began. Both fluff-fluffs were happy kickin' back on Dutchey's canopy bed, enjoying their crunchies and drinks. A warm breeze blew the lacy curtains. Dutchey's room is decorated in pastel colors. Soft, velvety pillows add luxurious comfort and exquisite style to her bed. By the window is her climbing pole. On top of the pole is a landing, or as Dutchey calls it her "perch" where she has bird watched countless times over the years. The pole used to seem so high and challenging to climb when she was younger and smaller. She looked at it now with a feeling of ultimate maturity. She just decided to give it to her little sister Blossom, who is nine-years-old, because it's taller than Blossom's pole and the landing on top is bigger. Along one wall is a collection of pictures of Dutchey and her friends, dating all the way back from kitten hood to the most recent photograph of her on top of the pyramid that won the cheerleading competition. Her gold trophy sits on a little shelf next to her squads' photo. Against the opposite wall is the vanity where she spends a lot of time in front of the mirror. However, right now she is content with her best friend, her cat-soaps, and thoughts of growing up.

There was a scratch at the door. Dutchey's mother, Ming, entered and the room filled with the exotic scent of lilac. Ming is an elegant Siamese feline with beautiful violet-blue eyes.

"Hi, fluffs. I thought I heard noises up here. Why are you home so early?"

"Half day, Mom," replied Dutchey. "Graduation rehearsal, remember?"

Mom teased, "Oh, that's right. Graduation… I almost forgot."

The fluff-fluffs looked at each other with blank faces. Mom laughed and jumped on the bed. She pawed through the pillows to get comfortable and settled into *All My Kittens*.

Dutchey commented, "Chico sure is a hunk!"

"Absolutely delicious!" replied Mom.

"He is sooo purrfect!" added Lashes. "From the tips of his furry little ears to the tip of his fluffy little tail!"

Power purr!

5

After *Veterinary Hospital* was over, they stretched out on the bed and listened to the birds singing in the trees.

Mom asked, "Have you arranged your beauty appointments for tomorrow?"

The fluff-fluffs chimed together, "Yes, Mom."

Ming smiled, "I'm so proud of both of you."

Lashes boasted, "I made the scarf my mom is going to wear tomorrow night. It's Belgian lace and very pretty."

Ming commented, "I have seen your creations, dear. You should stick with it. Designing fashion accessories may be your calling."

Dutchess nodded in agreement, "I keep telling her that."

Lashes replied, "I have so many fashion ideas! Sometimes I can't sleep at night because I'm so inspired."

Mom commented, "Pearl (Diamond's mother) tells me your party at the club tomorrow night is going to be quite a bash. You both will just *love* the theme!"

"Theme? What theme?" perked up Dutchess with eyes as big as saucers.

"I promised not to tell," teased Mom.

"Tell us, Mom," begged Dutchey. "Please!"

"I took the oath of secrecy."

"Okay," snarled Dutchey, "I'm starting to get hissy. Diamond knows everything and he won't tell. You know, and you won't tell." She looked at Lashes and asked, "Are we getting hissy now, fluff-friend?"

Lashes snapped, "Yes! Very hissy."

Mom laughed with delight and rolled on the bed.

Dutchess looked over at Lashes, "How can she be doing this to us?" They both looked at Mom and expected an answer, but just got her beautiful upside-down smile.

"You have a canary feather hanging out of your mouth, Mother!" laughed Dutchey.

The fluff-fluffs were laughing with Mom when all of a sudden; there was an unexpected *crash!* They looked up just in time to see two furry cats fly through the open window. Diamond made a perfect landing on the floor, but Kool slammed his head right into Dutchey's climbing pole. He shook his head several times and muttered, "Hey, who moved the pole?" Lashes and Dutchey jumped off the bed and rushed over to him.

Lashes commented, "That was real cool, Kool Katt." Kool was dazed and confused. He sat down and rubbed his head with his big paw.

Ming said, "Hi, toms. That was one fabulous entrance, Kool. Are you alright?"

"I think I'm getting a bump on my head."

Diamond greeted Ming, "Hi, Mrs. Woo. He's really graceful, isn't he?" He looked over at Kool and teased, "Hey Grace, how's charm school?" Kool responded with a very long hiss.

Cautiously, Lashes rubbed Kool's head with her paw. He lay down and closed his eyes, enjoying the attention. When he opened his eyes, he realized he was eye-to-eye with the bulletproof climbing pole. He leaped back and shook his head again, then looked around the room for a safe place to lie down. He spotted a spacious area in the corner, so he got up, slowly padded over to the spot he picked out, and plunked himself down. The fluffs followed and sat down beside him. "I guess I missed the target, didn't I?"

"Oh, you totally hit the target," laughed Diamond. "Dead on."

"Ha-ha," snarled Kool. He shook his head and his ears flapped together.

"Are you going to be okay?" asked sympathetic Lashes.

"Maybe in an hour or so. Thank *you* for *your* concern, Lashes." He glared at Diamond.

Dutchey looked over at Diamond with a glare of her own. "My mom knows your big secret about tomorrow night's bash and she won't tell us either."

Diamond boasted, "This party is going to be the best one yet!"

"Tell us!" begged the fluffs.

Ming and Diamond winked at each other.

The fluffs looked at Kool, as if he knew anything. "Don't look at me. I have amnesia." He rubbed his head against the wall.

Lashes looked at Diamond and demanded, "We *have* to know and you *have* to tell us!"

Diamond responded with, "You will just *have* to wait. You remember what curiosity did to the cat, don't you?" The fluffs hissed and growled.

"We can't wait!" Dutchey was so exasperated she slapped her tail on the floor.

Mom howled with laughter. "This is so much fun!"

Dutchey demanded one more time, "Tell us, or else… "

Mom pulled her tail, "You, my darling, will just *have* to wait until tomorrow night. Are you toms thirsty?"

"Oh yeah!" said Diamond. Kool was still in a daze.

Ming suggested, "Come downstairs and I'll ask Miss Fancy to whip us up a pitcher of seafood soda cocktail on ice." She knows that's Kool's favorite drink. "And, an ice pack for you, Mr. Kool Katt, poor kitty."

6

$\mathcal{T}$he warm breezy day called the cats to the backyard. Of course, there is a sparkling pool with a bridge, floating pads for sunning, and a shady white gazebo with vines, climbing roses, and colorful flowers hanging in pots. From the gazebo, there is a picturesque view of the ocean. They gathered in the gazebo and talked and laughed as they enjoyed their cocktails to the tranquil sound of waves breaking in the distance. They were feeling very grown up.

Ming toasted her precious Dutchess and friends for, "A job well done! The future is at your claw tips!" They clinked their bowls together and drank. "Okay kittens, I'm going inside to telephone Lily (Lashes' mother) to ask about the flowers for the party."

Lashes snarled, "Now, don't tell me my mom knows about party details, too!"

Ming and Diamond grinned and winked at each other.

"You've got that feather hanging out again, Mother," said Dutchey. "You too, Diamond!"

"See you later, Mom," the grown-up cats sang as Ming leisurely padded across the grass toward the mansion.

"How was the workout?" asked Dutchey. "Where's Jett?"

Diamond answered, "The workout was great!"

"Oh yeah?" questioned Kool sarcastically, balancing the ice pack on his head. "How would you know? You were talking to your mom and dad most of the time while we were pumping the sweat." Kool appeared to be getting back to his old feisty self.

Diamond ignored Kool and answered, "Jett went to the airport to pick up his auntie, uncle, and cousin Cleo from Pintac."

"Oh yeah, that's right," remembered Lashes, "they're coming for our graduation. How long are they staying?"

"For a month, I think," said Kool.

7

$\mathcal{J}$ett is a strong tom. He is toned, sleek, buff and black; he also has amazing gold eyes. He's easy-going and doesn't say too much, he's actually pretty laid back. He just hangs out with his buds and takes life as it comes, never making a fuss. He is an athlete though, and he has goals. He enjoys a high-spirited game of tennis. In fact, he is actually very good, quick on his paws. He is definitely going to be captain of the tennis team at Heavenly Hills High in September. There is no question about that!

Jett and his family are on their way to the airport in their black stretch limo. His auntie, uncle, and cousin are coming for graduation and a month long vacation. Jett is close with his cousin, Cleocatra. They exchange c-mail regularly. Cleo's family is tight with the Royal family of Pintac and she has told him all about her exciting and sometimes wild adventures with her best friend, Princess Jade.

Jett sat back in his seat, yawned, and dozed off. Finally, the limo arrived at the airport and the Stone family headed to Sky Cruise Airlines terminal to wait for their family.

At last, the jet landed and the weary travelers came padding down the long hallway. Jett looked the crowd over, hunting for his cousin. Cleo saw him first, ran ahead of everyone, and jumped him from behind for the tackle. They laughed and played while everyone greeted each other.

Jett's and Cleo's fathers, Dumont and Sanford, are twins. They are also black with gold eyes. Jett's mother, Ginger, has chestnut fur and brown eyes. Cleo's mother, Frangelica, has auburn fur and mauve eyes. They greeted each other in the usual fashion: touching noses.

"Hi, Auntie Frangelica and Uncle Sanford," laughed Jett, rolling on the floor with Cleo.

"Hi, Auntie Ginger and Uncle Dumont," said excited Cleo. "Hi, Starr. You're next!"

"Hi, Cleo," giggled Starr.

Cleo is a beautiful spunky black cat with a bit of chestnut brown fur speckled in, black whiskers, a black nose, and mauve eyes, just like her mother. She is fourteen-years-old and lots of fun.

With all the cat play going on, Jett didn't notice anything else, especially the regal beauty standing nearby. She was wearing a green scarf around her neck that matched her green eyes. She was also wearing a gold tail ring and a delicate gold chain around her right front paw. Her whiskers are black with white tips and her fur is velvet black. She is the same age as Cleo. Remembering her friend, Cleo jumped to her paws and ran over to get her.

"Where'd she go?" Jett asked himself, feeling abandoned. He was lying on his back playing catch with his tail. All four legs were going this way and that, and his view of everything was upside-down.

Cleo took her friend's tail with her tail and they padded over to meet her family. She hugged and tickled her nine-year-old cousin, Starr.

"Jade, this is my little cousin, Starr."

"Hi, Starr. It's nice to meet you."

Starr stood there in awe, but managed, "Hi, Princess Jade. It's very nice to meet you, too. I've never met a Princess before." They exchanged a royal hug.

Jett could hardly believe what he was seeing! She is the most superb, beautiful, lovely, upside-down cat he has ever seen!

Cleo tilted her head upside-down and looked at her nutty cousin. "Jett, this is my best friend, Jade. I've told you about her. Jade, this is my crazy cousin, Jett. I've told you about him."

Jade looked down at Jett, who was making a great first impression. He was still on his back with all fours in the air, looking quite silly. *Whoa Tom!* No cat ever moved so quickly! He spun to his feet, tripped over his tail, lost his balance, and landed on his side, looking even sillier. After that little display of grace and agility, he managed to pull himself up and stutter a feeble, "H... H... Hi." He was completely awestruck by this beautiful feline and hopelessly suffering from a brain freeze.

Cleo whispered quite loudly in his ear, "You're supposed to kiss her paw."

Jett reached for her paw and thought, "Even her claws are beautiful." He kissed her paw and their eyes locked. The world was spinning a million miles per microsecond.

"You can let go now, lover tom!" teased Cleo. She just couldn't pass up the opportunity to give good ol' cuz a bad time. Starr giggled at her *suave* older brother.

Jett forgot everything, even his own name. Trying to regain his composure, he stuttered, "Hi. I'm… I'm… um… ?" There was a tense moment of silence while everyone waited for Jett to think.

Cleo laughed hysterically and teased, *"Jett! Your name is Jett!"*

He continued holding Jade's paw and stated very mannerly, "Hi, I'm Jett and I am very happy to know you, your Highness."

"You don't know her yet, cuz!" teased unrelenting Cleo.

Without losing eye contact with Jade, he replied, "I plan to remedy that."

Jade smiled at him and in her most sophisticated voice purred, "Hello, Jett."

He wanted to greet her in the usual fashion, that nose touching bit, but after thinking twice, he decided that might be too forward for the first time meeting with a Princess, and he might blow it too early in the game. As for Princess Jade, she wouldn't dare let on that her heart was skipping beats. She wouldn't want to be too forward so early in the game either.

Jett's head was racing. He thought, *"Wow!* I think I'm seeing fireworks!" There were bright colors, rockets blasting, lights flashing, in fact, there *were* lights flashing! The paparazzi is here! And they're taking hundreds of pictures! Since Princess Jade is Pintac Royalty, of course the press has to show up to cover her arrival, and they are hot on their tails!

Cleo's father stated in a concerned voice, "This was not supposed to happen! Jade's arrival was supposed to be top secret! Who leaked this to the press?"

8

$\mathcal{R}$omance Interrupted!

Jett's father quickly issued instructions, "The limo is waiting for us in front of the terminal. Let's make a run for it."

Jett grabbed Jade's tail and Cleo grabbed Starr's tail. The two families ran like wild fire through the terminal, down the moving catwalk, past the baggage and ticket lines, out the door, and into the limo.

Whew! They made it. Except for one little thing… after everyone jumped into the limo, they sped off, leaving Princess Jade's bodyguard, Q, on the curb, behind the press.

Jade looked around the limo, "Oh, no! Where's Q?"

"Who?" Jett asked.

"My bodyguard," said Jade. Cleo looked around the limo and laughed.

"Oh," he said. He thought to himself, "We left him back there in the dust! Who needs him anyway?" He wedged himself between Jade and the door in the back seat. Everyone was out of breath, huffing and puffing. Jett took a deep breath and asked her, "So… you have a bodyguard?"

She sighed, "Yes, my parents think it is necessary. I think of it as a bother, but Q respects me and my privacy."

Cleo added, "What she really means is that he's easy to ditch!" Jade smiled and everyone laughed. Cleo made introductions. "By the way, Auntie and Uncle, this is Princess Jade. We talked her parents into letting her come with us."

Auntie Ginger said, "Hello, honey. It is so nice to meet you." They exchanged a warm hug.

"Thank you. It's very nice to meet Cleo's family. I've heard so much about all of you."

Auntie Ginger asked, "How are your parents, darling?"

"They are fine and send their love."

Jett's father asked, "So Princess, what do you think of your vacation so far?"

"Well, I do love a good adventure!"

Starr asked, "So far so good, Princess?"

"So far, so good!"

"Stop the limo," Jett's Uncle instructed the chauffeur, "I'll go collect Q and the luggage. Circle around and pick us up in twenty minutes."

The limo circled the airport, but being such a flashy car, it didn't take long for the paparazzi to spot them and start the chase all over again.

Jade took control of the situation. "Stop the limo! Stop the limo! I will say a few words to settle them down and make them happy!"

Cleo's mother asked, "Do you really think that's a good idea, dear?"

"I will say all the right things, I promise. I will be very proper. Lower the window, please."

The limo stopped, and within seconds, there were countless cameras, microphones, and lights flashing all around the limo. Jett quickly looked out of each window and marveled, "Wow! What a wild ride!"

Jade leaned over Jett and spoke through the open window to the crowd of reporters. There were cats of all colors, shapes, and sizes holding out microphones and snapping pictures. It was quite a scene watching them pushing and shoving each other for a front row spot to get the best pictures.

Jade also marveled, "Wow! What a wild ride!" In her most proper, yet enthusiastic voice, she spoke into the microphones and declared, *"Hello, Everyone! I Love You!"*

9

With raised eye whiskers, Cleo's mother, Frangelica, commented, "That was *very* proper, dear."

Cleo laughed, "I just love going places with Jade! There's always so much attention!"

Jade blew kisses with her paws and shared her beautiful smile with the cameras, then asked, "Jett, would you please raise the window."

Jett complied knowing he would do anything she asked. If she asked for the moon, he would have it here in a jiffy, wrapped up with the biggest bow he could find. He is a smitten tom. For the first time in his life, Jett is in cat-love, never to be the same again. He has turned to jell-o, all shaky and wobbly. He did try his best to act suave and debonair, but Cleo saw right through that and let everyone else know, too. Jett loves his cousin a lot, but he was almost ready to hiss at her. He looked around the limo and thought to himself, "Let's see, how can I make just the right impression?" He padded to the cooler in the limo and opened the little door. He offered everyone, Princess Jade first, of course, sushi and sparkling water. He was hoping his host-with-the-most idea would score him some points in his quest to impress the Princess. He was happy to see his family and all, but this was not at all what he expected. This boring little trip to the airport was turning out to be quite an adventure! And they were creating quite a stir! Jett's not yawning anymore!

After twenty minutes of circling the airport, they spotted Cleo's dad and Q on the curb with the luggage. The limo stopped and the luggage was hastily loaded into the trunk. They sped out of the airport and headed straight for Heavenly Hills.

Q is a real big tom—taking up three seats. He has short gray fur, except for his left front paw, which is white. It seems he is always shaking his white sock at Jade and Cleo, scolding them for one reason or another.

Jett offered Q something a little stronger than sparkling water, "How about a seafood fizzle? You look like you need one."

Q was very apologetic to Princess Jade as he took the drink from Jett. She assured him no harm was done. Cleo told him about Jade's little interview with the press and blowing kisses. He shook his head and mumbled under his breath, still huffing and puffing.

Starr asked Jade, "What's he saying?"

Jade sighed, "Oh, he just doesn't know what to do about me." Jett gazed at her and was in complete awe of her beauty. He started purring.

Heavenly Hills… a place that will be new and different to Princess Jade. Hopefully, there will be many adventures. Definitely, there is a very handsome new friend. She has always been drawn to piercing gold eyes.

As the limo drove up to Jett's stately mansion in Castleberry Estates, there were radio news break-ins that reported sightings of the Princess of Pintac and *the mysterious stranger* kissing her royal paw. When they entered the mansion and turned the television on, every station presented a royal picture. There was Jett, kissing Princess Jade's paw, right there on the television for the entire world to see! What an unexpected turn of events!

10

While Cupid's arrow was piercing Jade and Jett, our other feline friends had a fun filled afternoon. Kool's headache subsided, so he challenged the fluffs to a game they have been playing since they were kittens. "Let's play hide and chase."

Dutchey looked at Lashes and snapped, "Okay—but I don't want to hear *any-thing* about that silly *fluff-fluffs* against *tom-toms* business."

Diamond said, "How about this? Now it's *fluffs* against *toms*. Do we have a deal?"

"Deal." They stood in a circle and did a paw stack.

Dutchey's backyard is purrfect for hide and chase. There are plenty of bushes to hide behind and several tall trees to climb. The very tippy-top of the gazebo is a good place to hide, too. The toms closed their eyes and counted to twenty while the fluffs took off running. They ran to the largest tree in the yard, a big old sycamore that has branches growing high in the sky. The fluffs started climbing, Lashes went first. She climbed higher and higher. When she came to a fork in the branch, she stopped to wait for Dutchey, who was climbing just as fast, if not faster. All of a sudden, the branch Dutchey was jumping from *snapped*. She clawed for another branch, but missed. She screamed terrifyingly loud as she fell and bounced off the branches on her way down, then, *"reow"*... *thud.* She landed right on top of Diamond. He heard her screaming and ran to the tree. He looked up just in time to see her coming down, so he lay down at the base of the tree to soften her landing. Her head and upper body landed on top of him, but most of her body hit the ground. She gasped for a breath, let out a groan, and just lay there, still and silent.

The snapped tree branch fell to the ground, landing right beside them. Horrified, Lashes literally flew down the tree, Kool ran over, and Diamond let out a groan of his own.

11

Very carefully, Diamond slid out from under Dutchey and began talking to her. "Talk to me, Dutchey, meow or something." She just lay there, unresponsive. Diamond was scared. "Kool, get a floating pad." Kool took off running toward the pool. He dragged a floating pad back and he and Diamond slid her onto it and pulled her across the yard and into the house. Lashes ran ahead and opened the door.

"What happened?" Ming screamed.

Lashes cried out, "The branch snapped and Dutchey fell out of the old sycamore tree."

"Oh, no," screamed Ming. "I'll call Dr. Fitt."

Diamond rubbed Dutchey's ears and pleaded, "Wake up, Dutchey!" She just lay there, still, almost too still.

Ming talked to Nurse Hissy, then to Dr. Fitt. She hurried over to Dutchey and listened to her side. "Yes, her heart is beating. Yes, she's breathing. No, she hasn't coded. Yes, I'll bring her right in."

The cats were in sheer panic. This was a definite crisis. Dutchess was not waking up and her breathing was shallow. The toms carefully slid her through the house and out the front door. They were extremely careful as they lifted her onto the back seat of Ming's sports car. She drove *tout de suite* to the Furrball Vet Clinic. Miss Fancy watched in despair as Dutchey was taken away. She began to cry as the car screeched around the corner.

12

$\mathcal{D}$r. Fitt took a full body M.R.I. to check Dutchey's head, ribs, her back, and all four legs. He also checked for internal injuries. After studying the films, he diagnosed, "No broken bones, but her right back leg is swollen and she has lost consciousness." He looked up at the clock and noted the time on her chart. He put smelling salts under her nose, but she didn't move. He listened to her heart with his stethoscope. It was still beating and she was still breathing, but she just would not wake up. "I believe she has gotten the wind knocked out of her, too," added Dr. Fitt.

Everyone watched her intently. The waiting was absolute torture. Lashes was sobbing, Ming was frantic, Kool was trying not to panic. Diamond was pacing the floor in despair, muttering under his breath something about not being in the right place at the bottom of the tree. Kool had his paws full trying to reassure him that he did the best he could, and at the same time trying to comfort Lashes. Tears streamed down her face as she slowly ran her paw along Dutchey's tail. Kool wiped her curly whiskers with his big paw. This was an awful accident. In fact, this was tragic. What if Dutchey *never* woke up? What if Dutchey, well, they didn't dare think the unthinkable.

"Please wake up, my little kitten," Ming whispered softly to her precious Dutchey, gently scratching her head. "Please wake up, honey." They continued their vigilant watch.

Diamond whispered in her ear, "Please wake up, Dutchey. Please wake up, little pal. Wake up. Wake up. Wake up."

13

Lashes looked up at the clock and sniffled. "A long time has passed, Dr. Fitt…"

Dr. Fitt looked up at the clock and frowned. Ming was nervously pacing the floor now.

Finally, with a twitch and a moan, Dutchess took a deep breath, coughed, and opened her eyes. Everyone cheered except Dutchey, she growled. "What happened?" she mumbled and tried to move. "Grrrr."

Lashes replied, "Remember, we were climbing the Old Sycamore? The branch snapped off and you fell down the tree. Diamond broke your fall."

Diamond was staring at her, very much relieved. He could never imagine life without his best fluff-friend. He whispered into her ear, "You scared me half out of my fur."

Dutchey had a sad face and tried to change positions. "Grrrr. Hiss."

After the cheering and sighs of relief, Dr. Fitt stepped forward. "Welcome back, Miss Dutchess. You took quite a fall, little one." All eyes were on Dutchess, ready to respond in case of a relapse. Dr. Fitt continued, "I'm afraid I may have some bad news though." He looked up at the clock again and noted the time. Everyone turned to Dr. Fitt and listened. "You may have lost one of your nine lives." Everyone shrieked in horror. Poor Dutchey growled.

"Are you sure, Dr. Fitt?" asked Ming, her eyes welling up with tears.

"Yes," he said softly, "any feline who is unconscious for more than sixty minutes has lost a life." Everyone shrieked again. This is close to the most tragic thing that could ever happen to a cat. The most *cat*astrophic thing to happen, of course, would be to lose *all nine lives.*

Kool asked, "Has she lost a part of her brain, Dr. Fitt?"

"No she hasn't, Kool. She's still intact." Then Dr. Fitt looked closer at Kool and noticed the bump on his head. "What happened to you? Did you fall out of a tree, too?"

"No, I crashed into Dutchey's climbing pole."

Dr. Fitt shook his head. "Come with me. Let's take an x-ray of your head. Nurse Hissy, please keep an eye on Dutchess. Maybe she would like a drink of water." They padded into the x-ray room and Dr. Fitt instructed Kool to sit very still on the table while he took the x-ray. Kool waited on the table while Dr. Fitt went into the darkroom to develop the film. After a few minutes, he came out of the darkroom and hung up the x-ray film on a lighted view box. He held up a magnifying glass and looked closely at the film. After what seemed like a very long time, he said, "Great! No fracture."

"Whew!" Kool rubbed his head and was quite proud of his knot.

They both went back into the examination room and Dr. Fitt announced the good news. "Nothing is fractured. He does have a nice goose egg to be proud of, though. Nurse Hissy, would you get Kool an ice pack? And one for Dutchess too, please."

Dutchey tried to move her leg. "Grrrr."

Nurse Hissy scratched Dutchey's chin and replied, "You kittens! Will you please stay in one piece for your big night? It seems you can go all year without a scratch, and then the day before your big ceremony, you fall apart! Kittens... " her words trailed off as she padded out of the room.

Diamond asked, "Now that Dutchey woke up, can she go home, Dr. Fitt?"

Dr. Fitt looked at Dutchess, listened to her heart again, and observed her breathing. "This leg is a bit larger than the other one. Does it hurt, Dutchess?" He gently poked it.

"Yes. It's pretty sore. Is it broken?"

Dr. Fitt replied, "No, but you do have a bad sprain. You'll need to take it easy, little one."

Anxious Lashes inquired, "Can she go to Graduation tomorrow night?"

"Well, she took a nasty fall," warned Dr. Fitt. He looked at his patient long and hard and twitched his whiskers. "You are not the young, lightweight little kitten you used to be, Missy. You have to be very selective of the branches you trust to hold you. Will you promise me you will take it easy and not climb trees so fast anymore?"

"I promise."

Dr. Fitt observed her a bit longer and listened to her heart again. "Well, your heart is steady and your breathing is even now. Nothing is broken so there is not much more we can do here. You will be more comfortable in your own bed at home. You need to rest tonight and see how you feel in the morning. You should be able to participate tomorrow night. Call me if you need me."

"Okay," replied Dutchey. "Thank you, Nurse Hissy and Dr. Fitt."

"You're very welcome, little one," replied Dr. Fitt. Nurse Hissy rubbed her ears.

Lashes commented, "You know Dutchey, Diamond is your hero." Everyone looked at Diamond, including Dutchey. He put his whiskers next to hers for a moment or two.

"Thank you, Diamond," she whispered, sadly.

"You're welcome, but I still didn't save one of your lives."

Everyone was sad. Using up your nine lives, one-by-one, *can* add up.

Dr. Fitt asked Diamond, "How's your tummy feeling after Miss Dutchess landed on it?"

"I'm fine. Really."

Ming shook paws and graciously said, "Thank you so much, Nurse Hissy and Dr. Fitt." She looked at the toms, then at Dutchess. "Diamond and Kool, will you help her to the car?"

"Sure." The toms carefully slid her onto a little bed on wheels and rolled her outside the door. Nurse Hissy placed the ice packs across Lashes' neck.

The ramp down to the car was a bit steeper than the toms had anticipated. The bed on wheels was starting to pick up speed. There goes Dutchey down the ramp with Kool and Diamond chasing after her. She put her head up just in time to see a dense hedge coming at her. Kool ran super-fast, leaped into the air, and landed on the back left corner of the speeding bed causing it to swerve to the left and tilt sideways. Dutchey was sliding from one side of the bed to the other and was now facing backwards. She cried, "Save me, Kool!"

"I will! Just hold on!"

The speeding bed was about to crash into the hedge when the right front wheel ran over a rock. This caused the bed to swerve even more to the left and make a u-turn. Diamond caught up just in time for the bed on wheels to run over his front paws. Dutchey put her claws out and her head down. She was sliding all over the bed, which was now heading for the street. Kool held on to the bed with his right front paw and skidded with his other three paws until finally, the bed stopped, just short of hitting a fire hydrant. Dutchey slid forward and almost fell off. When Diamond finally caught up, her hurt leg was hanging off and she was scratching and clawing to get herself back on the bed. He pushed her up as she growled and hissed. She put her head down and closed her eyes. Her injured leg was hurting so bad, she didn't know if she could take the pain.

"Whew!" Kool said as he huffed and puffed. "Where's Dutchey's mom?"

Diamond and Kool looked over at the door. Lashes was standing in the doorway watching the whole thing. *"Toms, what are you doing?"* The ice packs smacked her in the face as she ran down the ramp to the bed on wheels. "Are you okay, Dutchey?"

Dutchey put her head up and cringed, "I think so. Did Mom see that?"

"No, she's still inside," answered Lashes.

"Whew." The four cats looked at each other with bulging eyes.

Lashes gave orders, "Kool, Diamond, the car is over there." She pointed her claw in the opposite direction. "Do you think we can get her there safely?" She pierced them both with blue-eyed daggers.

"Sorry, Dutchey," apologized Diamond, "the ramp didn't look *that* steep."

"Sorry, Dutchey," apologized Kool. Dutchey growled. Kool and Diamond turned the bed on wheels around and slowly pushed it to the car. Diamond was limping now.

After Dutchey was safely loaded in, they took off for home. On the way, Ming stopped for Siamese take-out, Dutchey's favorite. Everyone was very quiet in the car on the way home except for an occasional "grrr" from the injured patient.

As they pulled up the driveway, Blossom was at the front door to meet them. "What happened, Mom? Is Dutchey okay?" Miss Fancy was right behind her, anxious for answers.

Mom replied, "Dutchey fell out of the tree out back and hurt her leg, but she's going to be just fine. Come, little one, help us with dinner." As the three padded off to the kitchen, Blossom and Miss Fancy heard all about the visit to the vet.

14

$\mathcal{L}$ashes, Diamond, and Kool were in deep discussion about how they were going to get Dutchey upstairs.

Lashes had an idea, "We need an elevator."

Diamond suggested, "You should talk to your dad about that, Dutch."

Dutchey looked up the spiral staircase, at what seemed like a million steps, and started crying, "There's just too many steps."

Kool said, "Now don't cry, Dutch. We'll get ya up there."

Diamond had an idea, "Put her on my back and I'll carry her up."

Kool and Lashes helped Dutchey climb onto Diamond's back. Dutchey warned, "Don't drop me now."

"We won't."

Diamond took three steps up and Dutchey slipped sideways and almost fell off. Quickly, Lashes and Kool helped her get back on. Then they stood on each side of her to brace her. The ice packs were left behind on the marble floor at the bottom of the stairs.

Kool said, "Okay, we've got ya. On three, let's all go up together. One, two, three…"

They took a step, and that turned out okay. Then another and another. Dutchey wrapped her front legs around Diamond's neck to hold on. "Grrrr."

Diamond gagged, "Not so tight, Dutchey."

"Sorry."

Lashes was trying to hold up Dutchey's injured leg without actually touching it.

"Careful, Lashes," she cried.

"Sorry."

One step at a time, they carefully climbed. At last, they reached the top of the stairs and Dutchey slid off Diamond's back.

"Whew!" gagged Diamond. "You were kinda chokin' me there."

"Sorry."

Lashes ran back down the stairs, bit the corners of the ice packs, and pulled them up the stairs backwards. Kool and Diamond helped Dutchey up and stood on both sides of her. They helped her limp across the catwalk balcony and into her room. She dragged her bad leg behind her like *the mummy*. They boosted her up on her bed and she plopped down beside her pink velvet pillow with gold embroidery that said, *Future Queen*. "Grrrr." The toms sat down beside her. Nurse Lashes carefully placed Dutchey's ice pack on her swollen leg and Kool's ice pack on his swollen head. Then she sat down and supervised. Ming and Miss Fancy brought the dinner upstairs and served everyone. Blossom heard the news of Dutchey's lost life and tears were streaming down her face. Dutchey said, "Come up here, little sis, and be with me." Blossom jumped on the bed and lay down next to her sister. Dutchey licked her wet face and then Blossom licked Dutchey's ears.

Mom commented, "I called your father, Dutchey. He doesn't want me to come to the club tonight and I don't want to leave you either."

"Thanks, Mom," said sad Dutchey. "I'm sorry I lost one of my nine lives."

Mom looked at her precious kitten and felt sympathy for her. After all, she is behind three lives herself, and her beloved Siam Sam is behind four. "I love you and your father sends his love, too." She gave Dutchey a big kiss and rubbed her ears. "You are going to be just fine, little one."

Dutchey smiled a weak smile. She was sad and her leg was cramping. "Grrrr."

Half way through *Fluffy, the Rodent Slayer*, Dutchey and her friends fell fast asleep. Even little Blossom wanted to stay with her big sister.

Ming turned out the light, padded downstairs and called their mothers to tell them what happened and where their kittens are, "...and Pearl, how are the plans for the party coming along?"

15

Morning has broken!

Jett woke up with this strange, happy feeling. Then he remembered why, he remembered Jade. *Princess* Jade—that is. His stomach rolled over when he remembered her green eyes and her black velvet fur. He thought about teaching her tennis and all the cool places he wants to take her. He can't wait to introduce her to his friends. He is a smitten kitten and just doesn't know quite what to do with himself! He stretched out on his pillows and thought about the airport chase and the limo ride. He reached for the remote and turned on the television. The news was still reporting about the Princess Jade sighting. And, there he is, his picture splashed all over the television. The reporter referred to him as, "*The mysterious stranger* who kissed the paw of the Princess from Pintac last night at the airport."

"Isn't there anything else to report?" he grumbled. He switched channels and saw himself again kissing Jade's paw. He said out loud, *"Dude! Does everyone have to know?"* He turned off the television and a goofy grin covered his face. Full of energy, he got up, stretched, and yawned clear down to his socks. He strut over to the mirror and looked long and hard at his reflection. He commented to the mirror, "I need to work out more. Intense training is what this flabby bod needs." He hulked up and every toned muscle showed. His stomach growled at him and he growled back. No one was up yet so he decided to go downstairs and raid the kitchen. He peered out the kitchen window at the quiet backyard. Q was sound asleep beside the steps of the guesthouse where Cleo and Jade are staying. His heart leaped. After a moment, he padded over to his bowl and lapped up some fish oil with a water chaser. He was so excited he had no time for chow-chow. He has to find his buds right away and tell them about his wild adventure last night! Without one more second of hesitation, he bolted out the window and ran like the wind to Diamond's house.

16

At the same time Jett was watching himself on television, Princess Jade was lounging on the bay window in the tri-level guesthouse where she and Cleo are staying. She yawned as she watched the brilliant orange and yellow sunrise over the mansion. She peered out the window at the backyard and noticed a black bottom pool with a high dive. "How fun to jump from that!" She looked over and saw the tennis court with a very high fence around it. She smiled as she looked around at all the plants and beautiful flowers in bloom. "It's so pretty here," she thought as she yawned and lazily watched the magnificent sunrise. The bright sunlight poured in through the windows and Jade curiously looked around her new home for the next month. "It's contemporary and very beautiful," she thought. "And so clean." The kitchen is on the first floor, the living room is a few steps up, and two fabulous bedrooms with ocean views are another few steps up. The guesthouse has a beach décor, complete with seashells and sand candles. A conch sits proudly by itself on a glass table. An old fishing net hangs in the corner next to a portrait of the infamous Captain Squid on his fishing boat, boasting a proud smile while holding up a fifty-seven inch swordfish. The walls adorn gold-framed pastels and oil paintings of gorgeous sunsets with waves crashing on the rocks. The pillows and curtains are custom designed from the same satin fabric: seashells and fish. One pillow is shaped like a starfish.

"Hey, fluff-friend," yawned Cleo as she padded down the steps from her bedroom. She jumped up on the bay window seat and stretched on the long comfy pillow.

"Good morning, my dear friend. How did you sleep?"

Cleo replied, "My room is heaven! I love it! I slept like a snug bug in a rug! There was even a slimy oyster on my pillow! Yum!" She licked her paw and washed her face. "How was your nap?"

Jade sighed, "I couldn't sleep a wink."

"Why not?"

"I just couldn't stop thinking about last night."

"And my cousin?" teased Cleo. She giggled and yawned.

"You never told me how nice looking he is. So mannerly, too."

"He's a pretty cool cousin, even though he acted kind of dorky last night!" They both laughed. "Starr is fun, too. You'll just love her to pieces."

"She seems very sweet."

Cleo commented, "He's taken with you, you know. And you know I'm always right about these things." Jade looked at her with her head tilted to the side and slapped her tail rather hard on the window seat pillow. "Remember Prince Dane Gerous from Anut?" reminded Cleo.

Jade smiled and sarcastically said, "Oh, Great Dane... " Both fluffs snickered and rolled.

"What a saga that was!" said Cleo.

Jade laughed, "Talk about dorky!"

"Wasn't he just a bit much?!" replied Cleo, licking her other paw and washing the other side of her face.

"That's putting it ever so mildly!" replied Jade.

"He was *so* over the top!" laughed Cleo.

"Clear over to the other side!" agreed Jade.

"And he calls himself a Prince!" chided Cleo.

"He should be ashamed!" scolded Jade. They rolled on their backs and looked at each other upside down. She asked Cleo, "Ya know that on/off switch in your heart that tells you how to feel?"

Cleo sighed, "Yeah."

"Well, it just never went *on* for ol' Prince Dane Gerous." They busted out laughing.

"He sure didn't live up to his name, did he?" yawned Cleo as they laughed and rolled. She reached for the remote and turned on the big screen t.v. They saw more royal photos. Jade watched intently and smiled. She liked doing the interview. The connecting tail-run through the airport with Jett was fun. The *mysterious stranger* thing is really good stuff, too.

The news reporter stated, "We have no idea where the lovely Princess is staying, but we welcome her to Heavenly Hills and hope her stay is enjoyable."

They noticed Jett jump through the window and run away.

Jade perked up. "Where's he going so early?"

"Graduation rehearsal at Paw Valley Middle School." A few moments passed. The fluffs were thinking up something.

"Cleo, *dear*, do you remember the way to Paw Valley Middle School?"

"Of course I do, *dear!*"

The fluffs looked out the window and noticed Q sound asleep by the steps up to the door. He looked quite comfortable lying on his back with all fours in the air.

"I feel so safe and secure. Don't you, Cleo?" Cleo laughed and had a gleam in her eye. Jade had the same gleam. They looked at each other and nodded. Jade whispered, "Are you thinking what I'm thinking?"

Cleo whispered, "Let's get something to eat, sneak past Q, and go down to the school."

Jade smiled mischievously. "Do you think we should?" They smiled at each other, nodded, and without another word, jumped off the window seat. They raced down the steps to the kitchen so fast, they slid right into their breakfast bowls.

Cleo said with delight, "Oh good, fish oil. I have been feeling a bit dry lately. My auntie thinks of everything!" They quickly ate their chow-chow and washed it down with fish oil. After they finished breakfast and licked their whiskers, they padded upstairs and pawed through their luggage to find the lavender perfume. Jade found the slimy oyster on her pillow and slid it down. Then she sprayed Cleo with perfume.

"Spray behind my ears," Jade instructed. Cleo sprayed behind each ear. "Where's the minty fresh?"

Cleo pawed through the luggage. "Here it is."

"Spray my tongue." spritz spritz

"Spray mine, too." spritz spritz

Jade opened the curtains and exclaimed, "Cleo, look at the view of the ocean. It's incredible!"

Cleo agreed, "I know. I have the same view from my room. I love it here."

They put the perfume and the minty fresh on the vanity and Jade scribbled something on a piece of paper and put the corner of it in her mouth. Then they snuck out the back door. They crept behind the ivy and between the hedges, being as quiet as they could. They crept over to Q, who was snoring so loud it was surprising he didn't wake himself up. They spotted a bird feather by his ear.

"He gets an A+ in hunting," whispered Cleo.

"Shhh," whispered Jade. She quietly crept closer to slip the note under the feather. She was biting the note so hard, it had pierced over her fangs and she couldn't get it lose. "Help me, Cleo," she whispered. "The note is stuck in my teeth." Cleo tried hard not to laugh as she bit the other end of the note to free it from Jade's sharp fangs. She spit it on the ground. Jade picked up the feather with her teeth so she could put it on top of the note. Now the feather was stuck. "Cleo, help me." Cleo laughed out loud, then put her paws to her mouth. "Shhh," whispered Jade, with the feather dangling from her mouth. "He's gonna wake up."

"Him?" whispered Cleo. She bit the end of the feather and spit it on top of the note.

"Shhh," whispered Jade.

Q sniffed his nose and shook his back leg. The fluffs froze in their tracks. He rolled over on his side.

Snore … Snore … Snort

"He's such a *good* bodyguard," whispered Cleo.

"Shhh!"

Q's tail twitched and he snorted again. The fluffs stared at each other, afraid to move.

"I don't want him to catch us…" whispered Jade.

"Shhh!" whispered Cleo. They looked at each other, then at Q, then back at each other. Very quietly, they slinked away from him. They quietly jumped the fence and were in the front yard, home free. They ran at top speed to the end of the street. They stopped to look back. No Q. They burst out laughing. "We are so bad!" panted Cleo, catching her breath.

Jade warned, "When Q catches up with us, he is going to be so mad! Oh well. We left a note. Lead the way, my friend." They took off for Paw Valley Middle School.

17

When Jett arrived at Diamond's house, he climbed the tall tree and jumped through Diamond's bedroom window only to find… no Diamond. He jumped back through the window, flew down the tree, and ran to Kool's house. "Great workout!" he thought. "Great day! Great Life!" He ran past a newspaper stand and there he was, bigger than life, all over the front page! When he reached Kool's house, he scaled the tall tree, jumped through the bedroom window, and was greeted by Kool's mother, Dora.

"Good grief, tom-tom!" she exclaimed. "You scared me out of my fur! What are you doing here so early?"

"I'm sorry, Mrs. Katt. I'm looking for Kool and Diamond and I didn't find them at Diamond's house."

Dora sadly replied, "I guess you haven't heard about Dutchey's accident."

Jett snapped to full attention. "What accident?"

"She fell out of a tree, hurt her leg, was unconscious past the time limit, and lost a life." Jett slumped down with sadness and hung his head to the side. Dora padded over and rubbed his ears. "She's okay though. Kool, Diamond, and Lashes spent the night with her. You will find them at her house."

"Thanks for telling me," he said, heading for the window. He ran back and gave her a whisker kiss, then darted through the window and down the tree.

As he ran across the yard, Dora yelled after him, "Your picture is plastered all over the front page of *The Morning Chew.*"

"I know… I know… " his voice faded off as he ran top speed to Dutchey's house in Castleberry Grove, the hilly part of the city that displays a glorious view of the ocean on the left and a gorgeous view of lush green mountains on the right. The early morning was beautiful, not a cloud in the sky. He could think of nothing now, but Dutchey. He reached her mansion, leaped over the fence, scaled the maple tree, and vaulted through the bay window. As usual, his landing was superb and graceful. He was a little out of breath so he sat on the window seat to rest for a moment. He gazed around the room and observed his sleeping friends. His eyes landed on Dutchey. Something peculiar was happening. Her back leg was twitching. Sometimes a small twitch, sometimes a wild twitch. He quietly jumped off the window seat and crept over to Dutchey's bed. He jumped up and sat down beside her to observe her. He noticed a melted ice pack lying next to her *Future Queen* pillow. After a moment, he looked at his other friends. Lashes was curled up in the corner and looked like a furry fluff ball. There's little sister, Blossom, sound asleep up high on the perch. Diamond was lying on his back between two satin pillows with all four paws in the air. Jett looked closer and noticed tread mark lines across his front paws. Kool was stretched out on his side and resembled a multi-colored beached whale. Jett noticed a melted ice pack next to him, too. He shook his head and thought, "What happened here? I can't leave these cats alone for two seconds!" A few moments passed and Jett's mind drifted back to Jade. His heart skipped a beat as he remembered her exquisite features, her exotic green eyes, and her long legs. He felt a dragonfly twinge in his stomach when remembering kissing her paw. He lay down next to Dutchey and closed his eyes to daydream. There he goes again, floating away on cloud nine, when, without warning, Dutchey's leg cramped and she kicked him on the jaw! He jumped backwards in the air about three feet, fell completely off the bed, hissing, spitting, and of course, he woke everyone up. "Phftt. Phftt."

18

$\mathcal{D}$iamond rolled over, yawned, and stretched. He looked over at Jett, "Hey, dawg. What up?"

Jett jumped back up on the bed and rubbed his jaw with his paw. "I heard about Dutchey's accident, so I came right away. What happened?"

"Diamond's her hero," yawned Lashes. "He broke Dutchey's fall when she fell out of the Old Sycamore. What a saga that was. We had to go to Dr. Fitt for a full body and head scan and everything. She wasn't waking up so Diamond was sayin' real sweet stuff to her."

"Then she woke up," piped up Blossom, yawning and stretching up there on her perch.

Jett asked, "What's up with her leg?"

"Apparently," yawned Kool, "her leg took the brunt of the fall."

"It's twitching so bad, it looks scary. And her kick didn't feel that good either." He opened his mouth several times to see if his jaw still worked.

Dutchey was waking up now, groaning and hissing. "Oh… my… gosh… I feel like… I fell out of a tree or something." She yawned a long one. Everyone gathered around her as she tried to stand up. "My leg feels funny. *Reeoow!* Hiss."

Jett held her up, but she started falling anyway. "Oh, my poor little pal." He put his head next to hers, then got out of the way as she collapsed on the bed. He tilted his head and said, "I'm sorry about your accident, Dutchey."

"Thanks, Jett, and thank you for coming to see me. My leg feels funny," she said again as she and her friends watched it spasm out.

Jett turned to Kool and pointed at the ice pack. "What happened to you?"

"Umm… I had a little disagreement with Dutchey's climbing pole."

Diamond added, "And the pole won!"

"Ha-ha-ha," snarled Kool. He rubbed the lump on his head, feeling quite proud of it. He showed it off to Jett.

Jett inspected the lump, but wasn't impressed. "I've seen better goose eggs than that after your soccer games. And what's up with the tread marks, Diamond?"

Diamond looked over at Dutchey with a goofy grin, "Sometimes a bed on wheels isn't a good idea, huh, Dutchey?"

"No," she quickly agreed.

Jett shook his head and remarked, "You cats just fall apart when I'm not around."

Lashes declared, "I'm still in one piece!"

19

$\mathcal{T}$here was a scratch at the door. Ming entered the bedroom and jumped up on the bed beside Dutchey. "Good morning, kittens."

"Morning," everyone yawned.

"How are you this morning, darling?"

"Sore, Mom," replied Dutch, licking her leg.

"That's to be expected, dear." She hugged her precious kitten. Everyone was staring at Dutchey, but no one mentioned her lost life. As Mom licked Dutchey's ears, she noticed Jett opening and closing his mouth and moving his jaw side-to-side. "Hello, Jett. How are you this morning?"

"Hi, Mrs. Woo. I'm fine. I'm sorry about Dutchey's accident."

"Thank you, Jett. Blossom, honey, turn on the television."

And what could possibly be on? Oh, but of course, there it is again! There is the picture of Jett kissing the Princess' paw. The same picture is on the front page of the newspaper. All eyes were glued to the television.

Ming asked Blossom, "Change the channel, honey."

There were even more reports of the Princess and *the mysterious stranger.* Every channel was reporting something about the lovely Princess. The news reported, "The Princess of Pintac honors us with her lovely presence and truly surprising visit. We hope her stay is enjoyable and memorable."

"Jett, is that *you?*" asked Diamond, sitting up, not believing what he was seeing. "Are *You the mysterious stranger?*"

"Well, yeah," answered Jett, scratching his ear with his back paw.

Ming smiled. "What have you been up to, dear?"

Jett just sat there with a goofy grin on his face. His eyes were glued to the t.v. Each station continued splashing pictures and details of the arrival of the Princess of Pintac. They reported a wild airport chase with the paparazzi, a get-away limo, and *the interview* through the darkly tinted window when Jade announced how much she loves everyone!

"Who is that?" they all asked in unison, staring at Jett in total amazement.

Jett casually replied, "Oh, just this fluff who came with Cleo."

"Just this fluff?" exclaimed Diamond. "He calls the Princess from Pintac *just this fluff!*"

Jett was rolling on his back now. "She is the most amazingly exotic cat I have ever seen!" He quickly flipped over and looked around the room at all the pretty felines staring at him. "Except for the beauties here with me now, of course. Not that you fluffs aren't, well, umm, amazing."

Lashes twirled her curly whiskers with her claw, waiting for her compliment about being the most beautiful feline in the world, Dutchey's leg twitched, Blossom giggled, and Ming just smiled at poor love-struck Jett.

Jett was up on his paws now and very excited! "I couldn't wait to tell all of you about her! I cannot wait for you to meet her! You will meet her today! I can't wait for her to meet all my best friends! I think I'm in love!" He rolled on his back again and played with the end of his tail.

Everyone looked at Jett and then each other. After a few seconds, they all burst out laughing and blew kisses in the air.

Kool made loud smooching sounds and teased, "I think the love bug has bitten our *mysterious stranger.*"

"And there's certainly no cure for that," added Ming, winking at Jett.

Everyone laughed at Jett as he rolled on his back and stared out the window at nothing. Kool shot a fake arrow at him.

"I don't think I can stand him this way!" declared Diamond. "He's sickening!"

Everyone agreed.

20

Ming and Miss Fancy served up a grand graduation breakfast of french roast with tuna oil syrup. Then the graduates headed off to school in the limo. There are no classes scheduled today, only a half day for rehearsal. Dutchey's friends held her up as she limped and twitched her way across the soccer field.

"You've got quite a power twitch there, Dutchey," Diamond commented as they watched her leg jerking around.

"I'm having a cramp," she replied. "And just to let you all know, I am not enjoying this at all. Grrrr."

"Good thing rehearsal is only a few hours," Lashes said to her buddy, trying to be reassuring.

"I know," she sighed. "What am I going to do? This is so embarrassing. I'm supposed to be cool and poised tonight, not twitchy and jerky." Her friends looked at her with sympathetic faces.

Everyone is to meet on the soccer field, just like yesterday. On the stage are a podium, a microphone, and a few benches. Behind the stage are colorful tinsel streamers that sparkled as they blew in the warm morning breeze.

"All cats, take your places in line," announced Principal Fitt (Dr. Fitt's twin brother). "Just like yesterday."

21

As rehearsal got underway, Jett became antsy. He's excited and he can't wait for life to happen! He wasn't paying very much attention to Principal Fitt and his instructions for the ceremony because he was daydreaming about last night and her beautiful green eyes. He was heading off to some other galaxy when he noticed something jumping up and down on the bleachers. He squinted his eyes to look closer, and who did he see? Cleo, jumping up and down like a red-hot chili pepper on fire! "She's so crazy," he mumbled under his breath. He looked around and spotted Jade sitting on the very highest bleacher, staying clear of Cleo's jumping spree. Jett's heart began pounding, and without thinking, he stood up and waved his front paws wildly in the air. Cleo finally stopped jumping and sat down to pant. Jade was smiling and waving. Jett leaned over to his friends and in a loud and embarrassing high-pitched voice, he yelled, *"There she is! There she is!"* Every cat on the infield looked over at Jett, then up at the bleachers. They saw Princess Jade, smiling and waving, so everyone waved back. Word was spreading fast about the exciting front page of *The Morning Chew.* Jett sat down. His heart was racing and he was feeling a bit dizzy.

The Bully brothers were sitting a row ahead of Jett and his friends. The Bully brothers are triplets. They all have long yellow fur with various white markings and green eyes. Bull was first born and is the largest, Chip was second born, and Fangy is the runt of the litter. They play on Paw Valley's undefeated soccer team, as well. In absolute astonishment, the Bully brothers looked up at the bleachers and saw the Princess, then looked back at Jett, then looked back at Princess Jade.

Bull said in a loud, sarcastic voice, "Are you *the mysterious stranger* caught kissing the royal paw?"

"Yeah," Kool said, "that's him."

"*You?*" Bull looked Jett up and down and grinned. "Well then, give me some paw, dude!"

Jett high pawed the Bully brothers and other toms sitting around him. The fluff-fluffs blew kisses in the air and the tom-toms made smooching sounds. Jett laughed, even though he was a bit embarrassed. Then a thought came to him, "Where's Q? Did those fluffs ditch him? Who is protecting the Princess?" He looked down the field and there was out-of-breath Q running and shaking his white paw at Jade and Cleo. Jade ignored him and continued waving and smiling at the enthusiastic collection of whiskers on the infield. The whole graduating class was buzzing about Jett and Princess Jade, and now no one was listening to Principal Fitt. Sweet Secretary Hissy (Nurse Hissy's twin sister) padded up on stage and whispered something in Principal Fitt's ear. He listened intently and nodded.

"Quiet, quiet, everyone," said Principal Fitt, "I understand we have royalty among us this morning."

The graduates stood up, cheering and whistling because this was very exciting!

Exasperated Jett muttered under his breath. "*Dude!* A tom just can't keep anything private these days." He sat down.

Principal Fitt continued, "We are honored to have Princess Jade from Pintac watching us rehearse this morning. Now I know we all want to impress her with our best manners." All the cats howled, mannerly of course. "We have also been given word that she will honor us with her royal presence at this evening's ceremony."

Everyone cheered euphorically! The lovely Princess sat on the highest bleacher smiling and waving, looking every bit the celebrity she is. What a happy day for her! "This is so exciting!" she said to Cleo. "Your cousin must be extremely proud."

"I know he's proud of *you!*" teased Cleo.

"And how do you know that, my little friend?" Jade pierced her with her green eyes.

"Well, I've been watching him and I have never seen him like this before, and I've known Jett forever. He told me he has *never* been interested in any fluff, but I can tell, he is love-struck over you. He's acting so silly. That's the first sign. And you do remember how I'm never wrong about these things, don't you?!"

"Oh, I don't know… " she sighed. "He probably has a list of fluffs that goes on forever. Every good-lookin' tom does, ya know."

They were both silent for a moment and surveyed the competition. Jade thought to herself, a bit disappointed, "There sure are a lot of pretty fluffs in his class, but… wait a minute. There are plenty of good lookin' hunks of fur too, and they are all my age. Big cats, small cats, geeky cats, cool cats, tough cats, prissy cats… but… no cat quite like Jett. Gold eyes have always been my weakness. When I looked into his amazing eyes last night, I felt as though I was looking into his heart. This trip is very exciting, so far! All that happened during my arrival, all that will happen! I can't wait!" She looked over at Cleo and said, "My parents were right when they said I needed a change of culture!"

"Definitely!" agreed Cleo.

They watched everything that was happening on the infield during rehearsal. Everyone seemed to be having a nice, yet serious time. The bright sun was bouncing off the tinsel streamers, displaying reflections of every color in a rainbow. Jade looked around the field and commented, "The decorations are so sparkly and beautiful!"

"Very purrtty!" agreed Cleo, looking around.

Q was sitting on the bottom bleacher, panting.

Principal Fitt announced over the microphone that he would like Princess Jade to say something motivational to the students as they say farewell to Paw Valley Middle School and begin a new life at Heavenly Hills High.

The Grads whistled and howled as Princess Jade glided down the bleachers and floated over to the stage. Overprotective Q was right at her side, being all big and bad, acting as though he were in charge. Jade stood behind the microphone and looked out over the infield at the sea of cats watching her and cheering her on. She searched for Jett and found him, smiling ear to ear. Then she began her profound words of wisdom. She greeted them with, "Wow! Look at this great lookin' group of graduating cats!"

Cheering and howling echoed across the field. The Grads were so excited they could hardly contain themselves. The insightful Princess was still talking, but her voice faded in the roar of the crowd.

Principal Fitt motioned to his graduates to sit down and maintain control. "Manners everyone, manners… "

Finally, they calmed down and she was able to continue.

"Now, we all know that academics and athletics are what make or break a cat. You are here today because all of you cats have accomplished great things in your lives. You should be very proud of yourselves! So, go for it, Graduates! Take Heavenly Hills High by Storm!"

There was plenty of cheering and inspiration at this morning's Graduation rehearsal. Principal Fitt was very pleased with his eighth grade class. He gave them last minute instructions for the ceremony tonight and reminded them to take their naps. Then he bid them all a happy day, *after* he summoned Dutchess Woo to the stage.

22

It was a grueling walk up to the stage for Dutchey. She had already walked the long walk twice during rehearsal and she was tired and sore. Her friends accompanied her to the stage. Diamond and Lashes each took a side and propped her up.

"Yes, Principal Fitt?" Dutchey asked as they approached the stage.

"My poor student..." said Principal Fitt. "Dr. Fitt told us what happened yesterday. I am so sorry, but I'm very pleased you made it to rehearsal this morning. How are you feeling?"

"My leg keeps cramping, but I think I'll be able to come tonight," she replied, being brave.

"Very good, very good," encouraged Principal Fitt.

Q and Jade were waiting next to the stage. Q told her, "Ya did good, kid, but... "

Jade thought, "Lecture time... " She looked the other way, uninterested.

Q continued in a low voice, "You know I don't like it when you don't tell me where you and Cleo are going."

"We left you a note."

"How do you two always get so close and not wake me? You know I don't like that."

Jade shrugged.

Q is resigned to the fact that he is a little older now and a little bit overweight, so he tried to reason with the independent Princess. "We are in a foreign country, you know."

Jade sighed, "I know, I know. I won't do it again." She crossed her tale over his as she said this.

Q looked back at his tail and swiped it out from under hers. "You know I don't like it when you cross tails. It makes me think you don't mean what you say."

"You just looked so comfortable this morning; we didn't want to wake you."

"You know I don't like it when you use that as an excuse."

"Okay then, I will wake you up all the time and interrupt your much needed beauty sleep."

Q snarled at her. He knew she was too much for an old feline like him to watch over, but that is his job, so he will do it! With pride and honor to the King and Queen of Pintac! He imagined himself saluting the King, wearing a superbly engraved solid gold badge on his collar. He was so absorbed in his daydream, that when he eventually looked over at Jade with a goofy grin covering his face, she was gone. He frantically looked this way and that and worked himself up into a total panic attack before he finally spotted her over by Cleo and Jett, quite a distance away. He watched as she and Jett locked eyes then looked away with shy smiles. He grumbled, but no one was paying any attention to him at all.

"You were phenomenal!" Jett whispered to her. "I mean *are* phenomenal!" He scolded himself, "Can't I say anything right?"

"Thank you," she whispered back.

Sympathetic Principal Fitt said, "Dutchess, you take care of yourself this afternoon, young fluff, so you will be able to participate this evening. And keep your chin up." He knew about her lost life, too.

"I will. Thank you, Principal Fitt."

Miss Hissy gave her a warm hug and stroked her whiskers.

Principal Fitt turned to Jade and said, "Thank you, Miss Jade, for speaking to our over-excited Graduates."

"You're welcome, Sir."

Miss Hissy added, "Welcome to Heavenly Hills, Princess Jade."

"Thank you very much."

"Have a nice afternoon, kittens," said Principal Fitt, "We'll see you tonight." He and Miss Hissy padded away leaving Jett to make formal introductions of his new friend to all his best friends.

23

Jett began introductions. "Jade, meet my best friends: Dutchess, Lashes, Kool, and Diamond. Everyone, this is Princess Jade from Pintac."

Jade smiled and greeted everyone and they excitedly greeted her back.

"Hey, what about me?" asked Cleo, feeling left out.

"Everybody already knows you," replied Jett, head bumping her.

"Hey, Cleo," said Diamond, "How have you been?"

"Great! And you?"

"Good," Diamond replied. "How was the flight?"

"Exciting!" replied Cleo.

"Hi, Cleo," said Kool, "you've grown up."

"So have you!" she said in amazement. "All three of you toms are huge!" The three toms puffed out their chests.

"Hi, Cleo," greeted inspired Lashes. She gave her a hug.

"Hi, Lashes. Hi, Dutchey. What happened?" Cleo asked as she gave Dutchey a hug.

"Oh, I fell out of a tree yesterday," she sighed.

Lashes announced, "Diamond's her *Hero!* He laid down under the tree and broke her fall! I witnessed the whole thing!"

Diamond tilted his head to the side. "Awww. It was nothin.' Just everyday stuff." He scratched his ear with his back paw, then sat there, embarrassed.

Dutchey snarled and head bumped him. *"Not every-day."* Then she turned her attention to Jade. "Hi, Jade. Welcome to Heavenly Hills."

"Thank you." Both Lashes and Dutchey exchanged hugs with her.

"Great on-the-spot speech!" gushed Lashes. "It was very inspiring!"

"It was fun! This is Q, my bodyguard. He goes where I go."

"Hi, Q," they said together, inspecting this portly cat that doesn't look like he could do anything a bodyguard could do, let alone do it fast.

Q nodded his head as if he were too important to say hello.

Diamond broke the silence and suggested, "Come on. Let's take Cleo, Jade, and Q to our spot and rest for a while. You heard Principal Fitt's orders about our naps."

Dutchey looked at Diamond with a pitiful face, "I don't think I can walk that far." She sniffled and started to cry.

Diamond reassured her, "Don't you worry about that, my friend. You will just ride on my back, like yesterday, when we went up the stairs. Remember? Now, climb aboard."

Kool added, "I'll help, too. Dutchey can ride across both of our backs, sideways." They loaded her up and slowly padded to their spot by the shore.

24

While on the way to this unknown spot, Jade looked out over the ocean and thought, "The water is so clear and sparkly, just like a twenty-four-carat diamond tail ring! And the air smells like fish!" She took in a deep breath and decided, "Life couldn't be better!"

Their spot is near an alcove of rocks, back a bit from the splashing waves. Once they arrived, Kool swished his tail across the sand and made a smooth place for Dutchey to lie down. Everyone lay in a circle, facing each other, yawning.

"Take a load off," Jett said to Q.

"Okay," he bellowed, flopping down in the shade beside the rocks, as if he were released of all responsibilities.

"It's very peaceful here," Jade commented, "I love the ocean."

Dutchey said, "We've been coming to this spot since we were kittens. Now, tell us what it's like being a princess."

"Well, it is lonely sometimes. I don't get to leave the palace very often, and when I do, it is only for speeches and dedications. Cleo comes to visit often and she makes life fun."

Cleo smiled and nodded her head up and down.

Kool teased, "You looked like you were having fun last night at the airport... " Jade and Jett exchanged goofy looks and laughed.

Lashes asked, "Do you go to school?"

Jade sighed. "I am educated at home, but I am very excited for all of you and your ceremony tonight!"

Dutchey added, "Following the ceremony, there's a party at Diamond's country club!"

"Really? Are we going? Are we going?" Cleo asked Jett, piercing him with her mauve eyes.

"You better believe you're going!" exclaimed Jett.

"Yesss!!!" howled Cleo. Jade wore a happy smile and slapped her tail on the sand. "Tell us about the party, Diamond," begged Cleo. Diamond lay there being annoyingly smug. Yes, maybe even aggravatingly smug. He started power purring.

Dutchey spat, "See... that's what he does when he wants to get out of something, he purrs—loud like that. Will you stop acting so secretive over there? You and all your... secrets."

"What secrets?" asked Jade.

Lashes spoke up. "There's a theme for tonight's party and he knows all about it and won't tell us."

"Oh, tell us," begged Jade.

Diamond cheerfully smiled, teasing everyone. He purred even louder and swept his tail back and forth across the sand.

"Tell us," begged Cleo.

Diamond quoted, "You know what curiosity did to the cat, don't you?"

"But satisfaction brought us back!" snapped feisty Dutchess.

"So tell us right now!" Lashes demanded. Diamond changed positions to get comfortable for his nap.

"Oh, don't bother with him," said Dutch, "he's so tight whiskered, he won't tell." She looked the other way and put her chin in the air, acting mad.

Diamond sighed, then got up and padded over to the yellow flowers that grew wild beside the rocks. He bit some off with his teeth and dropped a few in front of each fluff. As he dropped the flowers in front of Dutchey, he said, "I can't wait to see the expressions on all your faces tonight! So don't be mad, because tonight you will be glad!"

Dutchey looked up at Diamond and smiled. "You are tight whiskered, but cute!" Their eyes locked for a moment.

"Her eyes... " dreamed Diamond.

"His eyes... " dreamed Dutchey.

There was a brief pause. The air was... fishilicious.

Jade broke the silence. "I love the idea of school outside the palace! You felines are so lucky! What classes do you take?"

Kool said, "Hunting."

Diamond added, "Fishing."

Lashes said, "Poise and Balance."

Dutchey added, "Literary Expression."

Jett said, "I love Math."

Cleo asked, "Why? So you can count all your money?"

"Yep."

Lashes anxiously suggested, "You should both stay here and go to school with us? We would have a great time!"

Jett nodded enthusiastically. He liked that idea.

Jade replied, "That would be wonderful!" Then she sighed, "I wonder what my father would say… " She looked up at the cloudless blue sky, ready to pass out. She was running on empty.

Kool yawned, "Remember what Principal Fitt said about our naps."

"Diamond," yawned Dutchey, "purr us to sleep."

"We're kind of spoiled," yawned Lashes.

"Help me out, lazy cats," Diamond said to Kool and Jett. There's always that edge of competition between the three tom-toms. They were purring so loud, no one could fall asleep. Finally, Dutchey stretched out her leg, moaned, and nodded off on the warm sand. Lashes rested her head on Kool's side. He makes a good pillow— so soft and furry. Q was already snoring. Cleo stretched out and rolled on her back, and Jett admired Jade's black velvet fur shining in the sunshine. Everything seemed to stop whenever he looked at her. Even the fishing boats stopped in their wake. Her delicate gold anklet sparkled in the sunlight.

As he stared at her, he thought, "She is simply exquisite." He was the last one purring as his heavy eyelids finally dropped. Within moments, they were all fast asleep in the sunshine, surrounded by the tranquility of twenty-four-carat diamond waves breaking on the rocks and the wonderful aroma of fish.

25

*L*ashes woke with a start! The tide was coming in and her tail was getting wet. She jumped up and as she shook the sand off, she remembered their beauty appointments with Mickey Manx. She woke everyone up by jumping over their heads.

"Wake up, everyone! Wake up! The tide is coming in and we have appointments to get beautiful!"

Kool yawned, "Why bother? You're already beautiful."

"Well, I know, but we have to get *more* beautiful. We have to go now!" she insisted. The sand was flying.

"Okay, okay," yawned Diamond, "we're up, we're up." Everyone shook and stretched. Then they loaded up Dutchey and took off to The Pampered Paw Beauty Salon. This is the glamour palace where fluffs are luxuriously pampered with pedicures, flea dips, fur blow-outs, and of course, massages. After the brisk ride on Diamond and Kool's backs, Dutchey definitely needed a massage.

As they arrived at the salon's front door, breathless Lashes looked at the clock and gasped, "Whew. We made it just in time."

"Hi, fluffs," greeted Tootie, the pretty feline behind the reception desk. "Hi, toms."

"Hi."

Out-of-breath Lashes panted, "We have appointments for a massage, blow-outs for both of us, and I think Dutchey needs a major pedicure." She picked up Dutchey's paw and inspected her claws. "Yes, definitely a pedicure for this fluff! Her claws are all split and traumatized. Look...."

Dutchey added, "I think I need a paw pad soak, too."

Kool was admiring his skid marks from yesterday's incident. "Paw pad soak!" he spat. "It is so uncool to soak your pads!"

Lashes replied, "Maybe for you, macho tom."

"Actually, it does feel kinda good," commented Diamond, "you should try it sometime." The toms burst out laughing. Even Q let out a big belly laugh.

Lashes added, "I think my tail needs a little help, too." She pointed at her wet and sandy tail to show everyone. "And I know Jade and Cleo would appreciate a pad soak." She looked over at the fluffs and tilted her cute head to the side. They nodded in agreement. "Tootie, can you squeeze in my two friends for the works? Please? Please? Please?"

"Of course," said Tootie. "Who are these beautiful felines?"

Jett stepped up, "This is my cousin, Cleo, and this is our friend, Jade."

Tootie said, "Hi, Cleo. It's very nice to meet you."

"Hi. It's very nice meeting you, too."

"Is this *the* Princess Jade from Pintac that we've been hearing so much about?"

"Yes," answered Jett, "but we're keeping that little bit of info under wraps."

"Are you *the mysterious stranger* kissing her paw?"

"Yes, but we are keeping that on the down low, too. Right Princess?"

He winked at Jade and she put one claw up to her mouth as if to say, "shhhh…"

Tootie grinned and twirled her whiskers like she was tying her mouth closed.

Mickey Manx came in from the back room and looked at Dutchey. "Oh, my little kitten, I heard about your accident yesterday. Come back to my massage table and tell me all about it." He helped her onto a table with wheels. Dutchey turned and looked at Diamond and Kool, remembering the bed-on-wheels fiasco that happened yesterday. They looked back at her with goofy grins and gave her the claws-up sign. Mickey wheeled her through the curtains and into the back room.

Lorenzo announced, "Come, you gorgeous creatures. Let me make you royally gorgeous!" He escorted the fluffs behind the curtain.

"See you tonight, toms," said Lashes, "I'm so excited!"

"We couldn't tell," the toms said together.

"Lashes, just look at your tail! Did you fall asleep on the beach again?" scolded Lorenzo.

"Yes… " her words faded out from behind the curtain.

The toms found themselves abandoned at the front desk while the fluffs blew kisses and disappeared into the back room. Q flopped down on the couch.

Diamond said, "Well, we can't hang around here all day. We have things to do."

They split.

26

$\mathcal{T}$he three toms were leisurely trottin' down the streets of Heavenly Hills when, all of a sudden, Jett got excited! With an overload of enthusiasm, he said, "I have an idea! Let's stop by the flower shop and get corsages for the fluffs to wear tonight!"

"That's a great idea!" replied Diamond. He nodded his cute head and swished his fluffy tail from side to side.

Kool looked at Diamond and smirked, "Haven't you given enough flowers today, lover tom?"

Diamond scoffed, "Stand back and learn from the pro!" He strut down the street with his nose and tail in the air.

"Oh yeah, that's it," laughed Kool as he and Jett strut behind him, imitating him. Kool teased Diamond by saying in a snobby voice, *"Hello. My name is Mr. Snobby Cat. How are you today?"*

"I am ever so fine! And yourselves?"

They laughed and kept on struttin.' They were in high spirits as they came upon The Pretty Petals Flower Shop. The three looked at each other and then padded through the front door. A dainty bell chimed and Lily padded in from the back room, out of breath.

Lashes' mother, Lily, is a beautiful Persian with blue eyes, a white face, and soft tan fur. Her whiskers are very curly. "Oh, thank you, thank you," she said, panting. "Will you strong toms help me load the rest of the flowers in the van? I'm running late and I just want everything to be purrfect for you tonight."

"Just tell us what to do," said Diamond.

"Three toms at your service," smiled Kool.

"Where do we start?" asked over enthusiastic Jett.

"You toms are heaven sent!"

There were flowers here, flowers there, flowers everywhere. They finally finished loading all the flowers into the van while Lily ran around, muttering to herself and checking off things on her list. "Don't forget that box labeled balloons."

"Okay."

"Or the boxes labeled *Top Secret.*"

"Got it."

Finally, the van was packed full and ready to go. Lily complimented them, "Good job! Thank you very much for helping me, but I know you toms didn't come all the way down here to look at my beautiful fur. What's up?"

Jett asked, "Would it be too late to ask for corsages for our friends to wear tonight?"

"How many do you need?"

Kool extended his claws and started counting, "Let's see... one... two... three... four... Four—right, buds?"

"Yep!"

"Will miniature white roses do?"

"Purrfect!"

Lily padded to the back room and returned with miniature white roses in her teeth. She proceeded to attach them to white ribbons to hang around the fluffs' necks. As she worked she asked, "How's Dutchey doing?"

Diamond replied, "Hmmm... her leg has a nasty twitch sometimes. I'm hoping the massage she's getting right now will help."

"Poor little kitty. Jett, did I see you on the television last night? Something about a royal Princess?"

Jett nodded, "Yes. That was me. Princess Jade from Pintac came with Cleo for our graduation. It was a big surprise!"

Lily exclaimed, "I can't wait to meet her!"

"I'll introduce you tonight."

"Promise?"

"Promise."

"How's Cleo? It's been a few years since she's visited, hasn't it?"

"Yeah, three, I think. Anyway, she's great. Her and Princess Jade are best friends."

Lily whispered, "Don't tell Lashes or Dutchey, but I have a big surprise for them, too! Don't tell now."

"We won't."

After a bit more fussing, "Here you go, toms." She proudly presented them with four little boxes, each with a lovely corsage inside. "This is on the house because you are so good to me, but I've got to run now." She rubbed whiskers with each of them. "You will all sparkle tonight! I love you three toms! See you tonight. Lock the door on your way out, please."

"Okay, thank you," said Diamond.

"Thank you, Mrs. Holcomb," said Jett.

"Thank you," added Kool.

"You're welcome… " she said, leaving them in a cloud of pollen.

They were standing in the open doorway holding the little boxes when Kool suggested, "Do ya think we should turn the *Open* sign to *Closed?*" They put the corsages on the floor.

Diamond agreed, "Yeah, I'll turn it around." To reach the sign, he had to go between the window and the display table. The first thing he accomplished was snagging his back claw on the sheer fabric that lined the display. To unsnag his claw, he yanked on the fabric and knocked over several vases of flowers. Water was dripping all over the floor.

Jett yelled, "Diamond, get out of there. You're too big and you're making a mess of everything."

Diamond looked over, "Don't worry, I've got it under control. Throw me a towel." He moved and knocked over another vase of flowers.

Kool said, "Bro, get out of there or you're gonna bust up the place and Mrs. Holcomb is gonna get mad at us. Back out slowly, dude. Just back away from the flowers." Since Diamond was obviously too big to turn around, Jett had to slip in and pull him out by his tail. As soon as he was out of the display window, Diamond shook the water off. Jett slid under the display, cleaned up all the water, fixed the sheer fabric, and lined up the vases. Kool was outside now, yelling at him through the window, instructing him how to arrange the flowers. "Put the yellow flowers over there and the red bouquet goes over here." Diamond was standing in the doorway laughing. He looked down at the boxes and decided to play soccer with them. He shuffled them out the door and onto the sidewalk. The door accidentally shut on one box, giving it a tweaky appearance. Kool started playing too, shuffling the boxes around on the sidewalk.

Jett was still fussing with the sheer curtain when he looked out the window and saw his buds playing corsage soccer. He quickly backed out of the display case, opened the door, and yelled out, "Hey!"

Diamond and Kool jumped and smacked their heads together. They sat down to pant and looked over at Jett. *"What?"*

Jett snarled, "What are you two doing? These boxes are special!" He gathered the boxes up and fussed over them.

"We were just getting them out the door," said Diamond.

"No, you weren't. You were playing soccer with them." He made sure the door was locked and closed it. The three toms picked up the boxes with their teeth and trotted right past the display window, forgetting all about the sign that still said *Open.*

27

$\mathcal{J}$ett dropped his corsage boxes on the sidewalk and said, "I have another idea. Let's race!" He was bursting out of his fur! Diamond and Kool dropped their corsage boxes, too.

"Where to?" Kool asked, looking over at Diamond.

Jett suggested, "Let's go to the iron gym. I need to work off some energy."

Diamond agreed, "I could use a good whisker scratch and a blow-out. You could use a blow-out too, Kool."

"What are ya sayin,' dude?" asked Kool. "You sayin' I look scruffy?"

"Scruffy Katt. That's your new name," laughed Diamond.

Each tom picked up a box in his teeth, Jett had to take two, and they took off running. They raced to The Eye of the Tiger, the heavy-duty iron gym that focuses on muscle building and strength endurance. The corsages took a bit of a beating, especially the boxes that were poked with sharp fangs. They reached the door at the same time and tagged it as if it were theirs.

"Hi, toms," said Mia, the fluff behind the reception desk. "Are you here to pump up or did you come to look at me?" She fluffed her fur and straightened her silk scarf.

"We're here to pump up and look at you," said Diamond.

She smiled and said, "Sign in, please."

Diamond asked, "Do you have a cooler to put these flowers in so they won't wilt?"

She looked through the see-through-tops of the mangled boxes. "Oooh, purrtty. Sure. I'll take care of it." The three toms grinned from ear to ear, feeling quite proud of themselves for getting corsages for their fluff-friends.

The gym has high vaulted ceilings to accommodate the extra high climbing posts that are used for speed climbing.

"Beat ya to the top," challenged Jett. He headed for a post. The race was on. Let's guess who won. Maybe the one with the most energy? And who might that be? Jett is just so energized lately. You'd think a lightning bolt named Jade hit him. They raced down the posts and jumped to the floor. Jett continued his climbing marathon, but Diamond shook out and padded over to the row of combs attached to the wall. He scratched, and scratched some more.

Kool ran two miles on the cat run. "Come on, Diamond. Get on the cat run and roll your lard."

Diamond was just being lazy. "I don't feel like very much exercise today. I'll get too exhausted." He was thoroughly enjoying scratching his chin. "After all, I *am* Master of Ceremonies tonight, in *two* places! I have to conserve my strength." He yawned.

Jett continued giving the tallest climbing post the total workout. Up and down and down and up.

Kool got off the cat run and headed over to the combs to scratch his long fur. A sign overhead said: *Please remove your fur from the combs when you are finished.* Diamond just kept scratching his face and chin. His tight whiskers are so itchy. Kool scratched his face and ran his body along the combs. He was starting to smooth out. He observed himself in the mirror and commented, "I need a coat cut."

Diamond checked himself out in the mirror and he was happy with his reflection. Honestly, he was about to jump out of his fur, too. He has been planning tonight's special party for the past six months, but he can't tell a soul about it. This is ultra secret stuff. Not even Dutchey knows anything. He thought to himself, "I can't wait to see her face when she sees who will be there tonight!" He wore a silly grin. He can't even tell Kool or Jett. It has to be a surprise! So many secrets. It will be worth it, though. He smiled and twitched his whiskers, then sneezed three times.

"Let's blow-out," said Kool.

"Okay."

They clawed their fur out of the combs and added it to the big furrball in the corner bucket.

Kool tried to get Diamond to talk. "So dude, now that it's just you and me, tell me about the party tonight. Fill me in on every detail."

"Well... you already know about the flowers and balloons."

"Yeah, and, what about all those sealed up boxes marked *Top Secret*. What's so *secret?*"

"Well, everyone has to wear something tonight. That's what's in the boxes marked *Top Secret.*"

"And... ?"

"Well, all your favorite foods will be there."

"Yeah... and... ?"

Diamond was tempted, but he can't wait to see Kool's face when he has to wear this... nope. Can't tell! "You know I want to tell you, bud, but I can't, and you'll be glad I didn't, because you will be so surprised. You understand, don't you, bud?" He looked at Kool and tilted his head to the side. Kool glowered at him. "You do under-stand—don't you?"

Kool snarled, "Dutchey's right! You are tight whiskered!"

Diamond yawned and stretched. "I just want all of you to be sur-prised to the *Maxx!*" He laughed. Another secret he can't tell.

"Okay, okay, Mr. Secrets." Kool shook his head, disappointed. "This party had better be good, that's all I can say."

"It will be, I promise." They entered the blow-out room and a few minutes later they came out all fluffy and handsome.

"Are ya ready, partner?" Kool asked Diamond.

"I am, but I don't think we're going to get him to slow down," said Diamond, referring to Jett and his maniacal climbing.

"Bud," yelled Kool, "you're gonna give yourself a heart attack."

"Come on, dude," yelled Diamond, "we gotta go."

Jett was all the way to the ceiling. "Okay, I'm coming down," he promised. He was about six feet from the floor, jumped to another pole a few feet away, and then jumped to the floor with a purrfect landing. "Look at me. Not even out of breath."

"You're so crazy, show-off," laughed Diamond.

"One quick scratch and I'm ready," said Jett. He headed over to the combs.

Diamond said, "Come on, Kool. Let's get the flowers."

As they approached the front desk, Mia looked up from her *Good Catkeeping* magazine.

"Wow, Toms! You look great!"

"Thanks," replied Diamond.

"Thank you," said Kool.

"Would you like your corsages now?"

"Yes, please," answered smiley Diamond.

Mia padded to the back room and returned with the cold little boxes. "Lucky fluffs!"

Diamond asked her, "By chance, do you have a piece of string?" Mia pawed through her desk drawer and found a long piece of string and gave it to Diamond. "Thanks, Mia."

"You're welcome. Bye, toms."

Kool said, "Later, Mia."

"Have a great night, Grads!" she said smiling and waving her paw.

Jett was waiting at the door. "Thanks, Mia. Come on, buds! What are ya waitin' for?" Kool and Diamond looked at each other and frowned.

"Sorry *we* kept *you* waiting, dude," remarked Kool as they went out the door.

Once outside, Diamond told Jett, "Here bud, you're in charge of the flowers." He tied the string around the mangled boxes to connect them and hung the string across Jett's neck.

"See you there," said Jett. He took off for home, leaving them in the dust.

"Later, dude."

Kool and Diamond cruised down the streets of Heavenly Hills saying, "hey" to every cat that passed by.

"Congratulations, Toms!"

"Have a great ceremony tonight!"

"Go, Toms!" someone yelled from a passing car.

"Tonight is going to be a total blast!" said excited Diamond.

"Still won't tell me, bud?" asked Kool.

"You know I want to. Quit tempting me!"

28

Meanwhile, the fluffs were thoroughly enjoying their royal pampering.

"Ahhh," moaned Dutchess. Mickey was massaging her legs, paws and, "Oooh! Not too hard, Mickey," she cried out as he massaged her sore leg.

"I think a little ice should help this old leg," suggested Mickey. He left the room and returned with an ice pack wrapped in a thin towel. He gently placed it on her leg. "How is that, my little friend?"

"Okay, I guess. Thank you." Her smile was upside down.

"Now, how about that paw pad soak?"

"That would be lovely," she sighed.

Mickey inspected her paws and scrunched his nose. "Your claws are nicked and split. Just look at your pads. You have a deep crack in this one."

"It hurts, too."

"What a mess." He shook his head. "You will need my premium oil. Wait here."

"Okay."

He returned with a small bowl of warmed oil that smelled sweet, like wisteria, and he gently placed her front paws in the bowl. "Ahhh. This feels wonderful. You are too good to me, Mickey."

"Nothing is too good for my little friend," Mickey replied with a sympathetic smile. He felt bad about what happened. "Okay, Miss Graduate, you just relax while I go and check on your friends."

A few moments passed as Dutchey lay there with her paws in the bowl and an ice pack on her leg. She thought about her fall and her lost life, and she felt a bit lonely. Then, suddenly, out of nowhere, she felt enlightened. She spoke out loud to the mirror, "I have eight lives to live and I am more determined than ever to live the rest of my lives to the fullest! I promise myself I will not let this ruin my celebration or take away any of the wonderful memories waiting to happen!" She nodded her head and smiled at the mirror.

"Hey, fluff-friend," said excited Lashes, parading into the room. She looked around and asked, "Who ya talkin' to, Dutchey?"

"Uh, just myself. Lashes, you look beautiful! You are so fluffy! Your tail looks a lot better, too."

"Thank you!" Her fluffy tail was straight up and she was wearing a great big smile. "May I introduce Princess Cleocatra and Princess Jade." The two fluffs from Pintac made a royal entrance.

"Wow!" exclaimed Dutchey. "Fluffs, you look wonderful! Let me see your claws." They held out their claws for inspection. "Very nice! I just love a French pedicure! It's so classy."

Jade asked Lashes, "Do you perm your whiskers, or do they naturally curl like that?"

Lashes answered proudly, "These babies are all naturelle! That's how I got my name."

"I love the look!" said Jade.

"So do I!" agreed Cleo. "We should perm our whiskers."

Lashes said, "I love your whiskers, Jade. White tips, are they naturelle?"

"Definitely," replied Jade.

Dutchey complimented Cleo, "Your mauve eyes are so beautiful! Nobody in our class has mauve eyes."

Cleo batted her eyes. "Thank you very much."

Lashes asked, "How's your leg, Dutch?"

"Okay, I guess, but enough of that. I have made an important decision."

"What?" everybody asked.

"I've decided I'm not going to let what happened yesterday bring me down or ruin my big night!"

"That's my fluff!" exclaimed Mickey as the fluffs cheered. Cleo whistled and Lashes did an impressive cheerleading jump.

Dutchey snarled, "I won't be doing that jump for a while."

"We are going to have such a blast tonight," exclaimed very excited Lashes, "I can't wait!"

After her massage and paw pad soak, Romeo, the pedicurist, gave Dutchey a French pedicure and Lorenzo blew out her fur.

Mickey announced, "Okay fluffs, it is time for your mist."

Dutchess stood up and stretched out her sore leg. "Ahhhh. My leg feels much better. Thank you, Mickey. You are truly magnificent!"

"It is my pleasure, Miss Dutchess." He smiled and pinched her whiskers.

"Come, come fluffs. Your mist is waiting," rushed Lorenzo. "Shall I call your chauffeur, Miss Dutchess? We don't want you to be late for your big night."

"Yes, please."

The fluffs padded into another room and stood under the mist that smelled like lavender. They admired themselves and each other in the full-length mirrors.

As they padded out of the misting room, Mickey asked, "How does everyone feel?"

"Wonderful!" the fluffs said together. "Thank you! Thank you!"

"You are all so gorgeous!" exclaimed Lorenzo.

"Congratulations and have a great evening!" added Mickey.

"Thank you," replied Lashes and Dutchey.

"It was very nice meeting you, Cleo and Jade," said Tootie.

Cleo said, "Thank you so much for squeezing us in!"

Jade added, "I feel royally pampered! Thank you!"

Tootie replied, "You're very welcome. Enjoy your big night, fluffs!"

"We will! We will!" exclaimed excited Lashes and Dutchey. The four exquisite fluffs blew kisses as they went out the front door.

"See you tonight at the party," said Dutchess.

"Bye," said the fluffs.

"Bye, ladies."

Q was asleep on the couch in the waiting area. Jade was deciding whether to leave him there... or not..."Wake up, Q," she said, "let's go." Q follows her wherever she goes. Jade likes him, but she enjoys her privacy, too. "Why have a bodyguard?" she wondered. "No one bothers me. No one even knows where I am. The news reported that. Life is so much more fun here than in Pintac."

29

"I feel great!" said Cleo as they padded out into the sunshine.

"I needed that massage," said Dutchey.

"Is it behaving any better?" asked Lashes, pointing at her leg.

"I think so," replied Dutchey as she put her ears back trying to be brave.

As they strolled down the street, they peeked through the windows of the fashion boutiques and the fine jewelry stores.

Jade exclaimed, "Wow! Look at that tail ring with the emerald gemstone!" She pointed her freshly pedicured claw tip at the gorgeous piece of jewelry in the display window. Green must be her favorite color. "Just look at the detail and the sparkle."

"Oooh, awww," agreed the fluffs.

A white stretch limo with gold trim pulled up to the curb. Dutchey announced, "Our limo has arrived! Come on, cats." Q opened the door and everyone hopped in.

"Thank you for picking us up, Jeebs," said Dutchey.

"You're welcome, Miss Dutchess," replied Jeebs, the family chauffeur who has served them for years and years.

Dutchey asked, "Jeebs, would you please drive by The Sphinx, so Jade, Cleo, and Q can see our club?"

Jeebs nodded, "Sure thing, Miss."

"What's in the cooler, Dutchey," Lashes asked as she padded to the cooler and opened the little door.

"Good stuff, I hope," replied Dutchey, "I'm hungry."

Lashes found a six-pack of squid squeeze. "Mmm. This is good stuff." She passed out a bowl and a straw to each cat. She tossed a bag of crunchies to Q and then sat down next to Dutch.

Jade held up her bowl, "I'd like to make a toast. To the most beautiful fluffs in Heavenly Hills!"

"Here! Here!" agreed Cleo. They drank to their new fluff-friends, Lashes and Dutchey.

Jade and Cleo stared out the window as the limo cruised through the exciting streets of Heavenly Hills. As they approached The Sphinx, Dutchey announced, "Okay, everyone, we're almost here!"

Jade exclaimed, "Wow! Wow! Wow!" Her eyes opened wider as she lowered the window. "Stop the limo! Stop the limo!"

Cleo laughed, "That's her favorite saying, 'Stop the limo! Stop the limo'!"

"Well, just look at that!" Jade paused in admiration. "Cleo, look at that beautiful blue sequined building shaped like a cat on the hunt! Oh look! The mouth is wide open and there's a pink carpet that looks like a tongue, and look—the fangs are pillars!" She looked over at Dutchey, bewildered. "Does one go into the mouth to get inside?"

"Yep!" laughed Dutchey. "That's my father's idea. He's crazy!"

"It's amazing!" said Jade. "I've never seen anything like it! Look how it sparkles in the sunlight."

"It's very cool inside," agreed informative Lashes, "very exotic and trendy."

"We'll have to crash it one night while you fluffs are still here," Dutchey said with a gleam in her eye.

"That'll be fun!" said Cleo.

"Big fun!" agreed Jade. Q glowered at Jade and Cleo. "Don't worry, Q. You can come, too," assured Jade.

"Okay, let's go," Dutchey instructed Jeebs. "We're dropping Cleo, Jade, and Q at Jett's, then to Lashes' house, then home."

Jeebs nodded as he drove the spotless limo over the bridge and up the hill to Jett's mansion in Castleberry Estates. Everyone ate, drank, and admired their claws.

"I'm just so excited!" burst out Lashes.

Everyone laughed at her, even Q, who was scarfin' down his crunchies, as if there was a race.

As they pulled up in front of Jett's mansion, Jade and Cleo admired the front yard. Surrounding the circular drive are carefully trimmed hedges, enormous trees, and colorful flowers. The long driveway is bordered on each side with lavender lily of the nile. The limo stopped at the end of the driveway. Jett's family must already be there because there are three limos lined up in the driveway. Q and the fluffs jumped out and Dutchey and Lashes said their good-byes with promises to see them later this evening. During the ride to Lashes' house, she and Dutchey lay down on the black leather seat and sighed. They both closed their eyes and were soon sound asleep.

"Fluffs... " coaxed Jeebs, "we're here... fluffs... "

Lashes yawned as she got out of the limo and padded into her mansion to collect her graduation cape. Dutchey just lay there. It's been a long day already and she was finally comfortable. Lashes is supposed to meet her family in the parking lot by the gymnasium in ninety minutes. Her father, the Mayor of Heavenly Hills, is going to make a speech at the Graduation ceremony as well. Mayor Malcolm Holcomb is pure Silver Point Persian. He is big, silver, and hand-some. He has a twin brother, Zachary, who is just as big and just as handsome. Uncle Zach and Auntie Consuelo serve up a delight-ful meal at their underwater restaurant, Below Sea Level. Lashes has twin cousins, Taffee and Toffee, who are two years older. Pure Persian and absolutely lovely!

30

After a few minutes, the limo arrived at Dutchey's mansion. Her family was there too, because there are four limos parked in the long driveway.

"Hi, beautiful fluffs," praised Ming as they came through the front door. No more up the maple tree for Dutchey. Ming hugged the decked out fluffs.

"Wow!" exclaimed Blossom. "You both look great!" She sniffed the air, "Smell good, too! Like a flower garden!"

"Thank you," replied Dutchess.

"Thank ya, little sis," said smiley Lashes.

"How are you, darling?" Mom asked her oldest.

"Great!" Dutchey replied. "A massage and blow-out, a little nap in the limo, I feel great!"

Mom requested, "Let me see your claws, fluffs." They held out their paws and extended their claws for inspection. "Nice. Very nice," smiled Mom.

Dutchess turned over her paw. "Look, I have a split in my paw pad."

"Meowch!" said Blossom.

"Meowch!" repeated Mom. "You may not be at your best dear, but you look wonderful!"

Dutchess beamed. She knew she looked good, in spite of everything that happened yesterday. She commented, "Mom, you look amazing tonight!"

Lashes added, "Your jewelry is stunning!"

"Thank you, darlings. You are both very sweet. Dutchey, your Grandfluffs and Grandtoms, aunties and uncles and cousins are here.

We're already sitting at the grand dining table. Would you fluffs join us for liver soufflé with giblet sauce and sardine surprise topped with whipped crème for dessert?" Lashes and Dutchess looked at each other and licked their whiskers.

"Yes," said Lashes.

"Lead the way," agreed Dutchey.

As they entered the formal dining room, the family yelled out, "Congratulations Dutchess and Lashes!"

The fluffs went around the table, hugging and kissing everyone. The Grandfluffs reminisced about, "How it seems just like yesterday that you were little kittens. Where did all the time go?"

"I'm so glad all of you could come!" said Dutchey. "This is going to be a fantastic night!"

Adoring statements were said, such as, "We wouldn't miss it! We're so proud of you! Our baby kittens!"

"I can't believe how beautiful you both look!" exclaimed Dutchey's Auntie Maya. "Well, really I can. Look at your breeding!" She held up her paws and looked around the table. Everyone laughed with her.

Lashes said with her biggest smile, "I'm just glad you're all here to party with us! As for me, I am so excited!" Her tail fluffed out as well as the fur on her back.

"I can't wait to see your family," said Dutchey's Grandfluff. "It's been far too long!"

"Yes! It has!" agreed Lashes.

"Sit down, fluffs," said Dutchey's dad, Siam Sam.

The fluffs sat down and Lashes turned to her buddy and teased, "Now Dutchey, don't mess yourself up!"

Dutchey replied, "Just don't make me laugh! And that goes for all of you!" She stuck her tongue out and everyone laughed at her.

The party has already started!

31

After dinner, Lashes helped Dutchey limp up the stairs to do final touches: smooth fur, make sure they were minty fresh, and apply a bit more lavender perfume.

"More perfume, Dutchey?" asked Lashes.

"Yes, my dear. Just a bit more," she replied with a snobby flair. They helped each other put on their white satin capes and admired themselves in the mirror.

"I'm so glad we're doing this together," Lashes said to Dutchey.

"Me, too. I'm so glad we're best friends."

"Through thick and thin!" added Lashes. They exchanged hugs, big smiles, and their friends forever pinky claw hook.

"I hope we can be cheerleading co-captains next year," said Dutchess.

"We will have so much fun!" agreed Lashes.

"We will go to all the games and cheer on the *tom-toms!* Oops, I mean the *toms.*" They burst out laughing.

"We'll have to be careful about that *tom-tom* bit," said Lashes.

"We will, won't we?" agreed Dutchey. Ming was watching from the doorway and snapped a picture. Dutchey complained, "Mom, we weren't ready! Take another one!" The fluffs stood together and posed, looking very snobby with their noses in the air. Mom snapped a picture.

"How about a nice pose this time, fluffs? Say lobster."

"Lobster."

"Was that nice?" asked Lashes.

"Yes. That was very nice."

Siam Sam yelled up the stairs, "Come on, fluffs. We gotta go or we'll be late."

"Coming, Dad," the fluffs said together as they padded along the catwalk balcony and reached the top of the staircase.

Dutchey looked at Lashes and said, "Come on, fluff-friend, let's get our purr on."

Excited Lashes replied, "Let's do it!"

"Say mice," Dad said, snapping pictures.

"Mice."

The whole family looked up the stairs expressing oooohs and awwwws. The young fluffs wore beautiful smiles as they carefully padded down the spiral staircase in their lovely white graduation capes.

32

Meanwhile, Diamond was in his bedroom checking out this cape he has to wear tonight. It's shiny and a nice shade of royal blue, it has snaps and elastics, it's square, but there is just no rhyme or reason to it, and no directions. He was sitting on his bed, studying it when a big ball of fur blasted through the window, appearing to be chased by a similar blue cape.

Diamond laughed, "Hi, Kool. Having a problem, dude?"

Kool gagged, "I'm choking in this thing and it's giving me a wedgie!"

Diamond unsnapped the collar snaps, but Kool managed to get even more tangled up in the leg elastics. He wound up on his back, growling, hissing, and spitting. "Phftt. Phftt."

Diamond held one of the corners steady. "Easy now, bud. Lift your legs out, one at a time."

Kool lifted his legs out and leapt backward. "That thing tried to kill me!"

Diamond laughed, "Where's the video camera when you need it? Okay, let's figure this out." He studied it for a few moments and decided, "I think if we snap the collar first, then put our legs through the elastics, it will fit better. Put the cape over my back. Now snap the collar." Kool snapped it on the very last snap. Diamond stuck out his tongue and stretched his neck. "Now hold the corners and I'll step into the elastics." He stepped into them. "See, nothing to it." He jumped on his pole and climbed straight to the top. "Look. I'm *Super-Cat*." He jumped to the floor and ran in circles around the room, his cape waving in the wind.

Kool put his ears back and shook his head. "Okay show-off. Help me get into mine, but I'll tell ya right now, I know I'm not gonna like it."

Diamond centered the cape on Kool's back and snapped the collar. Kool stuck out his tongue and put his ears back. This next step was where he had gotten into trouble. Diamond held the corners as Kool awkwardly flopped his furry legs into the elastics. He calmly collected himself, but as he turned to look in the mirror, *boing!* The end of one of the elastics popped free and shot him in his other leg. "Well," Kool sighed as his cape slid down, "maybe it's not meant for me to wear a cape tonight. You don't think Principal Fitt will mind, do you?" He grabbed at the cape around his neck, popped the snaps, and yanked it off.

"Yeah, I think he'll mind," replied Diamond, pawing through his desk, searching for the stapler. Kool picked up his cape and smoothed it out on the bed. Diamond stapled the elastic band back onto the cape. There were a few tiny rips, but he stapled it anyway. He looked over at Kool's big fat furry legs and decided to staple all of the elastics. "Just to be sure. Okay bud, let's try it again."

Resigned Kool sighed, "I guess a tom's gotta do what a tom's gotta do." He stood limp as Diamond put the cape over his back and snapped the collar. He took a deep breath and reluctantly stepped into the elastic bands. "Do I dare look in the mirror? Do I dare even move?" he asked Diamond.

"Well, if I do say so myself, you look, um, cool, Kool Katt! *Well, actually,*" he said in a snobby voice, "*You look intelligent and studious!*"

"*Oh yes,*" Kool replied, as he reluctantly turned around and spied his reflection. "*That's the look I was going for.*" When he looked in the mirror, he was actually quite pleased. "Hey, it fits a lot better your way. I do look *good!*"

"You sure do."

They posed macho poses in front of the mirror and agreed, "*We look good!*"

They shook their complicated macho paw shake and Kool remarked, "It sure would be great to be co-captains of the soccer team at Heavenly Hills High in September."

"We'll show èm how it's done," nodded confident Diamond. "Practice starts in three and a half weeks."

Kool nodded in agreement. "I can't wait." They exchanged looks of mutual admiration and then looked at the clock.

"Time to go, bud."

33

The Big Night Has Finally Arrived!

The soccer field at Paw Valley Middle School has been transformed into a fragrant ceremonial wonder. The grassy field now has white squares arranged in straight rows for each graduate to sit on. Gold braided rope surrounds the graduate seating area, the center aisle, and the stage. Accompanying the sparkling streamers from this morning are balloons and floral arrangements, courtesy of The Pretty Petal. Family, friends, and guests are directed to sit in the bleachers surrounding the field. The Graduates are to meet in the gymnasium, with their capes on, one half hour before the ceremony is to begin.

Miss Hissy is in the gym, running around like a maniac, adjusting, smoothing, and helping with those pesky elastic leg bands and collar snaps. "Kittens, stop that!" she exclaimed as Paw Valley's elite graduates were running around the gym, snapping each other's elastics.

The bleachers are filling up fast with Heavenly Hills' finest: Big cats, little cats, in between cats, old cats, young cats, and baby kittens. This is definitely a family celebration.

As Jeebs drove the limo into the parking lot, Dutchess pointed her snaggle claw, "There's Jett's limo. There's Jett and his family. Where's Diamond and Kool?"

"There they are," pointed Lashes. "Where's my family? They're supposed to meet me here." The fluffs looked in every direction.

"Look. Your limo is over there," said Blossom. "Where's Honey?" (Lashes' nine-year-old sister and Blossom's best friend).

As the limousine came to a stop, Diamond and Kool ran over and mannerly opened the door for their fluff-friends.

Dutchey admired the toms as she stepped out. "Well now, don't you toms look spiffy?"

Kool and Diamond broke into song, "We're too macho for our capes, too macho for our capes… "

Ming laughed and rubbed whiskers with them. "Knock èm out, toms!" she whispered in each of their ears and gave each tom a kiss on their head.

"We will! We will!"

Diamond said to Dutchey's parents, "I want you and your family to have an especially good time tonight. Let your fur down and have some fun!" He and Siam Sam shook paws.

"Thank you, darling," replied Ming, "we intend to. Where's your family? We want to sit with them."

"They're saving seats for you."

"Great!"

Lashes' family found her and quickly padded over. She greeted her Grandcats with whisker kisses and hugs while her dad (Mayor Mac) and Uncle Zach snapped family pictures. Her mom, Lily, and Lily's younger sister caught up.

Lily said, "Lashes, Dutchey, I have a surprise for you!" The fluffs turned around and saw someone unexpected.

Lashes exclaimed, "Auntie Rose, you're here!"

Auntie Rose gushed with excitement, "Surprise! Surprise! Kiss! Kiss!"

"We didn't think you were coming!" exclaimed Dutchey.

"And miss your big night? I wouldn't dream of it! Congratulations fluffs!" Lashes and Dutchey received big hugs and whisker kisses from Auntie Rose while she gave special instructions. "Okay fluffs, as you *gracefully* pad up the center aisle, keep your heads up and do not look at the ground. And by all means *smile!*"

The fluffs took Auntie Rose's advice very seriously. "Okay."

"We'll catch up later, little nieces! I have so much to tell you!"

Auntie Rose is just beautiful. She has soft and fluffy cream-colored fur, and caramel-colored legs, ears, and tail. She looked positively stunning wearing a purple sequined, wide brimmed hat with a lavender plume. The seventeen-carat amethyst necklace she was wearing made her eyes look lavender. Her whiskers are quite curly, too. At twenty-four-years-old, she is a super model who travels the world.

Lashes exclaimed, "Auntie, I love your hat!"

Dutchey added, "I do, too! You look very fashionable!"

"Thank you, fluffs. You both look positively lovely in your white graduation capes!"

Lily poked Mac in the ribs. "Mac, don't just stand there. Take more pictures."

Lashes, Dutchey, and Auntie Rose posed for a very snobby picture. Auntie Rose gave her other niece, Honey, a big hug. Then she hugged Lashes' cousins, Toffee and Taffee. "Where's my nephew?" Mac II is Lashes' older brother by two years. He is quite large, as handsome as his dad, and has blue eyes with an amazing sparkle. Mac II gave Auntie Rose a swing around hug and her hat went flying. "Wheeee! You are getting so big and strong my macho nephew!" He put her down and she put her hat back on. "Now, where are my other handsome grads?" Auntie Rose hugged Diamond and Kool, exchanging whisker kisses with style and flair, even though her hat kept falling off. Dutchey's family greeted Lashes' family with whisker kisses and hugs. All that kissing, purring, and accidental whisker pulling, lots of love was being spread in the parking lot by the gym. Dutchey's and Lashes' Grandfluffs greeted each other with a whole bunch of compliments about, "How well they are holding up at such old ages." One of them remarked, "It's that miracle vaccine that keeps us so young and beautiful." The Grandtoms greeted each other with paw shakes and chatted about the latest sports event and score.

The rest of Kool's family finally arrived. His Grandcats have come quite a distance to be here for the ceremony and celebration. Kool's auntie, uncle, and cousins escorted them out of their limo and the whole family padded over quickly to exchange hugs and take pictures.

Jade wedged herself between Cleo and Jett as the family headed over to where all the families were gathering. She thought Jett looked outstanding in his cape. For some reason, she did not want to let him out of her sight. It seems as though the love bug has bitten her, too. Everyone congratulated Jett and he made introductions.

"You all remember my cousin, Cleo."

Smiley Cleo greeted, "Hi, everyone!"

"Hi, Cleo." All the mom-fluffs hugged her.

Jett continued, "Jade, I mean, Princess Jade, this is everyone!"

"Hi, Everyone," Jade said with a lovely smile. There were so many cats staring at her, she didn't know who to look at first! She thought to herself, "Wow! Big families!"

Ming commented, "So, this is the lovely young fluff we've seen all over the television. It is so very nice to meet you."

"Thank you. It's very nice meeting all of you."

"Are you enjoying your stay, dear?" asked Lily.

"Yes. I love it here. Everyone is very kind to me."

All eyes turned and stared at Jett. His face changed from a content cat to a cat in the headlights. "What?"

Everyone teased him at the same time, *"Mysterious Stranger!"*

"Oh," he said as he relaxed and scratched his collar area with his back leg. "I know," he said, a bit embarrassed, "caught red-pawed on film, kissing the paw of the Princess from Pintac." He looked over at Jade. "We sure did make spectacles of ourselves, didn't we?"

"That's an understatement!" she replied with a grin.

"Enjoy your stay, Princess," said Mayor Mac. The dad-toms in the group nodded their heads in agreement.

"Thank you. I am having a fabulous time."

Handsome Mac II piped up, "It's an honor to meet you, Princess Jade. I'm Lashes' older brother, Mac."

"It's very nice to meet you, Mac."

Jett grit his fangs. Mac II sensed a hint of jealousy. Quickly he said, "I've gotta find Crystal." (Diamond's cousin who is two years older). "Looks like Mom and Dad will be a while. Happy Graduation, everyone! Don't trip. See you after." He ran away.

"Bye, Mac."

All eyes were now focused on both graduating fluffs. Each fluff was given a little box from their mothers. They looked at each other with anticipation and opened the lids. They each carefully lifted out a gold chain with a gold square. One side of the square was smooth, the other side jagged. The engraving on one square said *Best* and on the other said *Friends*. They fit the gold squares together like puzzle pieces. "Awww," they said together, all misty. They helped each other put them on, and then they stood together, whisker to whisker, holding the gold squares together with their claws while their dads snapped pictures.

Ming yelled, "Wait! Wait! Change places, fluffs. It's not supposed to say *Friends Best.*"

"Oh!" The fluffs quickly switched places and fit the squares together the right way. They smiled pretty for the camera and then hugged each other and their parents.

Dutchey exclaimed, "Thank you for our necklaces."

Lashes dramatically added, "We will never take them off."

"We are very proud of you, sweetheart," Mac said to his daughter. Lily dabbed her eyes with her lovely new scarf.

"I love you, Mom and Dad," Lashes replied. She dabbed her eyes with her mom's scarf, too.

Proud Siam Sam said, "Our hearts are filled with love and pride as we watch you graduate this evening, Dutchess."

"We love you so much, Dutchey," said proud mother Ming.

Dutchey replied, "I love you both, too."

"Wish I was graduating," commented Blossom.

The pre-teen cats all nodded their heads in agreement, "Us, too!"

"Soon enough, my little kittens," replied Lily. "Soon enough."

"Group picture. Group picture," Sam said, directing the grads together. "Smile."

"Purrfect!" said Ming. "Have a great ceremony, kittens. We will see you afterwards. Come on, everyone. Let's find Diamond's family."

Dutchey's Grandfluff addressed the other Grandfluffs. "Ladies, walk with us. We have so much to catch up on."

Lashes' Grandfluff began, "Well, did you hear what happened at last weeks meeting of The Society for Dramatic Felines…?" Her words faded into the crowd heading for the bleachers. Everyone waved as the families disappeared into the crowd. Mac II, Crystal, and Bobby (Kool's cousin two years older) had met up with each other and ran over to the fluffs.

"I don't know if Heavenly Hills High is ready for you two," laughed Mac II, hugging them both.

"You go, fluffs!" said Bobby. He squeezed them both with strong hugs.

"Don't you worry, fluffs!" reassured Crystal. "I'll show you the ropes. You both look lovely tonight! So grown up." She is quite lovely herself, with those intense, turquoise Castleberry eyes!

"Thank you," gushed the fluffs as they exchanged hugs.

Crystal inspected their new necklaces. "So purrty." The three exchanged hugs again and then she demanded, "Where's my cousin?"

"Here I am," said Diamond, padding over. Crystal gave him a big hug and he clicked claws with Mac II and Bobby.

Kool padded over, "Hey, cats!"

At the same time, the older teen cats said, "Congrats, Kool Katt!" They exchanged hugs and paw shakes, too.

"Jett!" Mac II yelled. He looked over and Mac II gave him the claws-up sign. "Have a great night!"

"I will!" He returned a double claws-up sign.

Crystal waved and yelled, "Jett, congratulations!"

"Thanks, Crystal."

Mac II whispered in Crystal's ear, "There's the Princess of Pintac."

"Really? Introduce me! Introduce me!"

"I will at the club. Come on, let's get to our seats."

"Okay," said Crystal. "Have a great ceremony, foxy cats!"

"See you at the club," said Bobby.

"Thanks, cats!" the graduate cats said together as they watched them run away.

Lashes looked at her buddy and said, "Mac's right, you know. Heavenly Hills High may not be ready for us!"

Dutchey replied, "I may have to agree with you *friend best!*" They looked at their necklaces and laughed.

34

$\mathcal{J}$ade and Cleo were watching from a distance and ran over at the last minute.

"Let's see your bling-blings," said excited Cleo. "Awww, how sentimental! Your parents are so sweet."

"You fluffs look outstanding!" complimented Jade. "What kind of fabric are these capes made of?"

"Satin," replied Dutchess.

Inspector Jade ran her paw pads along the smooth satin cape. She commented, "Just lovely! I love the gold thread stitching."

"It's so beautiful!" agreed Lashes.

Kool's fluffy neck was unbearably itchy underneath his extra-small cape. He squirmed around and tried to adjust it with his back leg. Naturally, his claw got stuck and made a long snag. Lashes gave him the once over inspection and smoothed out his cape. She checked and made sure the collar *really* was on the very last snap around his neck. "Sorry it's so tight, Kool. Extend your neck. Maybe that will help." He did that and looked quite funny. Lashes laughed, "Maybe you shouldn't extend your neck." Kool was helpless, but in his heart, he knew he looked *good!*

Diamond whispered to Jett, "Do you have those boxes, bud?"

"Yesss!" He ran over to Q and retrieved the mangled boxes.

Diamond instructed, "Fluffs, close your eyes."

The toms fumbled with the boxes while the fluffs waited anxiously with their eyes closed. Jett looked up, "No peeking now." He was having a particularly difficult time with the two boxes he had to open because the string was in a knot. He was so nervous he was shaking. Finally, he removed the corsages from the boxes and held them up to decide which one was the best. "Well," he thought, "this one has one more little rose bud on it, but this one has more roses that are blooming now." He looked at the corsages and frowned. "I… don't… know… " Quickly he decided both were equally beautiful, put the ribbons in his teeth, and padded over to his cousin and his new friend. After a bit more fumbling, the toms looked at each other, nodded, and together they draped the corsages around the fluffs' necks.

"Okay," gagged Kool, "open your eyes."

"Wow!" exclaimed Dutchess. She sniffed and looked down at her beautiful white rose corsage. "I love you toms!"

"You are the best toms ever!" said Lashes. "We really are so spoiled!" She lifted up her corsage with her paws and put her nose in it.

"How beautiful!" exclaimed Jade.

"Jett, you're the best cousin in the world," said Cleo, giving him a hug.

"I'm glad you're here, cousin," whispered Jett.

"Me, too." She whispered in his ear, "Are you shaking?"

"I'm nervous," he whispered back.

She gave him a big kiss on his head. "You'll be great!" She gave him another hug.

"Thanks, toms," the fluffs said together, all misty.

Miss Hissy was at the door of the gym whistling for all graduates to come in and form a single file line.

Jett addressed Jade and Cleo, "I'll be looking for both of you up in the bleachers."

"I'll be looking for you, too," Jade replied. They exchanged intense looks and shy smiles.

"Come on, Jade and Q," said Cleo, "we should find everyone and get to our seats."

"Okay," said Jade. "This is so wonderful. Enjoy every minute, promise?"

"We promise!" the gang said.

"Wait! Let's have a group huddle," insisted Cleo. They all got into a huddle and power purred. Even Q. "I love this part," said Cleo.

Diamond's enthusiasm was catching, "Here's to accomplishing goals!"

"Yeah!" They all did a paw stack.

Miss Hissy whistled again. "All cats. Come into the gym and line up *now*."

Diamond pointed the way to the soccer field. Cleo, Jade, and Q bid the graduates good-bye and joined the crowd heading to the bleachers. As they trotted along, with Q several steps behind, Jade thought about her recent eighth grade graduation. It was dinner at the palace with her family. It was nice and all, but the only thing different from any other dinner was that there were jellyfish crepes for dessert. There was no official ceremony. Certainly not like this. No big party. No group huddle. No paw stack. No big memories. Oh well. Maybe someday…

The cats in the gym were all hyped up! Thank goodness Nurse Hissy just arrived to help her twin sister, Miss Hissy, who was having a very difficult time calming down all the excited cats. The sisters agreed they were all out-of-control. When Principal Fitt arrived, he shouted to his Graduating Class several times to get in line, but no one paid any attention. He hopelessly stood there and watched 333 cats chasing each other and popping leg bands. He shook his head and looked up at the ceiling, for it was all just too much. He looked over at the clock and realized they only had seven minutes to get it together. He let out several piercing whistles in an effort to get his excited Graduates' attention. Miss Hissy was frantically looking for staples.

"Line up. Line up. Just like rehearsal," instructed Principal Fitt, who was looking quite dashing in a black top hat and bow tie.

35

The bleachers were packed with hundreds of colorful classy cats wearing brilliant diamond collars and platinum tail rings, silk scarves, hats, bow ties, bangles, and beads. The felines of Heavenly Hills were decked out and ready to celebrate!

Paw Valley Middle School's award winning band began playing the traditional ceremonial song, "Pomp and Circumstance."

As the Graduates began their walk across the field, the audience gave them a standing ovation full of cheers, howls, and plenty of whistling. The proud graduates walked in single file. Fluff. Tom. Fluff. Tom. White cape. Blue cape. They looked great! They continued their walk across the track, padded down the aisle of gold braid, and passed through the floral archway into the center of the field that was decorated just for them, all 333 of them. They each stood on a white square and waited for the last graduate to take their place. Principal Fitt stood behind the microphone and declared, *"Don't they look fabulous?"*

The audience cheered and howled for them. Mac II, Crystal, and Bobby were competing in the, "Who Could Howl the Loudest" competition. Jasmine, Heather, Taffee, Toffee, *and* Auntie Rose all joined in.

"Everyone, please take your seats," instructed Principal Fitt. The Graduates waited for his signal and all sat down together. No one was allowed to lie down and no one was allowed to fall asleep.

The cats in the bleachers finally calmed down as the Graduates sat proudly on their white squares, paying full attention to the stage. Principal Fitt spoke, "First we have a little business to take care of. We have speeches to make and awards to give! I am honored to introduce our Mayor of Heavenly Hills, Mayor Malcolm Holcomb. Will you please say a few words to our special graduates?"

Mayor Mac stood behind the microphone and looked out over the colorful audience in the bleachers and the proud Grads sitting on their white squares. He looked striking, or maybe it was the diamond accented Rolex collar he was wearing.

"Graduates, Congratulations! I am very impressed with all of you, the goals you have reached, and all the wonderful accomplishments you have made! You are fine, young cats who should be very proud for realizing how important education is in your life and for striving to do your best! Education is the most important gift you can receive. Once you are full of knowledge, it will never leave you. I am extremely proud of all of you, and, of course, my lovely daughter, Lashes Holcomb. Have a wonderful ceremony, Graduates. You have earned it! I could not be more pleased. Congratulations!"

Lashes leaned across Kool and whispered to Dutchey, "My daddy loves me!"

The euphoric crowd cheered as he left the stage. Everyone loves the Mayor of Heavenly Hills! He is just so inspirational!

Principal Fitt stood behind the microphone, "Now, I would like your Class President, Diamond Castleberry III, to please come up to the stage."

Diamond stood up, paused to look back at his friends, and then trotted up the center aisle toward the stage. As he stood behind the microphone, he watched with pride, 332 cats howling, whistling, and making the biggest fuss ever. Diamond is well liked and very popular. Up in the bleachers, the teenage cats and the little ones were howling their loudest and stomping their paws. The adult toms were beaming with pride and the lady-fluffs were crying.

Diamond began, very, very seriously, "My fellow Graduates… " The audience quieted. It was so quiet you could hear a whisker drop. Without warning, he howled and yelled out, "We Did It!"

That got everyone up on their paws again.

36

The ecstatic Graduates cheered Diamond on. He continued, "We all know how important education is, and we have learned and accomplished so much here at Paw Valley Middle School. What I've personally learned from Principal Fitt is that when you believe in yourself, *everything* is possible!" The crowd howled louder than ever. "My wish for all of us is to pursue a life of happiness, success, contentment, and most of all, to kick tail at Heavenly Hills High!" The excited Graduates whistled and howled. "But, before we get any more out of control, I would like to recognize our great Principal and leader of our school, Principal Fitt. He is the greatest Principal in the whole world!" The Graduates stood up on their squares and cheered for their fearless leader. Diamond continued, "Whenever any of us had a problem, he was always there to listen and provide helpful suggestions and words of wisdom. He always attended every game or match, and supported us with his whole heart. When you're out there on the field during a game, all sweaty, tired, and muddy, and he's rootin' us on, well, his support just means everything! He provides a school where we feel good about learning and have fun, too. I think he should go with us to Heavenly Hills High! What do you think, Grads?" They howled their vocal cords off. As Principal Fitt stood next to Diamond, in front of the elite of Heavenly Hills, he felt very proud and important. Diamond jumped to the ground, reached under the stage with his paw, and pulled out a box wrapped in gold foil with a gold bow. His claw accidentally hooked into the fancy wrapping and ripped it. Everyone waited in anticipation as he pulled on the pretty bow to cover the rip, blew off the dirt and grass, and jumped back on stage with it. He spoke into the microphone, "All of us Graduates decided that you deserve this for putting up with us these past three years." They shook paws and he gave Principal Fitt his present. Piercing howls from the Grads filled the soccer field as Principal Fitt opened his gift. He slowly opened the box and lifted out a gold trophy. Then he looked at the inscription. Diamond said, "Let me read it, Principal Fitt. We all agreed that there should be a message on this gold trophy. It reads, *To Principal Fitt, the best leader 333 cats could ever have!*" Then he gave the trophy back. "Principal Fitt, you are the best, and this is just a little reminder of our years here together!"

Principal Fitt and Diamond exchanged a paw shake. He spoke to the stoic cats on their squares, "All my wonderful Graduates: These past three years have just flown by and I know why. It's because of great students like you that have filled my day with laughter and practical jokes. I must admit, you have gotten me a few times! Thank you very much for this gift. It will remind me of each and every one of you every time I look at it. It's going in my office, *not* the trophy case by the gym."

The proud Grads howled and whistled, and the audience stomped their paws. Diamond jumped off the stage again and fished for another present. He pulled out a little silver box with a silver bow. He blew off the dirt and grass and jumped back on stage. "Miss Hissy, would you please come over here?" The Grads howled and cheered as Miss Hissy reluctantly padded over to Diamond. It was her turn to receive a present. "Hey, I didn't tear this one!" Everyone laughed at Diamond as Miss Hissy opened her gift. "Miss Hissy, we wanted you to know how special you are. You have always been there, answering question after question. You even put up with us when we would come into your office all wet from the rain and shake all over your papers, but you never, ever got mad!" The Grads and audience laughed and Miss Hissy cried. She opened the silver box and peeked through the tissue paper. She lifted out a solid gold apple with a diamond worm poking its head out through the side. Diamond said, "We will never forget you, Miss Hissy, and we hope you will never forget us." He hugged her and she wiped her face on his cape. She was shaking. Diamond urged, "Look at the bottom."

She looked at the bottom and started to full on bawl. The tears were dripping off her whiskers as she sobbed into the microphone.

"The numbers 333 are engraved on the bottom. I love all of you kittens and will miss you so much. Thank you for brightening up each day, even when it was raining, and for remembering me with this. I will proudly place it on my desk and think of all of you when I look at it. Thank you everyone. You are all such wonderful cats! I wish all of you love and luck with your futures!" She blew a big kiss to the Grads with her paw. The Grads stood up, caught her kiss, and blew it back.

Diamond helped Miss Hissy and her gold apple back to her chair. He returned to the microphone and said, "I want her to come with us to Heavenly Hills High, too! Can someone please get her a hanky?" Principal Fitt tried to console her. The audience and Grads kept cheering and whistling.

Diamond continued, "Now I will give out awards for academics and athletics. First, I will acknowledge academic achievements. Will LuLu Brubaker please honor us with her presence on stage? LuLu has maintained a 7.0 grade point average for, well, ever since I've known her." The audience laughed as he draped the gold medallion around her neck. Everyone cheered for LuLu because she deserved it.

Diamond continued, "Kool Katt and Jett Stone, please come up to the stage."

The audience roared for the young toms as they trotted up the center aisle to the stage. Diamond and his buds did their fancy paw shake. Principal Fitt left weeping Miss Hissy and joined Diamond at the microphone because he had to announce Diamond as one of the top academic achievers, as well. The three young toms stood proudly as Principal Fitt announced their 7.0 grade point averages and draped gold medallions around their necks.

Principal Fitt stated, "Education is very important for all who have a strong desire to succeed in life."

The audience cheered with excitement, "Bravo! Bravo!"

Principal Fitt continued, "Next, we will give out awards for athletic achievements. Will Katya Bloobettey and Fangy Bully please come up on stage? Katya has led our fluffs Track and Tree Team to the National Championships and brought home the prestigious Speedy Kitty Trophy. We are all very proud of her—she's a fast little kitty—and wish her continued victories at Heavenly Hills High

School!" Principal Fitt draped a gold medallion around her neck. The audience cheered and howled for Katya and she was happy!

Principle Fitt continued, "Fangy Bully has shown outstanding fishing skills by winning the coveted Fishtail Trophy for catching 151 fish in 151 seconds, setting a new record here at Paw Valley!" Fangy beamed as his medallion was draped. The audience gave him a round of piercing howls.

Principal Fitt continued, "Jett Stone has proven himself to us at every single tennis match. As captain of our *undefeated* Tennis Team, he has led us to the National Finals, earning our school the National Championship Trophy. I see a great future for this young tom." He draped another gold medallion around Jett's neck. Jett beamed up a proud smile to a beautiful black cat sitting somewhere in the bleachers. Jade's heart skipped five beats and eventually skipped away. She and Cleo waved, but she couldn't tell if Jett saw her. One thing is for sure; she likes Jett and definitely wants to get to know him better. The on/off switch in her heart is *on!* And it's flashin' like a neon light! The audience cheered and stomped for Jett.

Principal Fitt turned to Diamond and Kool, "You two!" he began with a proud smile. The audience continued howling so loud, no one could hear. Principal Fitt held out his paws and stepped back from the microphone as if to formally present his outstanding soccer captains. He waited patiently for the crowd to quiet down. Finally, he was able to continue, "These two young toms have led our *undefeated* Soccer Team all the way to the National Playoffs, and won the coveted Championship Trophy for three, I repeat, three years in a row! In fact, our soccer team has earned so many trophies this past year, I think we'll need a bigger display case!" The energetic crowd only got noisier. "We have been honored to have toms with such talent, skill, and strength. We wish them the very best at Heavenly Hills High School. I know we are all very proud of these fine cats. They have great futures in front of them!" The cheering audience and Graduates were wild as the medallions were draped. Up in the bleachers, Crystal did her prowler howl and Mac II covered his ears with his paws. They both laughed and sat a little closer.

Principal Fitt continued, "We also have a couple of super cheerleading captains who have led our cheerleading squad to National Competition and won the highest honor, the Pom-Pom Trophy.

These two lovely fluffs will surely be missed! Will Dutchess Woo and Lashes Holcomb please come front and center!?"

The amount of whistling and howling was crazy! Mac II stood up, roared his prowler howl, and was joined by Auntie Rose who stood up and howled her prowler howl.

Mac II commented, "Wow! Auntie, I'm impressed!"

Auntie Rose laughed, "Oh yeah, I've still got it!"

Crystal said, "Let's howl together, Auntie Rose." They howled a loud and long prowler howl.

Mac II covered both ears. "Yikes! Ladies!"

Lashes and Dutchess gracefully padded up the center aisle toward their friends. Lashes whispered, "Keep your head up and smile. And try not to limp."

Dutchey gritted through her teeth. "I am. I mean, I'm not." She was trying her best to be cool and poised.

Lashes reminded, "Glide Dutch, like we're on the catwalk. And *smile!*"

"I'm trying," Dutchey replied, keeping her head up and counting the steps. She winced as she stubbed her bad foot on the first step up to the stage. No matter how hard she tried, her leg was not cooperating. Diamond rushed over to help her. Principal Fitt draped gold medallions around their necks and the audience roared. Miss Dubois, head cheerleading coach, was up in the bleachers whistling her loudest, and the squad sitting on their white squares were howling their loudest.

Principal Fitt introduced, "Here are our top achievers! These cats have demonstrated academic excellence, as well as consistently demonstrating great perseverance, a healthy desire for competition and excellent athletic achievements. Congratulations Graduates!" The audience was wild with excitement! So were the Graduates!

"This is so much fun!" Jade said to Cleo. They both looked around at all the cats whistling and cheering.

The Graduates on stage beamed with pride as they looked up at the bleachers to find their families. Cameras were snapping away.

Principal Fitt informed everyone, "The spectacular gold trophies won this year are on display in the glass trophy case next to the gymnasium. Okay Graduates, please return to your squares."

There was another standing ovation, "Bravo! Bravo!" the crowd roared and howled.

As she limped back to her square, Dutchey mumbled under her breath, "I'm ignoring you, you old leg." She finally got back to her square and sat down just in time to stand up again.

"Graduates," announced Principal Fitt, "your time has finally come. Will you please stand?"

The Graduates stood at the same time. Row after row, they padded up the center aisle and up the steps to the stage. They looked great! They felt great! As each cat graduated, Principal Fitt announced his or her name and draped a solid gold medallion around his or her neck as the photographer took a picture. The gold medallion is very prestigious. It has engraved 3-D profiles of the great *Professor and Mrs. Felinestein*, the inventors of the age slowing process vaccination essential for long living cats. Finally, it is the gang's turn to graduate and receive their medallions.

"Jett Kensington Stone." The audience cheered and howled.

"Lashes Leezette Holcomb." There was even more howling and whistling.

"Kool Bartholomew Katt." The audience was up on their paws.

"Dutchess Diana Woo." The audience was whistling like crazy.

"And, your Class President, Diamond Thomas Castleberry III."

The audience and Grads were whistling and cheering and hootin' and hollarin.' Crystal, Bobby, and Mac II were howling one continuous howl! Auntie Rose, Heather, Jasmine, Toffee, and Taffee were definitely keeping up with them, maybe louder! Even Q let out a roar! The audience was stomping their paws and making an unbelievable amount of noise!

Cleo turned to Jade, "This is so exciting!"

Jade replied, "I know. I love all the cheering. This is all so wonderful! I wish I'd brought my camera."

All of the lady-fluffs: moms, aunties, and grandfluffs were crying and blubbering, with pride, of course. The tween cats were giggling, but secretly can't wait for their turn in a few years. The little fluffettes and tommy-toms were howling the loudest they could.

"Are you getting pictures, Sam?" slobbered Ming.

"Yes, dear," replied Sam, clicking away.

"More, Sam. Don't stop clicking." She could barely get the words out.

Jade kept her eyes fixed on Jett as he and his friends trotted down the side aisle back to their squares. They looked very happy and quite proud of themselves. They gave each other congratulatory hugs and high paws. Jade and Cleo observed and commented about every tom as they graduated.

"He's kinda hunky," Cleo said about one cat.

"They're cute," Jade said about a set of twins.

"I wonder if Jett knows him," wondered Cleo.

"Hmmm," pondered Jade.

Finally, the last name was announced and the last gold medallion was draped. The audience quieted down as the sky turned into beautiful shades of pink, yellow, and orange. The sun was peacefully setting over the ocean.

At one end of the field was a big screen and large speakers. Music started playing and the video began. There were pictures of everyone doing something fun: the soccer games, the tennis matches, track and tree events, the fishing derby, an aerial shot of the cheerleaders in a circle with their pom-poms, looking up at the camera. Cute fluffs. There were pictures of cats snoozing on the quad, and cats racing to see who could run the fastest, jump over the highest fence, or climb the highest tree on the school grounds. The video ended with a group shot of Sweet Secretary Hissy and Principal Fitt being mobbed with affection by the eighth grade class.

Principal Fitt instructed, "Graduates, will you please stand one more time?"

The Grads stood at full attention. Each Graduate's gold medallion reflected the low afternoon twilight.

Principle Fitt declared, "Graduates, I wish you love and prosperity throughout your entire lives. Fluffs and Toms, I would like to present to you the Graduating Class of Paw Valley Middle School."

The soccer field was crazy with excitement! So much accomplished and yet so much to come! The Graduation was a huge success! No mishaps, no one tripped over his or her cape, no wedgies. There were only a few popped elastics, but no one fell asleep. What a truly rewarding ceremony it turned out to be!

37

Soon the soccer field was vacant and took on its normal appearance. All of the flowers and balloons were whisked away to the Heavenly Hills Country Club for *The Party of the Century!* A few tinsel streamers were left behind, caught in the soccer net, blowing in the breeze. The Graduates made their final stop at the gymnasium to turn in their capes, a gagging relief for some. Next on the agenda is Diamond's big surprise party. The Grads all crammed into one limousine and are on their way to the Heavenly Hills Country Club to party down. Everyone is in celebration mode now!

Diamond exclaimed, "Hey, fellow Grads! Wasn't all that recognition absolutely great?!"

"That was so awesome!" exclaimed Dutchey. "I feel so important!" She started purring.

"I loved it!" replied Lashes. Her purr was so loud, she was rattling. She wore a hanger smile.

Kool teased, "Can I take the hanger out of your mouth now?"

Lashes laughed, "I can't help it! I'm too excited!" She put her paws up to her whiskers and tried to squeeze her smile away. Kool laughed and playfully head bumped her. Power purr!

Jade exclaimed, "Cats, I'm so proud of you! You were purrfect during your ceremony! May I see your medallions, Jett?" He sat proudly as Jade held a medallion in her paw. She inspected the 3-D profiles of *Mrs. and Professor Felinestein* and rubbed her paw over it. "This is very impressive!" she complimented as they locked eyes.

Cleo inspected Jett's medallions next. She bounced one up and down on her paw, "A bit heavy, eh cuz? I'm so proud of you!" She gave him a big hug and kissed him between his eyes.

"Thank you, cousin." He took off one medallion and draped it around her neck. Then he took off the medallion Jade had been inspecting and draped it around her neck. Everyone was wearing big smiles! Jett thought he would take a chance and sit a little closer to Miss Princess, and much to his surprise, she moved a little closer too, *and* started purring! Jett balled up his paw, jerked it back, and silently said, *"Yes!"*

"This is so exciting!" exclaimed Lashes, inspecting her own medallions.

Diamond peered out the window. He was deep in thought now and feeling a bit nervous. Last minute issues—the food, the flowers, the special guest, Dutchey's leg... uh-oh! Nothing can go wrong tonight. He was so excited he was ready to burst out of his fur!

Kool B. Katt slid back in his seat and observed his happy friends. His eyes rested on loud purring Diamond. His best bud for, let's see—fourteen years now, his co-captain, his trusted confidant. He asked himself, "What's he got up his paw tonight? This bash better be *fantastic* since he won't even tell ME!"

38

The Grads laughed, purred, and chatted all the way to the Heavenly Hills Country Club. As they arrived, Lashes and Dutchey's faces were literally plastered against the tinted windows. The limo slowly drove into the entrance and cruised past the colorful fountain spraying water a hundred feet in the air.

"Wow!" exclaimed Dutchey. "Look, Lashes! Instead of white lights around the fountain, there's colored lights. Look! The water is spraying all different colors! Wow! What a show!"

"Wow! It's amazing how the colors change," replied Lashes. "It gives the fountain a different look, don't ya think?"

"I love it!" agreed Dutch, still staring at the fiber optic fountain.

Lashes looked at Jade and Cleo and proudly announced, "We painted the fountain bricks ourselves!"

Kool added, "Us toms wanted the bricks to be blue and purple, but the fluffs just had to have their pink."

Dutchey stuck her tongue out at Kool and said, "We used *dark* pink paint and I think it looks great!"

Lashes added, "We mixed the paint ourselves."

The animated, colorful fountain was Diamond's idea. He ordered the lights and hooked it up himself. "Hey fluffs," he proudly said, "check out the marquee."

The marquee said in large letters:

Congratulations Paw Valley Graduates

"Wow!" exclaimed Dutchey.
"That means us!" squealed Lashes.

Everyone was delighted with themselves! There was lots of power purring going on now.

The Heavenly Hills Country Club is a beautiful place anyway, but tonight the club seemed magical. The circle drive entrance is lined with day lilies, azaleas, yellow and orange snap dragons, hydrangeas, and gardenias. There are twinkle lights around the hedges and bushes. Tall palm trees swayed in the gentle breeze of the evening.

The limo came to a stop in front of the club. Q jumped out and held the door open. He really is a gentle-giant tom. Next, Diamond jumped out and helped the fluffs gracefully step out onto the purple velvet carpet leading into the club. Dutchey and her leg were especially graceful.

"Okay, my friends," he said, "close your eyes and hold tails."

"What? Hold tails?" snarled Kool. "Us toms, too?"

"You, too, my fellow toms." Kool and Jett groaned. They didn't want to, but closed their eyes anyway. Diamond led his friends up the purple velvet carpet, through the aqua glass double door entrance, and into the foyer.

Dutchess asked impatiently, "When can we open our eyes, Diamond?"

"In a minute. Don't look yet!" The fluffs' noses twitched. The foyer was full of fragrant sterling silver roses beautifully arranged in crystal vases.

"I'm so excited!" burst out Lashes.

Diamond quickly looked around to make sure everything was in place and looked just right.

"When can we open our eyes?" Dutchey asked again.

Diamond said, "Okay… now!"

"Look!" screamed Lashes.

There stood the premier poster that announced:

Welcome Kitty Maxx

Lashes and Dutchess screamed, "*Kitty Maxx!*" The fur on their backs stood straight up and their tails fluffed out as they looked at the poster of *Kitty Maxx*.

"I've got a chill back!" said Dutchey.

"I've got a chill tail!" exclaimed Lashes.

"I can't believe it," screamed Dutch. *"Kitty Maxx!* Here?!?!" They both jumped up and down and screamed like maniacs.

"I think I'm going to faint," Lashes panted.

"Or give yourself a heart attack," laughed Kool.

"I can't believe it! I can't believe it!" gasped Dutchess. The fluffs looked at each other and started jumping again. Lashes' medallions hit her on the chin. Dutchey's leg gave way and she landed with all four legs sprawled outward.

"Nice landing," complimented Diamond as he helped her up.

"Read it out loud, Diamond! Read it out loud!" demanded Dutch, shaking her fur out.

"Welcome *Kitty Maxx!*" announced Diamond. Scream. Jump. Splits.

"Yeah!" exclaimed Kool.

Jett, Jade, Cleo, and Q laughed as they watched our most proper fluffs become flat-out hysterical.

Diamond continued reading the poster, "They will be singing their #1 hits, "Falling For You," and "Blast." This is going to be one fabulous party!" The fluffs became even more unglued!

Jade looked at Jett and commented, "I've never heard of this group, *Kitty Maxx.*"

Jett asked, "You haven't? You definitely will be impressed, Princess. I promise."

"Okay," said Diamond. "Are you ready for the next surprise?" Scream. Scream. Leg twitch. "Close your eyes and join tails again." The toms groaned. Diamond led his friends outside through an archway of fragrant tropical flowers.

Eyes still closed, Lashes leaned towards Dutchess and whispered to the back of her head, "This is so exciting!" Then she padded right into the archway of tropical flowers.

Dutchey whispered, "I want autographs and lots of pictures!" Then she said out loud, "Can we open our eyes now, Diamond?"

"Not yet," he said, "and no peeking. I want this to be a night you will all remember! Dutchey... you're peeking! Keep your eyes closed!" He took four leis off the table and put them up to the fluffs' noses. Their whiskers twitched as he put the leis around their necks.

"Now?" asked Dutch.

"Okay... now!"

39

"Aloha, everyone!" greeted Diamond.

"A luau?!" exclaimed Dutchey. She looked around the club with curious eyes. "Wow! I feel like I'm in Meowie! Listen... there's even ukulele music playing!" She started purring.

Lashes asked Diamond, "Is this the theme you wouldn't tell us about?" She tilted her head to the side, looking very cute. She smelled her lei and power purred.

"Yep," he replied. The Heavenly Hills Country Club looked like an exotic tropical island paradise! Diamond could hardly contain himself. "The club looks great, doesn't it?" He didn't even wait for answers. "I'm hungry. Come on, let's check out the spread."

"Wait, wait," said Dutchey. She hobbled to the table, picked up a lei with her teeth, hobbled back, and put it around Diamond's neck. "There, you look great!"

"Thank you, purrty fluff. So do you. Now, let's get some food."

"Hold up," said Lashes. She whispered to Jade and Cleo and pointed to a sign above the lei table. They ran over to the table and brought back leis for the toms to wear.

"*Oh No No No!*" snarled Kool. "I'm not wearing *that!*"

"*Oh yes you are, Kool Katt!*" insisted Lashes. "Read the sign. You can't come to the luau unless you wear a lei." She tried putting it around his neck, but he hissed and backed up, ducking his head back and forth—anything to avoid the inevitable. Lashes chased him around and teased, "Now handsome, don't be all snarky!" Nevertheless, he was not giving in. He is way too macho to wear a lei. It's totally unthinkable. As he ducked and bobbed Lashes' advances, he backed into a tall basket of flowers and knocked it over. He rolled backwards over the basket and landed on his back. He tried to get up, but somehow he had managed to get himself tangled up in the long ribbons tied to the balloons attached to the basket. The fluffs were laughing hysterically! Poor Kool was helplessly trapped on his side with balloons bobbing all around him, some hitting him in the face. Hysterical Lashes tried to help him, but that only made matters worse. As she tried to untangle him, he saw the lei dangling from her teeth. He wiggled and twisted, this way and that. He tried to hide from her by crawling under the flowers in the tipped over basket. He figured if he couldn't see her, she couldn't see him. "Boo!" she teased, peeking into the flowers. He jumped and smacked his head on the basket. "Now Kool, you can make this hard on yourself, like you're doing right now, and hide under these flowers all night, or you can wear your lei and have fun with us!" He grumbled and tried to stand up. The balloon ribbons were so tightly wrapped around his legs, his tummy, and his neck, he couldn't move. There was a white daisy sticking out of his ear. Lashes was relentless. She pressed her nose rather hard against his nose and pierced him with a laser beam look. She was not about to give in. "Well?"

Diamond was hysterically laughing and yelled over, "Hey Kool, how hungry are ya?"

Kool hissed at him and mumbled, "Okay, get it over with. I *am* hungry." He lay there limp while Lashes untangled him and plucked off all the daisies.

She held up the lei. "Here it comes! Are ya ready?" He cringed. Finally, she draped him with his lei. It looked a bit beat up and was missing a few flowers now, and that was just fine with Kool. Lashes head bumped him and said, "Come on now, you big hunk of fur. Tonight's gonna be fun! I know I'm excited! Can I see a smile?" Reluctantly, he smiled—but only a half smile. She was happy with that.

Diamond couldn't stop laughing. He has been waiting for this moment all day! Kool shot him a dirty look.

Jade put a lei around Jett's neck. She could do anything she wanted! He didn't care.

Cleo reached high and put a lei around Q's neck. "I always knew you were a softy," she said. Q looked embarrassed, but didn't take it off or put up near the fuss Kool did.

Beyond the table piled high with lovely leis is an exquisite spread of food. The long banquet tables are set up by the club's snack bar, The Scratching Post. The gang padded over.

Excited Dutchey exclaimed, "Look Lashes! The Scratching Post is decorated to look like a cabana on a tropical island beach! And look at all the tiki torches!"

Lashes looked around and excitedly commented, "I love the tiki torches! This is so great! Let's see, what's there to drink?"

Kool read the menu, "Well, there's the ever-so-tasty squid squeeze, and there's your favorite, the oh-so-refreshing coconut slash."

Lashes put her word on it—"Chillicious!"

Cleo picked out her favorite. "I just love a seafood soda on the rocks! Look Jade, they're serving crabacinno and liver latté!"

"I love liver latté!" replied Jade.

Diamond asked, "So, you love liver? Look at the liver cake with chow-chow sprinkles." He pointed at the center table.

"Yum!" Jade licked her whiskers.

Kool looked over the food on the banquet tables. "What's there to eat? Let's see… there's lobster tail, tuna roll, cracked crab legs, anchovy pudding, whipped sardines in oil, crabby won-tons, salmon crepes… " He sniffed one of the trays and then licked it.

Lashes said, "Look, Kool! There's your favorite, the ever popular, mouth-watering fumanchu fish surprise!"

"Mmm!" Kool reached out and put his paw in his favorite dish.

Lashes slapped him, "Keep your paw out of the food," she hissed, giving him a plate.

Cleo said, "This is positively delightful! I love fish!"

Jett remarked, "Look at that big ice bucket with the giant rainbow trout."

"Nice eye," said Jade, licking her whiskers.

Jett laughed. "Nice crabby apple in its mouth!"

Lashes exclaimed, "Dutchey, look at all the colorful umbrellas and the twinkle lights in the trees! Look how purrty they look when they sparkle like that!"

Dutchey agreed. "This is awesome! I have never seen the club look so beautiful! Oh, look at all the flowers in bloom! There's my favorite, the lavender lily of the nile, and look at all the colorful hibiscus flowers!"

Lashes remarked, "The peach flowers are my favorite! And the orange trumpet flowers and the snapdragons! This is so exciting!"

Cleo looked at Jade and whispered, "Let's do our hula dance!" She and Jade picked a spot on the grass and began moving to the ukulele music.

Lashes joined in and urged, "Come on, Dutchey, move those hips." Dutchey tried. She moved her front legs back and forth, but the hips weren't going anywhere. Lashes commented, "This is great for my tummy. We should make it a mandatory cheerleading exercise!"

Cleo and Jade danced exactly alike, every flowing movement the same, as if they had practiced together forever. The hired photographer for the evening ran over and took pictures as they moved with the music. Their dance told a traditional story of the native islands. They were very entertaining and received a round of applause at the end of their performance.

"Thank you, thank you," the fluffs said to all who were watching. *The Hula Fluffs* just arrived and told them they danced beautifully!

Dutchey head bumped Diamond and said, "Diamond, this celebration is greater than great!" Was all this your idea, the theme, *Kitty Maxx?*"

Diamond Castleberry III's turquoise eyes sparkled. He replied, "Yep. This is definitely going to be a party worth remembering!"

Jade spotted the sparkling blue pool and padded over to it. Cleo ran after her. "Look, Cleo! The pool is heart shaped! Look at the pretty lily pads floating on top of the water! Wow! And look at all the big rocks around the pool!"

Cleo exclaimed, "I absolutely love the waterfall! You can swim through it and play games like Hide and Chase!"

Jade was so excited. "Look at the shallow end. Look how the sandy-colored slope goes into the water, and look how the water laps up like waves on a beach!" She padded over to the slope and let the water cover her paws.

"It is so cool!" replied Cleo. Diamond and Jett casually sauntered over to the awestruck fluffs from Pintac.

Jade looked out past the pool at the burning tiki torches and the huge trees that sparkled with twinkle lights. "I love all the tiki torches and the trees look so beautiful!"

Diamond pointed, "See the Old Oak? It's the tree all lit up with the landing on it."

Jett added, "There's a fantastic view from the landing."

Cleo commented, "I love how the Old Oak is decorated. I love the different colored hanging lanterns."

Diamond pointed his claw in the opposite direction. "All the way out there, as far as you can see, is the Eighteen Hole Championship Golf Course. It goes out onto a bluff over the ocean at the fourteenth hole. You have to hit the ball over the ocean to the other side of the bluff, or you lose your ball."

Cleo sighed, "It's so cool!"

Diamond continued, "There's a big Celebrity Golf Benefit here this weekend. Target Wood will be here and everything."

"Wow!" the fluffs said together, almost breathless.

"It should be exciting. Plenty of famous celebrities will be staying here at the club and at our resort down the way. We've been booked solid for months."

"Wow!"

Jade whispered, "Listen, you can hear the waves breaking in the distance."

Jett stood there, staring, in complete awe of the lovely Princess.

Diamond insisted, "Cats, let's eat!" They met the gang back at the banquet tables and picked over the enticing food. Then they took their selections of tasty treats to a grassy area by a big rock that has old faded initials, *D&D 4ever*, scratched on it.

"This food is delicious!" exclaimed Cleo. "I'm in heaven!"

As they enjoyed their treats, Diamond casually asked everyone, "Well, are you surprised?"

"Yes! This is the best party ever!" exclaimed Dutchey, licking her whiskers.

"Worth the wait?" he asked.

"Yes! Yes! A thousand times Yes!" exclaimed the fluffs without hesitation.

"This is really awesome, bud," Kool said with a mouthful of fumanchu fish surprise. He and Diamond opened their mouths and played, "look!"

"Eeewww! Stop it, toms!" scolded Lashes. "We don't want to see your chewed up food in progress. *Thank you.*"

Jett asked Lashes, "Did your mom make all these leis?"

Lashes looked over at Diamond, "It's your secret."

Diamond swallowed his food, looked over at Kool and stuck out his tongue, and answered for Lashes, "Yes. Her mom made all the flower arrangements and leis. Didn't she do a great job?"

Kool stuck his tongue out at Diamond. "Yes, she did."

Lashes smiled her biggest smile and Dutchey put her nose in her lei and smelled away. They were all very happy, even Kool!

Jade declared with a flair of excitement, "Everything looks fantastic! And the food is delicious! This is so wonderful!" She gobbled her food down as if she hadn't eaten in days.

Dutchey and Lashes shared a plate of lobster dripping in butter. They took a bite, looked at each other, and closed their eyes as if they were in paradise. Each cat licked their plate clean while swaying back and forth to the ukulele music.

Dutchey licked her whiskers and announced, "Now I'm ready for mousey mint pie."

"Me, too!" agreed Lashes.

"Look at all the handsome toms!" marveled Cleo, enjoying a mouthful of whipped sardines.

Screaming continued as more Grads saw the premier poster in the foyer. Groaning continued as more toms saw the—*must wear a lei*—sign.

What an exciting evening Diamond Thomas III has planned!

40

"What can we get you fluffs to drink?" asked host-with-the-most, Diamond.

"I'd like a coconut splash, please," answered Dutchess. The other fluffs nodded in agreement.

"That sounds great!" chirped Lashes. Surprised by that chirp, she cleared her throat.

"We'll be right back," said Diamond, "come on, buds."

The fluffs looked over at the pool and Jade commented, "The water is such a pretty color blue and I love the heart shape!"

"I love the lily pads," added Cleo.

"This is a very beautiful country club!" exclaimed Jade, looking around at everything. Dutchey buried her face in her lei and purred.

"This is so exciting! I can't wait for *Kitty Maxx!*" exploded Lashes.

The toms returned with little plates of mousey mint pie. Diamond pulled the tray across the grass with the desserts and Kool and Jett pulled the tray with the drinks. Each coconut splash drink was very fancy. It came in its own coconut bowl with a colored umbrella toothpick poked through a chunk of pineapple submerged in the drink. And what did the toms bring back for themselves? Snappy toms, of course.

"I'd like to sink a toast," announced Diamond. "To my best friends! To us! The Fabulous Snobby Cats of Heavenly Hills!" They clinked their bowls together, drank, and power purred.

As they sat on the grass and enjoyed their fancy food, they talked about the ceremony and now the luau at the club with *Kitty Maxx* and how great their lives are. The music started playing top 40 stuff. A little bit of country, too, but when "Waiting for the Great Times," by *Shakatra* blasted out, every cat there got up on their paws and moved to the beat.

"Come on, cool cats!" said Kool. "Let's dance!"

41

The paparazzi is here! Ms. Savannah Sizzleton, fashion and life-style specialist with *Feline Flair* is at The Heavenly Hills Country Club with her media camera crew, Felix and Oscar. She is here to capture the party following Graduation with a preview of Heavenly Hills' finest felines. Her crew, with video and still cameras, are set up on the purple velvet carpet entrance leading into the club so she can give an in-depth account of who's who and what's what.

Ms. Savannah Sizzleton is a beautiful twenty-four-year-old sil-ver tipped Burmese with aquamarine-colored eyes. She can wear every color in the rainbow and look fabulous. Tonight, she's wearing a summery floral scarf tied around her neck and a microphone pack tied around her tummy. Her crew, Felix and Oscar, are tabbies. When Savannah's eyes made contact with the camera, she came alive:

"Aloha, everyone! This is Savannah Sizzleton with *Feline Flair* reporting *Live* from The Heavenly Hills Country Club. I'm here to bring you all the highlights of this wonderful evening that cel-ebrates the accomplishments of 333 cats that have just graduated from Paw Valley Middle School. I'm here on the purple velvet car-pet at the entrance of the club where the graduates, faculty, fami-lies, and friends will party and be entertained by the exceptionally hot group, *Kitty Maxx*. This velvet carpet feels so nice on my paw pads. As you all probably know, purple is the color of royalty, and here comes Heavenly Hills' royalty now! The Castleberry family is the first to arrive! They are pulling up in three shiny black Lexus limousines. Allow me to give you a brief history about the head of the Castleberry dynasty, Diamond Castleberry I. He owns, well, pretty much most of Heavenly Hills. He's a visionary with business savvy and plenty of drive. He has even been on the cover of *$$$$$* Magazine countless times. For several decades, he has dabbled in real estate, building mansion after mansion in upscale Castleberry Estates and Castleberry Grove. Thirty years ago, he and his lovely wife, Mona, created Heavenly Hills Country Club with their great friend, Donaldo, who has since moved on to develop Cat-hatten.

Recently, Diamond I and his wife renovated the country club, giving it an ultra deluxe, extravagant Caribbean style. Celebrities come just to be cool and hang out. There is also the Eighteen Hole Championship Golf Course for all those who just can't get enough golf. The elite Castleberry's host major events and entertain celebrities and royalty from all over the world. Now, one mile down the road from here and adjoining the country club is their ultra lavish Heavenly Hills Ocean Resort. Felines flock there to take breaks from their hectic everyday lives and to relax and receive plenty of pampering with massages, warm mineral baths, mud baths, a sauna, and botanical treatments for smooth and manageable fur. The botanical fur treatment is especially luxurious. This family stacks and banks!" Savannah took a deep breath. "Diamond I and Mona Castleberry are stepping out of their limo now. They are such a wonderful couple." As they padded up the velvet carpet, she greeted them, "Mr. and Mrs. Castleberry, it's so nice to see you. You both look spectacular this evening." Diamond I and Mona are very generous felines. They know Savannah well and the three exchanged hugs.

Mona replied, "Thank you, Savannah. You look lovely tonight, too."

Diamond I shook her paw. "Good evening, Savannah. I'm glad you are here to cover this fantastic celebration for all these fine, young cats."

"Thank you, I'm happy to be here. You're both looking very relaxed."

"We just got back from Catiqua Falls," purred Mona. "It's so lovely there. We're celebrating our lives together." She gave her husband a kiss on his whiskers. He smiled and purred, as always.

"That sounds wonderful. Congratulations to you and your family, and of course, Diamond III. I heard he was magnificent at the Graduation ceremony."

Grandfluff Mona boasted, "Yes, he was, thank you. We are very proud of him."

"He is the apple of my eye," agreed proud Grandtom Diamond I. "This luau party was his idea, you know, and a grand one I might add!"

"Did I understand correctly? Is this a traditional luau?" asked Savannah.

Mona replied, "Yes, it's very exotic and just beautiful inside. I'd like you to take lots of pictures."

"No problem. Mrs. Castleberry, I love your *M* pendant! It's beautiful! How many carats?"

"Thank you, dear. I think this is about twenty-two-carats. My husband would know exactly. I love this color topaz! It's so... me!"

"It certainly is! It matches your turquoise eyes purrfectly. Mr. Castleberry, you look striking in this collar! I can't believe how much it sparkles!"

"Thank you, Savannah. My wife had this one-of-a-kind collar custom-made for me as a gift for my last birthday."

"It's a Rolex collar accented with diamonds from *Catiers*," added Mona.

Savannah spoke into the microphone, "Mona Castleberry looks stunning wearing a twenty-two-carat, turquoise topaz initial pendant, and Diamond Castleberry I looks especially stately in a custom-made, eye-catching Rolex and diamond collar! This couple looks like a million bucks!"

Mona smiled, "Thank you for your kind words, Savannah. You are such a doll. Please join us after you finish here."

Diamond I said, "Our doors are always open to you, Ms. Savannah. Please take a picture with us." They adore Savannah and graciously posed with her.

"Thank you. I am so honored. Have a great celebration Mr. and Mrs. Castleberry."

"Thank you, dear."

Savannah spoke into her microphone, "They are such a nice couple. Diamond Castleberry III, Class President of Paw Valley Middle School, is in charge of this evening's *Party of the Century*. Just a few moments ago, he was seen leading his friends into the club, making sure their eyes were closed. He must have a few surprises up his paw tonight. The rest of the Castleberry family have just arrived and are lighting up the purple carpet." As the group approached Savannah, she greeted them with, "Aloha, everyone and congratulations!"

Diamond's dad, Diamond II, greeted her, "Thank you very much, Savannah."

Diamond's mom, Pearl, commented, "Savannah, I see you in your magazine, on the television, and now here. You are working too hard."

Diamond's Uncle Beau added, "Savannah, we agree. You *are* working too hard. You must come to our resort and be our special guest."

Diamond's Auntie Sophia added, "Spend the day with us and you will feel like a brand new fluff! We just got a special new oil that does wonders for your fur! You must try it!"

"Aren't you so nice to worry about me? I could use a good mud bath, too! Fluffs, you all look gorgeous tonight!"

"Thank you, we think so," laughed Diamond's aunties.

Savannah turned to Diamond's mother, Pearl. The exquisite pearl necklace she was wearing caught her attention. "Mrs. Castleberry, is your necklace Mother of Pearl?"

"Yes it is, Savannah," replied Pearl.

"Classy and very lovely! Belle, I just love your shooting star dangle diamond earrings! How many carats?"

"These are three-carat champagne diamonds. Aren't they lovely?" beamed Auntie Belle, showing off her diamonds by shaking her head to make them swing.

"Yes, just gorgeous. You're my kind of glamour fluffs!" She turned to Diamond's dad and Uncle Beau and asked, "Are those collars what I think they are?"

Diamond's dad replied, "If you're thinking Rolex, you're right!"

Savannah remarked, "Very bold and stylish! You all look wonderful this evening. Please pose for my camera."

"Hello, Crystal, Sierra (Diamond's little sister who is nine), Brianna and Vienna (Diamond's cousins who are five).

"Hello, Savannah," said Crystal. "You look very pretty tonight."

"So do you. I love your crystal heart necklace. Look how it sparkles in the light."

Crystal said, "I received this lovely bling as a gift from my parents when I graduated from Paw Valley two years ago."

"It's very nice." Savannah addressed the younger fluffs, "You are all just adorable. Please pose for my camera." They posed very snobby, then very nice. The family all posed together and headed into the club.

Savannah commented, "The Castleberry family just wreaks of wealth, style, and glamour! Yet behind all the filthy-rich-eccentric-lifestyle, they really are a very down-to-earth and wonderful family."

Savannah sprayed minty fresh breath freshener. "Want some, toms?" They stuck their tongues out.

"Okay." spritz… spritz…

42

Savannah continued, "Oh look, the Mayor and his family have just arrived. They are pulling up in a pewter-colored Mercedes Benz limo. Mayor Malcolm Holcomb and his beautiful wife, Lily, add pizzazz and style to every event they attend. They are stepping out of their limo now and heading my way. Along with them are their children, Mac II and Honey. Aloha, Mayor and Mrs. Holcomb! You both look fabulous this evening! Congratulations to you and your lovely daughter, Lashes!"

Mayor Mac greeted Savannah with a power paw shake. "Aloha, Savannah and thank you. We are very proud of her."

Lily added, "Thank you, Savannah. Yes, we are very pleased!" They exchanged warm hugs.

"Mrs. Holcomb, did you have a paw in arranging all of the flowers for this evening's celebration?"

"Well, yes I did."

"The entrance here is breathtakingly beautiful! I can't wait to see inside!"

"Thank you, Savannah. It all came together very nicely."

"Your scarf is lovely! What kind of lace?"

"This is Belgian lace. My daughter made this beautiful scarf for me to wear tonight."

"Belgian lace is always so elegant!"

"Yes it is, thank you."

"Mayor, tell me about your stylish collar. Is it…?"

"Yes, it's a Rolex. My wife surprised me with it."

"Well, you two are one stylin' couple. Please pose for my camera."

"Mayor Holcomb's twin brother Zach, and his beautiful wife, Consuelo, and twin teenage fluffs, Toffee and Taffee, are heading toward me now. Congratulations to you and your niece, Lashes."

Uncle Zach replied, "Thank you, Savannah."

Auntie Consuelo added, "Thank you, my dear."

"Mrs. Holcomb, your bling is gorgeous. Would you tell me what kind of gemstones are in your necklace?"

"Of course, dahling. This is a diamond, mystic fire topaz, and amethyst tier necklace. It's new. My husband gave it to me."

"I just love it! Please pose for my camera."

"Aloha, Mac, Honey, Toffee, and Taffee."

"Aloha, Savannah," said Mac II.

"Aloha, Savannah," greeted Toffee.

"Fluffs, your silk scarves are lovely. I love the gold and silver metallic swirl. I want one!"

Taffee remarked, "I love your scarf, too."

"Thank you, Taffee. Honey, how are you this evening?"

"I'm terrific!"

"Well, you all look lovely this evening. Well, not you, Mac. You look very handsome, though. Well, you know what I mean."

Mac II winked at her. "Well, thank you, Savannah." She blinked with embarrassment.

"He knows what you mean, Savannah," laughed Toffee. "Stop teasing her, Mac."

Savannah said, "Please pose for my camera." She looked down the purple runway and spotted a classy limo pulling up. "I think your Grandcats have just arrived in a sharp looking pewter-colored Infiniti limo. Is that an Infiniti, Mac?"

Mac II was surprised she knew about cars. "Good guess, Savannah." On an impulse, he took the microphone from her, and then asked, "May I?"

"Sure," she replied. "You *are* the mayor's son."

He began commentating. "This is Malcolm Holcomb II, reporting *LIVE* from the purple velvet carpet. My Grandfluff Winter, my dad's mother looks exquisite tonight in emeralds and diamonds. My Grandtom Winston is sporting an equally sparkling emerald and diamond studded gold collar. Did you all know he was Mayor of Heavenly Hills many years ago?"

"Yes!" Everyone laughed at Mac II. He has a delightfully amusing sense of humor.

"Here comes my mom's mother, Grandfluff Camellia Somerset. She looks very elegant this evening wearing a gorgeous string of pearls and a white pillbox hat, placed just off to the side. She has extremely curly whiskers."

Savannah leaned over and said into the microphone, "I love the look!"

Mac II continued, "My Grandtom Calvin is looking quite dapper this evening, wearing a fine white silk bow tie."

Savannah said, "What a beautiful family! Thank you for commentating, Mac. You're hired!"

Still holding the microphone, Mac II stood close to Savannah and instructed her assistants, "Snap a picture of us, please."

Everyone laughed at Mac II as he gave her back her microphone.

Savannah said, "Aloha, everyone. Fluffs, you look divine this evening! And Toms, what can I say? You always look classy!"

"Thank you, Savannah," said retired Mayor Winston. "It's so nice to see you, dear."

Grandfluff Winter commented, "I enjoy your magazine column very much!"

"Thank you. You are so sweet. You must be so proud of your Lashes."

"Yes, we are," beamed Camellia.

"Well, you all look fabulous this evening and I hope you all have a wonderful celebration. Please pose for my camera."

Lily urged her husband, "Go inside and get her a lei. Hurry."

Mayor Mac hurried away, then returned with two leis and put them around Savannah's neck. "You deserve two leis. You're doing all the work while we're having all the fun!"

"These leis are beautiful! I love purple orchids! Thank you!"

"You're very welcome," beamed Lily. "Can you smell the plumeria blossoms?

Savannah put her leis up to her nose. "Yes. They smell exotic."

Lily added, "The plumeria is a traditional flower that is native to the islands. I put little hints of the fragrant blossom in each lei."

"They smell wonderful. You are so talented, Mrs. Holcomb."

"Thank you, Savannah. Enjoy and we'll see you inside." They posed for a picture with Savannah, and then headed on into the party.

Next, a wide-brimmed purple hat with a lavender plume grabbed Savannah's attention. She squinted through the growing crowd of cats to see who is last to step out of the Holcomb limo.

Savannah questioned, "Is that, no, it can't be…?" She yelled out, "Rose Somerset?!"

"Savannah Sizzleton?!"

The retired cheerleaders from Heavenly Hills High screamed and hugged and hugged and screamed. What a spectacle they made of themselves!

Savannah exclaimed, "It's so great to see you, fluff-friend! It's been such a long time! I just love your look! And your own calendar? Fluff, you are steppin' out, right into celebrity heaven!"

"Thank you, my dear fluff-friend! Just call me Miss February!"

"It's such a clever picture! You, swinging on a heart shaped swing, being shot at with cupid's love arrows!"

"Fluff, I get to do all kinds of crazy stuff! You would not believe it! But Savannah, you and your column in *Feline Flair!* I love it! It's all the rage! Catch up with me at the party. I have so much to tell you!"

They both jumped up and down and screamed, *"Who knew?!"*

"Would you give me a super model interview, my long-time friend?"

"Only if you'll do a prowler howl with me!"

"For you, dahling, anything!"

"Let's do it!" They both howled loud and obnoxious prowler howls. The camera crew cracked up.

"Did you get that, Felix?"

"Got it!"

Rose exclaimed, "I'm so excited to see you! Let's go and talk right now!"

"Okay, let's go!" They padded off, heading into the club.

Felix yelled after her, "Ms. Savannah… where are you go-ing?"

The fluffs laughed and Savannah said, "Just kidding. I have a few more interviews, but I promise, after I'm done here, I'm huntin' you down!"

"Okay. I'll save a smoked salmon won-ton for you! Work it, doll face! You look beautiful tonight."

They hugged again and Rose picked up her hat and put it back on. Looking extremely snobby, they both posed for the camera.

"Did you get that, Oscar?"

"Got it!"

"See you inside, dear," the lovely super model said as she fashionably padded into the club. The Mayor met her with a traditional lei.

43

Savannah went back to work. "A shiny white stretch limo with gold trim is pulling up. I wonder who this is. The Woo family is here! I love this family! The Woo family owns the most exotic nightclub in Heavenly Hills. It's called The Sphinx. It's shaped like a cat, you have to go into the mouth to get inside, and the kitchen is in the tail! What an imagination Sam Woo has! Here come the fluffs, shimmering and sparkling in brilliant gemstones. Let me begin by saying glamorous socialite, Ming Woo, has accessorized this evening with a ring that spirals around her left front leg. It has a brilliant gem insert that accentuates her beautiful eyes. Very lovely! I'm going to ask her exactly what kind of gem it is and how many carats. She's also wearing a matching tail ring. Sam Woo adds a flashy flair, sporting a rope chain. I'm going to ask if it's solid gold!" As the Siamese family padded up the purple carpet, they greeted Savannah with open paws.

"Aloha, Mr. and Mrs. Woo, it's so wonderful to see you! Congratulations to you and your Dutchess!"

Ming replied, "Aloha, Savannah and thank you."

Sam added, "We couldn't be more proud!"

"Mrs. Woo, I absolutely love your paw ring! What kind of gem is that, how many carats, and where did you get it?"

"This is a violet-blue, seventeen-carat, marquise cut, tanzanite gemstone. My husband got this for me for Christmas last year, as well as my matching tail ring, at *Sox Fifth Avenue.*"

"Absolutely, breathtaking! I adore your tail ring, too!"

"Thank you, dear. It's the cut of the gem that counts the most."

Savannah replied, "I'll remember that." Then she asked Sam, "Is your chain solid gold?"

"Platinum, of course."

"It's spectacular! And you both smell wonderful! What perfume are you wearing, Mrs. Woo?"

"Cool Breeze for Fluffs."

"And what are you wearing that smells so good, Mr. Woo?"

"Cool Breeze for Toms."

Savannah took in a deep breath, "You both smell intoxicating! Who is with you tonight?"

Ming began, "Both of our parents are here, as well as my twin sister and her husband. This is Sam's twin brother, and his wife. And this is our precious Blossom, our twin nieces, Heather and Jasmine, and our nephews, Cisco, Sly, and little Sammy. And, our wonderful Miss Fancy."

"Aloha, everyone!"

"Aloha, Savannah!"

"Fluffs, your blings are exquisite. Tell me about them."

Dutchey's auntie replied, "I'm wearing a nine-carat, oval cut purple sapphire necklace."

"It's magnificent!"

Dutchey's other auntie boasted, "This necklace is pastel jade surrounded by amethyst. I love it because it's just so different."

"It's beyond words! Fluffs, you look just gorgeous. Miss Fancy, what is this gorgeous gemstone you are wearing?"

"This pendant is a deep blue, emerald cut sapphire."

"It's brilliant! With a bling like that, what else do you really need? Toms, are these diamond studded collars gold or platinum?"

"Platinum."

"You all look amazing this evening. Please pose for my camera. It looks like your Grandcats have just arrived in a gold Cadillac limo. Here they come now. Fluffs, you all look stunning in diamonds. And toms, you look especially stylish this evening wearing polka dot bow ties."

The Grandcats graciously thanked Savannah for her compliments.

Savannah twitched her nose. "I love your choice of cologne. What's it called?"

"Chats," said Dutchey's Grandtom.

"I could smell you all night! And fluffs, you look amazing this evening!" She turned to Dutchey's ultra eccentric Grandfluff and asked, "How many carats?"

She excitedly answered, "Forty! It would sink to the bottom of the ocean!"

"And I'd be down there lookin' for it!" laughed Savannah. The Woo family laughed with Savannah and exchanged hugs. "It is so nice seeing all of you gorgeous and handsome felines. Congratulations and enjoy your party. Please pose for my camera." They headed into the club.

Savannah went off the microphone, "Felix, is my fur okay?"

"You look more stunning than any cat I've seen yet!"

"Oh, stop it, Felix! This scarf has got to go. Two leis and a scarf, it's a bit much." She untied her scarf and threw it over her back into the bushes. She fluffed her fur and took a deep breath.

44

The crowds of cats were arriving faster than Savannah could interview. Excited felines were running right past her to get their big chance to party at the most elite country club in Heavenly Hills. Savannah peered through the crowd to see if she recognized anyone from the old days.

"Here comes a silver Rolls-Royce. Those tinted windows make it so difficult to see who is in there. Oh, look! It's Principal Fitt, his twin brother, Dr. Fitt, and their dates, the Hissy sisters. Principal Fitt looks spectacular in a black top hat and bow tie. Aloha, everyone and Congratulations!"

Principal Fitt said, "Aloha, Savannah. It's been a long time." Savannah gave her former principal a hug and knocked his hat off.

"Sorry, Sir," she picked it up and awkwardly put it back on his head. "Principal Fitt, you must be very proud of your Graduates!"

"Yes, I am. They are all very fine cats. I will miss having them around next year. They've given me some very special moments."

"Sounds like you miss them already?"

"It's true. I do."

"Is this class special?"

Miss Hissy answered, "Yes, this class is special. They are smart, talented, fun-loving, and in general, just a wonderful group of young felines."

"Awww. Sounds like you will miss them, too."

Miss Hissy sighed, "Yes, I will."

"Fluffs, you look lovely tonight. What kind of pearls are these?"

Nurse Hissy replied, "These are rare black pearls plucked fresh from the ocean last week. We had them made into these necklaces for tonight's celebration."

Miss Hissy added, "These necklaces represent my students. They are all rare pearls!"

"That is so sweet," said Savannah, "I think I'm going to cry."

"Me, too," replied Miss Hissy.

Dr. Fitt asked, "Savannah, isn't your birthday coming up soon, along with your yearly vaccinations?"

"Um, yes."

"Don't forget to make an appointment for your booster shot. I have a needle with your name on it."

"I promise, Dr. Fitt. Have a wonderful evening, everyone. Pose for the camera. Oscar, make sure Principal Fitt's hat is on right and his bow tie is straight."

Oscar replied, "Okay, hat needs to go to the left, tie needs to go to the right. Purrfect." They headed into the club.

Savannah went off the microphone and complained, "Dr. Fitt always has a needle waiting for me. Meowch."

Oscar and Felix laughed. Oscar reassured her, "You're not alone. He has a needle with everyone's name on it."

Savannah laughed and took a breath.

45

Savannah continued, "The Katt family is arriving in a black Bentley stretch limo. The Katt family owns Duke's Club, a snazzy, jazzy little club on the docks. I've been there and I know for a fact how eccentric Duke's Club is. Every night of the week, something is planned for the audience. Wednesday is karaoke night, which can be very entertaining! I should know, I've been booed off the stage several times! Here comes the Calico family now! Aloha, Mr. and Mrs. Katt. Come and chat with me for a moment."

Duke greeted her with a paw shake, "Aloha, Savannah. How have you been? You haven't come to our club lately and we've missed you."

"Oh, Mr. Katt, I don't think I can ever show my fur at your club again, especially after my last performance!" Everyone laughed and joked with Savannah. "Congratulations to you and your son, Kool!"

Dora sweetly replied, "Thank you, Savannah. We are both very proud of him!"

"Mrs. Katt, you look stunning tonight! "Are these orange sapphires?" Savannah picked up the necklace with her paw and looked closer.

Dora commented, "Yes. Orange sapphires surrounded by citrine. Isn't it stunning?"

"It's magnificent! How many carats?"

"This is a nineteen-carat pendant. I think it goes well with the different colors of my fur. It's my all-time favorite!"

"I can see why! Who have you brought with you tonight?"

"This is Duke's twin brother, Surf, and his wife, Ruby."

"It is very nice to meet you both. Ruby, are those rubies and opals cascading around your hat?"

Ruby excitedly replied, "Yes! Isn't my hat just divine?!"

"Yes! I love it! The Katt family is sizzlin' tonight!"

Dora continued, "We have so many family members here tonight, I can't keep track." She was actually looking a bit frazzled. "These are our triplet's, Jacqueline, Jillian, and Jocelyn. Our nieces and nephews are here, too. This is Bobby, and these are the twins, Karly and Jessica." She looked around and frantically called out, "Little Smokey? Where are you? Come here, Smokey." He pranced over to her. "Stay out of the bushes."

Savannah asked Karly and Jessica, "How old are you?"

"Nine."

She asked Smokey, "How old are you?"

"Five."

She asked the triplets, "How old are you?"

"Five."

Bobby piped up, "I'm sixteen."

"How did you know I was going to ask that?"

"Lucky guess I guess!" Bobby Katt is very handsome. He has mostly black fur, but has a few tan and white markings on his body.

Savannah laughed, "Is it true that you're best friends with Mayor Holcomb's son, Mac?"

"Yeah, we're tight. We'll be playing on the varsity soccer team at Heavenly Hills High School in September."

"Well, you were undefeated this year! I know because I covered many of your highly energized games."

"Yeah, we have a good time out there, getting all gritty and dirty."

"Good luck next year. Well, by far, you are the most colorful family I have seen tonight! Please pose for my camera." The Katt family made a colorful picture.

Dora asked, "Our parents are here somewhere. Duke, did we lose them again?"

"Here they come," reassured Duke.

Savannah spoke into her microphone, "Duke and Dora's parents are stepping out of a white roadster. Both couples are wearing the same orange fire sapphires. Very classy! Aloha, everyone."

"Aloha!"

"Fluffs and Toms, you all look superb this evening!" Your blings are spectacular!"

Grandfluff Katt replied, "You can never go wrong with sapphires."

"I agree with you all the way! You all add glitz and sparkle to this wonderful event! Congratulations and have a very fun evening! Please pose for my camera."

They posed for pictures and headed inside to the luau for some fun.

Savannah fluffed out her fur. Next...

46

Savannah took a breath, "Here's Paw Valley's soccer coach, Coach Pinderton, and his lovely wife. Aloha, Coach and Mrs. Pinderton. You must be very proud of your soccer team and all they have accomplished these past three years."

Coach Pinderton agreed, "I am amazed at this great group of toms. I will miss them and all the fantastic moments of victory they have brought me."

"You may have to start coaching at Heavenly Hills High."

"That sounds like the best idea yet, Savannah. You never know…"

"You look lovely this evening, Mrs. Pinderton."

"Thank you, darling."

"Coach, be very proud, and enjoy this wonderful celebration. Please pose for my camera." They padded through the double door entrance.

Savannah took another deep breath, "Here comes Mr. and Mrs. Rockshire, who coach the tennis and track and tree teams. Mr. Rockshire coaches the tom's team and Mrs. Rockshire coaches the fluff's team. Coaches Rockshire, please stop by and chat with me."

Mrs. Rockshire greeted Savannah with a hug. "Hello, Savannah, my best tennis student. It's been so long since we've seen you!"

"Aloha, Mrs. Rockshire. It is so great seeing you, too! You look wonderful this evening, as usual. Always so trim."

"Thank you. Are you keeping up with your game, dear?"

Savannah was at a loss for words, "Well, yes, I suppose you could say that. I watch a lot of matches and report on them."

Coach Rockshire laughed, "Savannah, you and your career have just skyrocketed to the top and we are very proud of you!"

"I love your column in *Feline Flair!*" added Mrs. Rockshire. "I am a very loyal fan of yours."

"Thank you both. I appreciate that so much. You must be very proud of your tennis teams. They sure brought home a ton of trophies."

"I'm very proud at the growth and accomplishments of all of our athletes."

Savannah took a chance and asked the coaches, "I'd love to do a segment on athletics, fitness, and sports. May I call you?"

"Yes," replied Mrs. Rockshire.

"Definitely," agreed Coach Rockshire.

"It's so great seeing you both. Please pose with me for a picture." The coaches were draped with leis as they entered the party.

"Oh, look. Here comes my old classmate, Monique Dubois, with a very handsome escort." Savannah whispered into the microphone, "I'll try to get details!" She yelled out, "Monique!" Miss Dubois ran up the purple velvet carpet and knocked Ms. Savannah right off her paws and into the bushes. They laughed and screamed each other's name as they crawled out the hedge. Felix and Oscar cracked up as the fluffs shook themselves out, then jumped up and down and screamed.

"Savannah, my dear friend and partner in fun! Just look at you! All over the purple velvet carpet and everything! And your column in *Feline Flair*—it's the bomb!"

"Thank you, my old friend, but enough about me! Congrats to you and your fabulous cheerleading squad!"

"Yes, they are a pretty spectacular group of fluffs!"

"As good as we were?" asked Savannah, raising a whisker.

"Never!"

"Guess who I saw?" said Savannah.

"Who?"

"Rose Somerset!"

"Really? Our other partner in fun!"

"We howled our old prowler howl! Want to do one?"

Monique replied, "I'd love to!"

Felix shook his head and pointed the video camera at the fluffs. They howled obnoxious prowler howls, then laughed and hugged.

Savannah exclaimed, "I love your trio of diamond necklace! How many carats?"

"About three each. It's the princess cut. Isn't it purrty?"

"Wow! It is stunning! Who is this handsome tom escorting you?"

"This is Maurice."

"Hi, Maurice. It's very nice to meet you. Your diamond collar is amazing!"

"Merci très beaucoup." (French for thank you very much).

Savannah shrilled, "I just love French! Look at my chill tail!" She pulled her fluffy tail to the side to show everyone. Felix took a picture. "Congratulations Monique and have a very fun evening. I'll catch up with you when I get inside, but first, let's pose for my camera." Monique grabbed Ms. Savannah for a snobby photo together.

Savannah whispered in Monique's ear, "Your date is very handsome."

Monique excitedly whispered, "I know!"

"Any plans for marriage?"

"Maybe... "

"He's tailicious!"

They jumped up and down and screamed while Maurice waited patiently by the double door entrance. Miss Dubois and her handsome guest disappeared into the club. Savannah adjusted her leis and fluffed her fur.

"Here comes a black limo with gold trim. It's the Stone family. I'll share with you just a bit about them. They own the upscale restaurant, Moskitos on the Marina. Their three-story restaurant is located at the end of the harbor and has a gorgeous panoramic view of the ocean. I love sitting outside on the upper deck and watching the sailboats breeze into the harbor and glide into their slips. And the sunsets are breathtaking. The menu is delightful, too! I love Moskitos! Here they come! Aloha and congratulations, Mr. and Mrs. Stone, to you and your son, Jett."

Jett's mom, Ginger, gave her a hug. "Thank you, Savannah."

Jett's dad, Dumont, added, "We are very proud of him."

"How many trophies did he win this year?"

"Twenty-two," answered Jett's proud father.

"He's fierce on the tennis court. No one stands a chance. Mrs. Stone, what are you wearing and how many carats?"

"We're all wearing diamonds tonight. It's just that kind of celebration that calls for the sparkle of diamonds. Our diamonds are all around five or ten-carats, give or take a few."

Frangelica added, "You know what they say? Diamonds are a fluffs' best friend!"

"I agree, whole-heartedly! Who is with you this evening?"

Ginger began, "We've brought our parents, and this is my twin sister, Spicey, and her husband, Clovis, and their little twins, Copper and Pepper. This is our precious Starr. And this is Dumont's twin brother, Sanford, and his lovely wife, Frangelica, from Pintac. Their daughter, Cleocatra, is already inside."

Savannah said into her microphone, "The Stone family is drenched in diamonds this evening. Necklaces, paw rings, diamond studded collars, the works. They all just sparkle! Here come the Grandcats. What kind of car is that, Mr. Stone?"

"*That*, my dear, is a custom-made convertible Jaguar. Our parents insisted the top be down tonight."

"It's very impressive! I would look great riding around in that with the wind blowing through my fur! Aloha, everyone and congratulations!" she said to the wind-tossed Grandcats as they padded up the purple velvet carpet.

"Thank you," they replied. The Grandfluffs were busy smoothing their fur and adjusting their hats.

"You all sparkle brighter than the sun! Enjoy your evening and please pose for my camera." The Stone family headed in to the party.

At last, Savannah and crew found themselves alone. "Well, it looks like everyone who is coming to *The Party of the Century* is here. Congratulations to the eighth grade class of Paw Valley Middle School. Cheers to them for graduating and achieving their goals! Education is so important! Just look at what a journalism education has done for me! I have just had the most wonderful time greeting everyone this evening and admiring all the brilliant blings! This group of elite felines provides over-the-top glamour to any purple velvet carpet occasion! I didn't get to talk to every cat because they were all so anxious to get inside. Who can blame them? I can hear the music playing and it sounds like a rockin' party already! Now, it's time for us to see what's going on inside. Look for this segment on my new show, *Livin' the Good Life,* and look for my column in *Feline Flair* to find plenty of pictures of this evening's festivities. This is Ms. Savannah Sizzleton, temporarily signing off *Live* from The Heavenly Hills Country Club purple velvet carpet. See you inside."

Savannah sat down to rest. She said to Felix and Oscar, "I'll bet you both ten bucks Princess Jade from Pintac is here."

47

*A*westruck Savannah gasped as she and her crew padded through the double doors and entered the foyer. Savannah instructed, "Oscar, get some pictures of the sterling silver roses in the crystal vases. Roses add so much class. Take some pictures of the *Kitty Maxx* poster. Oh, just look at the floral archway!" She stepped under it and said, "Take my picture here." They hoisted their equipment and stepped outside. "Wow! Just look at everything! Have you toms ever photographed the club looking so tropical?"

"No," agreed Oscar.

"Nope." Felix shook his head.

They set their equipment down on the lei table. There were only two leis left, so Savannah whisked them off the table and put one around each toms neck. They groaned as if they were in pain.

"Read the sign, toms." They groaned even louder.

"I want to find Rose. Follow me." Roaming reporter Savannah and crew began circling the club and taking pictures. The enticing aroma of food filled the air.

Felix licked his whiskers and complained, "I'm hungry."

"So am I," said Oscar, twitching his nose and licking his chops.

Savannah looked over at the food and decided, "This would be an excellent time to review the spread of food. I'm starving, too. Come on, toms, let's check it out." They padded over to the fancy banquet tables. "Oscar, get a picture of the liver and chow-chow sprinkle cake. Get a picture of all the tiki torches and the tropical bar. Oh, get one of that huge pineapple over there. And take one of that larger-than-life fish in the ice bucket with the crab apple in its mouth. Ooh, I just love anchovy pudding! Felix, video me sampling all this fancy food!" She popped a salmon crepe in her mouth and closed her eyes, "Mmm, fishilicious!"

Felix complained, "When do *we* get to eat, Ms. Savannah?"

"Just a few more pictures, then, I promise, you can dive in." She licked her whiskers and looked into the camera.

"Aloha, everyone! This is Ms. Savannah inside the country club now, where this beautiful luau is already in full swing, complete with exotic leis, tiki torches, and a fish in a bucket of ice sporting an apple in its mouth. The Clubs' décor whisks us away to a tropical island paradise. There are flowers everywhere! The sound system is incredible and the dance floor is packed. I'm over here by the banquet tables and this is, without a doubt, the most fabulous display of food I have ever seen! Let's see, there's lobster tail, smoked salmon won-tons, cod in cider sauce, crab cakes, and fish loaf. Ooh, I love halibut salsa with toasted crunchies, there's saucy squid, pickled octopus legs... hmm... I don't think I'll try that... anything with suction cups... I just can't bring myself to eat. There's stuffed trout, savory whitefish bake, conch fritters, yellow tail jack, and mousey mint pie. Oh look! Fumanchu fish surprise. We had better get some before it's all gone." She scooped some surprise out with her claws and tasted it.

Savannah was no longer on camera because Felix had already passed out from starvation and Oscar has just joined him. But nothing gets Savannah down—she picked up the camera and snapped several pictures of the food. Then she picked up the video camera and pointed it on herself. "I'm sorry, everyone. My crew passed out from starvation so I suppose I should let them eat." She pointed the camera at her lifeless crew sprawled out on the grass with their tongues hanging out. "We'll be right back." She put the video camera down and started laughing. "Get up, toms, let's eat!"

Felix and Oscar jumped to their paws and dug in along with Ms. Savannah. The only place left to sit was way out on the grass, on the outskirts of the party. As they ate, Savannah observed the festivities. A limbo competition was happening next to the stage accompanied by cats beating on bongo drums. The Old Oak was lit up and the landing was packed with cats. Little kittens dared each other to see how far they could go out on a limb before falling off. Some may say this is a dangerous little game, but kittens are light and *always* land on their feet, well, most of the time. The bright tiki torches cast a yellow glow, adding to the ambiance of the party. The music was blaring *Jammin' Cats*, "Twist and Howl."

After savoring every last bite, Savannah licked her whiskers and yawned. She's working hard tonight. She looked up at the landing. "Oscar, Felix, can we get some aerial shots?" Felix and Oscar were still eating, but looked up at the crowded landing anyway, uninterested.

Oscar swallowed his food and suggested, "Ms. Super Reporter Sizzleton—why don't you climb up there and you get the shots?"

She thought about it for a moment. "Well, I am feeling a bit feisty tonight, so, why not? We can put the cameras in the bag and pulley them up to me, okay?"

Felix and Oscar looked at each other, surprised. "Okay, but can we finish our meal first?"

"Okay," she said, licking her plate one final time.

After Felix and Oscar licked their plates clean, the three picked up their gear and pawed their way through the crowd to the Old Oak. Just below the landing, two ropes hung from a pulley. Oscar put the cameras in a bag tied to the rope and Felix pulled down the other rope. Up went the cameras. Meanwhile, Savannah spit on her paws, inspected her razor sharp claws, and leaped onto the trunk. "Make way! Paparazzi coming!" she yelled, sprinting up the tree. She raced the camera bag to the top and won. Her silver tipped tail fluffed out as she climbed up on the landing and peered out over the edge. All the cats up there moved over for her, some climbing higher up the huge, lit-up branches of the old tree. "Wow! I haven't been up here in years! What a view! I can see everything!" She focused the camera and shot her aerial party pictures. Then she pulled out the video camera and filmed slowly from left to right. Savannah is very excited because *she* is a super reporter who will do just about anything for a great story! She has captured *The Party of The Century* from a magnificent birds' eye view. In fact, this was the most spectacular event she had filmed in a very long time!

48

$\mathcal{T}$he excited Graduates made a circle on the dance floor and moved back and forth to the blaring music. They were happy just being together and celebrating their magical evening.

"Hi, sweetheart," Ming said as she and Sam sashayed through the crowd over to Dutchey.

"Hi, Mom! Hi, Dad!" exclaimed elated Dutchey.

"Hi, kitten!" yelled Dad. He gave her a big hug and whisker kiss.

"Are you surprised, fluffs?" asked Mom, winking. She hugged Lashes and gave her a whisker kiss.

"Yes!" screamed Lashes and Dutchey.

"Worth the wait?" Mom asked. She gave her grown-up graduate a long hug and a big whisker kiss.

"Definitely!" replied Dutchey. "I love this! The theme is so purrfect! I can't wait to see *Kitty Maxx!*"

"I'm so excited!" Lashes added, her eyes darting everywhere, making sure she hadn't missed anything. "Are they here yet?"

Diamond answered, "No, not yet."

Dutchey's parents exchanged hugs and whisker kisses with Kool and Diamond. Miss Fancy squeezed in and hugged everyone, too. The rest of Dutchey's family danced over and inspected the prestigious gold medallions.

Ming spotted the mayor and his wife and waved. "Lily, Mac, we're over here!"

The glamorous couple danced over. Lily hugged the Graduate fluffs and wished them all the best. Mayor Mac shook paws with the Graduate toms and gave the fluffs big lion hugs.

Lily whispered, "You fluffs were spectacular tonight. I love you both so much." When they hugged her, she started to cry.

Lashes power purred. "Now Mom, you promised you weren't going to cry."

"I know. I know," she blubbered.

"You look very pretty tonight, Mom," Lashes said, changing the subject. "I just *love* your new scarf!"

She cried as she twirled her daughter's curly whiskers with her claw. She kissed her between her eyes. "I love my scarf, too! And I love you!"

"I love you back." Lashes dabbed her mom's super curly whiskers with the lacey scarf. "You can always count on my mom to get all wilty."

Dutchey smelled her lei, "The flowers and leis are amazing! And our necklaces are *the best!* Thank you for doing all this for us!"

"You're very welcome, sweetie. How's your leg feeling?"

"Good! No! Great!" They hugged again.

Mayor Mac congratulated Diamond and Kool, "You both were terrific at the ceremony! We're very proud of you."

"Thanks, Mayor," grinned Kool.

Diamond grinned, too. "Thanks, Mayor. You looked pretty good yourself, up there on stage, chattin' with the crowd."

The Mayor nodded and said, "And I return the compliment."

Diamond grabbed Lashes' mom and twirled her around the dance floor. He whispered in her ear, "The flowers and leis look great! You really helped me pull this party together with your special touch! Thank you so much!" He gave her a big whisker kiss and another twirl.

"You are very welcome, my dear," replied Lily, a bit surprised, but loving all the affection.

Diamond put her down and said very mannerly to her and the Mayor, "I hope you both have a terrific evening!"

"We are," said Lily, shaking out her fur and adjusting her lacey scarf.

Mayor Mac called over to Jett, "Jett, come over here for a second." Jett and Jade shimmied over along with Cleo.

"Congratulations, Jett," everyone said together.

"Thanks, everyone," Jett said, shaking paws and receiving hugs and whisker kisses.

Lily asked Jade, "Are you enjoying yourself, dear?"

"Yes, I am. This is a terrific celebration!"

Ming graciously added, "Welcome to Heavenly Hills, Princess! I hope you're having a royally good time."

"I am, thank you very much."

Lily asked Cleo, "Are you having a good time, sweetie?"

"Yes," replied Cleo. "The Club is beautiful tonight! The tropical paradise theme is so fun. I love it!"

Lashes asked her mom, "Where's Auntie Rose?"

"She's catching up with Grandfluff and Grandtom. She has so much to tell us about her photo shoot in Catcun. She left the shoot early so she could be here."

"How exciting!" gushed Lashes.

Dutchey agreed, "I can't wait to hear about everything!"

"Me, too," exclaimed Lashes.

Mom replied, "She has plenty to tell! What happened to your chin, Lashes?"

"I guess I got carried away. I've been jumping up and down and these medals are *heavy!*" She rubbed her chin with her paw. "Dad, would you wear one? Both medallions together are just too heavy."

"I'd love to," said Dad as he took a medallion off her neck and proudly placed it around his own.

Adoring Lashes said, "Thanks for the speech, Daddy."

"You're welcome, my little kitten." He gave her another lion hug.

"Dad, would you wear one of mine?" yelled Dutchey. Her dad was spinning on his head in the middle of the dance floor.

Mom shook her head, "I'll wear it, honey. He might hurt himself with it. I think his lei and chain have already choked him three times!"

"Dad's crazy!" exclaimed Dutchey.

"I know, dear. His Siamese-ness is coming out tonight. How's your leg?"

"Okay… terrific…" she grimaced.

Mom tilted her pretty head and smiled at her grown-up graduate. She gave her a kiss on her head and said, "Enjoy your wonderful celebration, my precious daughter. You deserve this."

"I will! I will!" sang Dutchey as Mom and company danced away.

Mac II, wearing his flowery lei, be-bopped through the crowd over to Lashes and friends.

He yelled, "Congrats, little sis! Congrats, Kool!"

"Thanks, dude."

"Thanks, Mac," Lashes snickered at big brother macho tom and his purrty lei.

"Congrats, Diamond and Dutchey."

"Thanks, Mac," they said together.

Kool asked, "Where's Bobby?"

"I don't know. I haven't seen him yet," answered Mac II, "I think we're supposed to share a dance together or something." Everyone who heard that laughed at Mac II.

"Where's Crystal?" asked Lashes.

"Eating," answered Mac II.

"Where's Heather, Jasmine, Taffee, and Toffee?" asked Dutchey.

"With her, eating!"

"Well, look who's here!" announced Jett. "It's the Bully brothers!"

"Hey, cats!" Bull said as he hip slammed Jett into Jade. "Introduce us *mysterious stranger!*" The fluffs giggled at the three roughians wearing leis.

Jett announced, "This is my cousin, Cleo, and this is Princess Jade. Fluffs, this is Bull, Chip, and Fangy Bully."

Fangy looked at Cleo and Cleo looked at Fangy.

"Hi," said Cleo.

"Hi," said Fangy, staring.

"Hi," greeted Jade.

"Evenin,' fluffs," Bull bellowed. Chip just stood there, speechless, in awe of such beauty. Bull hip slammed him. "Dance, dude!"

"Hi, toms," said Lashes.

Bull greeted everyone in a gruff voice, "Hey Lashes! Hey Dutchey! Hey Kool! Hey, Big Diamond. Rad bash! I just love the flowery leis!" he said sarcastically.

"You look about as tom as we do," laughed Diamond. He stuck his tongue out at Kool.

Just to return the favor, Kool and the Bully brothers stuck out their tongues at Diamond, who was laughing hysterically at his macho buds. He has been waiting for this moment all day, too.

The dance floor was smokin'! Fangy and Cleo were shakin' it up together. Jett, Princess Jade, and Chip were shakin' it down. Lashes and Kool were break dancing. Diamond, Dutchey, and Bull were doing the electric slide, or in Dutchey's case, the electric twitch. Big cats were dancing with little cats. Geeky toms with leis on, who would have rather been wallflowers, were dragged out to the dance floor by excited fluffs who just want to have fun. Q was literally shaking up the place. Other cats found it amusing to chase their own tails until they were dizzy. The Heavenly Hills County Club was packed and rockin' out!

The cheerleading squad: Jolene, Clairese, Blanche, and Coco hit the crowded dance floor and pushed their way over to their captains.

Clairese yelled over the loud music, "Fluff-friends!"

"Hey, fluffs!" Lashes shouted back, her voice cracking.

"Aloha, fluffs!" yelled Dutchey.

"What a great party!" Jolene exclaimed.

Coco complimented, "Diamond, this bash is fab! I love the leis and the whole luau theme!"

"Aloha," said proud Diamond, "are you fluffs having a good time?"

Everyone yelled together, "Yes!"

"Great!" Then he said into Dutchey's ear, "Let's move closer to the front. Pass it on."

"Yes!" She told Lashes and her friends, "We're moving closer to the front! Pass it on."

"Psssst. Kool," said Lashes, "we're moving closer to the front. Pass it on."

Kool nodded and yelled in Jett's direction, "Jett, we're moving to the front. Pass it on."

Jett was face to face with Jade, staring into her captivating green eyes, his stomach flipping and flopping to the beat of the music. Without looking away, he yelled, "Cleo, we're moving to the front."

Cleo looked over with a happy smile because she was hip hopping with all three Bully brothers now!

"Okay," she yelled, "come on, you good lookin' hunks of fur. We're movin' to the front."

49

$\mathcal{A}$s the gang inched their way closer to center stage, they danced into Diamond's family.

"Aloha, Mom and Dad," said Diamond III. "Aloha, family."

"Son, look at you," exclaimed Dad, admiring all three of his medallions.

Mom rubbed whiskers with her young tom and whispered in his ear, "You did such a wonderful job at the ceremony! I am so very proud of you!"

"Thanks, Mom."

"Don't trip over all your medallions," said Dad, beaming with pride. Diamond nodded and wore a toothy smile. "This is a great party! Thanks, Mom and Dad."

"You're very welcome, Diamond Thomas." Dad leaned closer and whispered in Diamond's ear, "Son, you're kickin' tail tonight and you're makin' me proud. You did an excellent job commentating the ceremony and in planning this luau—I am very impressed!"

Diamond III continued wearing his toothy grin. "Thanks, Dad, you helped." They hugged and shook paws.

Pearl addressed the fluffs, "Dutchess, Lashes, you both look so beautiful tonight!"

"Thank you," replied the fluffs, "so do you!"

Pearl asked Dutchey, "How's your leg, sweetheart?"

"Fine… " she said weakly, her ears were tweaked back and actually bending forward at the tips.

Pearl rubbed both their whiskers. "During your ceremony, I was so excited for you both! You looked so graceful as you padded up to the stage to receive your awards." Her eyes misted up. The fluffs smiled and gave her snuggles. She's another mom, too.

"Thank you for this wonderful party!" said Lashes.

Diamond's mom replied, "You've earned it. Congratulations to you both! I love you!"

"We love you, too!" the fluffs told her as they hugged her and whisker kissed.

Diamond's parents gave Kool and Jett hugs and paw shakes, too. "Congratulations, toms! We're so excited for you!"

"Thanks, Mr. and Mrs. Castleberry," Kool and Jett each replied.

Next was Auntie Belle's turn. She gave tons of kisses and hugs. "Congratulations, my kittens! I knew you could do it! And you will always be kittens to me, no matter how old you get! I love you all!"

"Thank you, Auntie Belle. We love you, too!" A growing crowd of cats surrounded Auntie Belle. She knows most of the students because they come by her after school hang-out.

Jett announced to Diamond's family, "You all remember my cousin, Cleo."

Pearl gave her a big hug. "Aloha, Cleo. It's so nice to see you again!"

"Aloha! It's great to see you, too. This is a fantastic party! I've always loved your club!"

"Thank you, dear," Pearl replied.

Auntie Belle squeezed in and gave her a hug. "How have you been Miss Cleocatra? I've missed you. Look at you... all grown up!"

"I've been terrific and I've missed you, too. I cannot wait to visit your seaside café. I love all the celebrity pictures you have hanging on the walls."

"Come and visit anytime, sweetheart."

"Thank you, Auntie Belle." They hugged again.

Jett yelled over the booming music, "Everyone, this is Princess Jade from Pintac. This is Diamond's family."

Diamond's mom welcomed her, "Aloha, sweetheart. We are so glad you could be here for this special celebration. You make it even more special!"

"Thank you so much. It is very nice to meet you. I love your gorgeous club!"

"Thank you, Princess," replied Diamond's dad. "You make sure to enjoy yourself, okay?"

"I am," she said with a great big smile.

Auntie Belle greeted Jade, "Aloha, Princess Jade. You must come with Cleo and the gang and visit my café. I have tables outside now and the view is fabulous!"

Jade replied, "I intend to visit. I have heard so much about your trendy café! It's called The Shooting Star, right?"

"That's right." She whispered in Jade's ear, "I've already framed and hung up the famous picture of you and Jett at the airport! It's the town buzz!"

"I think I like that," the Princess replied, winking at Jett. His stomach flipped all the way over this time.

"Don't forget about the group photo later on," reminded Diamond's mom as his dad whisked her away. "Have a great celebration…" Her words faded away as she floated across the dance floor.

The gang continued on their quest to reach center stage. On the way, they danced into Nurse Hissy and Dr. Fitt dancing with Miss Hissy and Principal Fitt. Dr. Fitt was spinning on his head, but took time out to talk to Dutchey.

"Dutchess," he said, getting up on his paws, "how's that leg feeling?"

"Okay," she replied, "but more importantly, are you having a good time, Dr. Fitt?"

"Yes, yes." Dr. Fitt nodded and shook out his fur.

"We're having a delightful time, dear. Just delightful!" assured Nurse Hissy.

Principal Fitt was busy trying to keep his top hat on while learning the four-paw-shuffle from Miss Hissy, but did manage to tell everyone, "Congratulations!"

"Thank you," everyone howled together.

"Take it easy, little one," Dr. Fitt instructed Dutchey.

"I promise." She whispered to Lashes, "He should talk!"

Lashes tried to laugh, but only a squeaky noise came out.

Dutchey laughed and commented, "Lashes, your voice, you went from chirping to squeaking!"

Lashes tried to laugh again, and nothing came out. She whispered, "I'm having such a fun time. Are you, Dutch?"

Dutchey whispered back, "I am having a *fabulous* time!" They pinky clawed.

Next, they danced over by the Tomlinson Twins, Tommy and Tony, who are handsome black and gray toms. Tony has a black circle around his left eye that makes him look bad! They also play on Paw Valley's undefeated soccer team.

Tommy yelled through the crowd, "Great party, big Diamond."

Diamond looked over at Kool and laughed. Sarcastic Kool said to his soccer mates, "Buds, purple orchids, it's so you!" They all stuck out their tongues at each other.

Bull was vibrating across the dance floor. He was on the move and everyone cleared a path. Q found a dance partner: Auntie Belle. Finally, the group reached the front at the same time Mayor Mac jumped up on stage and stood behind the microphone. The medallion he was wearing reflected the colorful lights flashing across the stage. He also was wearing a large *Key* hanging from a wide red ribbon. The music played softly so everyone could hear what the Mayor of Heavenly Hills had to say. Eager Savannah held up her microphone.

Enthusiastic Mayor Mac spoke into the microphone, "Graduates: Aloha and Congratulations! You were all terrific during the ceremony! I'm so proud of each and every one of you!" He paused while the crowd on the dance floor cheered and howled. "Graduates, you have all worked very hard and have earned this special celebration. I hope you will make wonderful memories tonight so you will have something great to look back on and remember, when you get as old as I am, that is!" The crowd responded with euphoric cheers. The mayor continued, "Now, I have been informed that we have a Royal Princess here tonight! Right here in our very presence!"

Savannah got a chill back and yelled, "I knew it! I knew it! Felix, Oscar, get it all!"

50

$\mathcal{J}$ade gulped. She was not expecting this at all. The crowd whistled and chanted, "Jade! Jade! Jade! Jade!"

Mayor Mac continued, "Would Princess Jade from Pintac please come up on stage?"

Jett helped Jade onto Q's back and then she high jumped to the stage. She looked out at the crowd of cats chanting her name and acting all wild and crazy! She thought, "Wow! These cats are *really* excited I'm here! For me, this is very exciting!"

Mayor Mac took off the gold *Key.* "Princess Jade, I would like to present to you this *Key to the City.* You are welcome anywhere here in Heavenly Hills. Just wear this *Key* and the doors of our city will magically open. On behalf of every feline in Heavenly Hills, we hope your stay is filled with good times and wonderful memories." He draped the *Key* around her neck.

Savannah asked her crew, "Are you getting this, toms?"

"Every word," whispered Felix. "Shhh."

Princess Jade took a deep breath and spoke into the microphone, "Thank you, Mayor Holcomb. I am overwhelmed by your graciousness. Heavenly Hills is lovely and I intend to investigate every inch of it!" The crowd roared with enthusiasm as she continued, "I want to congratulate everyone for achieving your goals and earning such an amazing ceremony and celebration. You all looked just splendid as you received your precious gold medallions earlier this evening. I know I will always remember this night as a wonderful memory and I hope you will, too. My good wishes and congratulations go out to everyone! Thank you again, Sir." She twirled her *Key* and flashed her gorgeous royal smile. The camera flashes were blinding. The music started up again when Mayor Mac jumped off stage. The crowd whistled as Jade jumped off the stage and landed beside her new friends, who immediately inspected her *Key*.

Jade exclaimed, "Lashes, your father is so generous!"

"Wow!" replied Lashes, "I don't think I've ever seen him give any cat *The Key to the City* before! You are very special!" She gave Jade a big hug.

Jett stood there silently admiring Jade. He had grand ideas of his own. He plans to take her everywhere and show her everything. Too bad she's only staying for a month.

Cleo ran her paw pad down the smooth *Key* and shook her head at Jade.

Jade asked, "What? What did I do?"

Cleo whispered in Jade's ear, "It looks like we may have to beg to stay, fluff-friend."

"We'll have to be very convincing," the Princess whispered back. The two fluffs from Pintac stared at each other and imagined how different life would be if they were to stay and go to school with the gang here in Heavenly Hills.

Fangy grabbed Cleo's tail by surprise and away they went.

The older teen cats danced over to Jett and Princess Jade.

"Introduce us, Mac," urged Crystal.

Mac II looked at Jett, "Would you please do the honors?"

"Of course," he yelled over the loud music. "This is Princess Jade from Pintac. Meet Diamond's cousin: Crystal, Kool's cousin: Bobby, Dutchey's cousins: Heather and Jasmine, Mac's cousins: Toffee and Taffee. They will all be High School Juniors in September. And this is Mac's Auntie Rose."

"It is so very nice to meet you, Princess," Crystal yelled over the loud music. "We'll have to take you out on the town while you're here."

"It's a pleasure meeting all of you and I would like that very much," Princess Jade replied.

"Aloha, Princess Jade," said handsome Bobby Katt.

"Aloha," she smiled.

Toffee suggested, "You'll have to come to our underwater restaurant, Below Sea Level, and dine with us."

Taffee added, "But we won't make you catch your own dinner like we usually do."

"I'd love to," laughed Jade.

Heather added, "And, you have to come to our nightclub, The Sphinx, and party down with us, too!"

Jade nodded, "Dutchey took us for a tour of Heavenly Hills today, and we saw The Sphinx! It is the most incredible club I have ever seen, from the outside anyway!" She paused and looked closely at the beautiful cat with the curly whiskers under the purple hat. "Are you Rose Somerset, the famous super model?"

"Well, yes, I am," said Auntie Rose, twirling her curly whiskers.

"I thought so. Were you on the cover of *Snooze* last month?" asked Jade.

"Yes, that was me. We had a blast in St. Coy. We shot at the Villa Le Coy Hotel and Resort. You must go there! It's beautiful!"

"Wow! It's a pleasure to meet you!" exclaimed Jade.

"It is an honor to meet you, Princess Jade." They shook paws, then hugged.

Savannah popped up and whispered in Rose's ear, "Is that Princess Jade from Pintac?"

Rose whispered, "Yes, shall I introduce you?"

"Would you be a doll?"

"Princess Jade, I'd like to introduce you to my dear friend, Ms. Savannah Sizzleton. She is the top fashion specialist of *Feline Flair* magazine."

"Hello, Ms. Sizzleton. Oh-my-gosh, I read your column all the time and I love it! You really keep us fluffs informed of the latest fashion trends and the very best vacation spots!"

"It is such an honor to meet you, Princess. How long are you staying in Heavenly Hills?"

"We plan to stay for one month."

"I would love an interview with you before you leave. Just to get your thoughts of your vacation to our fabulous city."

"Yes, I think that could be arranged."

Savannah screamed and got a chill tail, "Can I get a picture?"

"Sure." Jade squeezed next to Savannah.

"Do you want me in the picture?" asked Savannah, surprised.

"Of course. And I'd like a copy for my photo album, okay?"

"Wow! Okay! Get good ones, Oscar."

They posed pretty, then snobby.

"Thank you, Princess Jade. This has been such an honor!" said Savannah.

"The pleasure is all mine. I'm a big fan of yours!"

"Thank you," replied Savannah, "I look forward to our chat." She looked over at Jett. "Are you *the mysterious stranger?*"

"Yes, he is," answered Jade. Jett looked silly with one ear folded back.

"Can I have a picture of both of you together?"

"Sure," she replied as she reached over with her paw to fix Jett's ear.

"Oscar, get several." They put their whiskers together and smiled purrty. "Thank you, thank you... " Savannah's words faded as other cats squeezed her out, wanting their chance to meet the Princess of Pintac. But, that's okay. She's happy anyway. A thought crossed her mind, "I have not one, not two, but maybe even three very high profile interviews! I am so proud of myself!"

Diamond's dad danced over and secretly alerted Diamond, "They're here. They're unloading at the back entrance."

Diamond's turquoise eyes twinkled. "Do they need any help?"

"No. They have a crew of cats who seem to know just what they're doing."

"Okay. How much time?"

"Let's say about twenty minutes and then you announce them. Wait for my signal."

"Okay."

Anxious Dutchey asked, "Are they here? Are they here?" Diamond grinned and turned up the volume of his purr.

"Are they? Are they?" asked Lashes. Diamond purred louder than ever, if possible.

Dutchey put her ears back and yelled at him, "You are such a brat!"

Diamond just kept grinning and purring, but stopped when he noticed Dutchey holding up her back leg. "Do you need to lie down, Dutch?"

Dutchey fiercely replied, "No Way! I am not leaving this spot. It took us half the night to get here!"

"Okay, okay, just lean on me." He steadied himself to be the rock his friend needed to lean on tonight.

Kool pulled Lashes' tail. "Look at the *Prince* and *Princess.*"

Lashes looked over at Jett and Jade. "Wow! He went from *mysterious stranger* to *Prince* in less than twenty-four hours!" They both smiled at the royal couple.

Kool teased, "Awww," and shot a fake arrow in their direction.

Jade whispered into Jett's ear, "I'm having the best time of my life." She was standing so close he could smell her lavender perfume.

"So am I," he whispered back. "I'm very glad you came with Cleo." Their noses were about half an inch away from each other's when, all of a sudden, *wham!* Jett got hip slammed from behind and his nose crashed right into Jade's nose. And what a nose crunch it was! Jett's world was spinning! "Sorry," he said, licking his nose.

"That's okay. I really didn't mind," she said, rubbing her nose with her paw. Jade has never felt this feeling before. Butterfly City, that's where she is, a very long way away from the oh-so-protected walls of the palace. "It sure is fun just being a cat," she thought as she licked her nose, "I'm letting my fur down tonight, and I'm going to have the best time of my life! This is so fantastic!"

Jacqueline, Jill, Jo, Pepper, Vienna, and Brianna bounced over to Dutchey and friends.

Diamond teased, "Such big leis for such little fluffettes!"

"Aloha, little fluffettes," yelled Dutchey, Lashes, and Kool.

"Aloha," they yelled with big smiles and then bounced away.

"They're so cute!" commented Dutchey.

Kool's parents, Duke and Dora, and Auntie Ruby and Uncle Surf spotted Kool and his friends on the dance floor and danced over.

"Nice medallions, Kool," Dad said. Mom smiled at her handsome son and gave him a hug and many whisker kisses. Kool twirled her around in a circle.

"We're very proud of you," complimented Dad.

"Thanks, Mom and Dad." Kool put one medallion around his mother's neck and one around his father's neck.

Dora puddled up and blubbered, "I'm so proud of you, my little *tommy-tom.*"

"*Mom!*" snapped Kool. "*Do I have to keep reminding you?*"

"Of what, *tom-tom?*"

"Those names! No more tommy-tom or tom-tom. It's just plain old *tom* now!"

She sobbed loudly, "My *b a b y!"* Kool twirled her around and around until she was too dizzy to cry. They both laughed as they staggered around.

Auntie Ruby whispered in Kool's ear, "You were so handsome on stage as you received your medallions. Your uncle and I are very proud of you!"

"Thank you, Auntie." He twirled her around the dance floor too, and her fancy hat flew off.

Uncle Surf was dancing close by and yelled, "Congratulations, Diamond."

"Thank you," said Diamond as they exchanged paw shakes.

Kool picked up his Auntie's flashy hat and put it on. Someone snapped a picture.

"This is a beautiful party, Diamond," blubbered sentimental Dora, "and you were just purrfect at the ceremony." She wiped her wet face with the back of her paw.

"Thank you. I hope you are all having a great time and enjoying the entertainment!" He twirled Dora around and around. As Diamond dizzily staggered around, laughing with Kool's mother, Kool took off Ruby's hat and put it on Diamond.

Auntie Ruby yelled, "Congratulations, Diamond. You were fabulous tonight!"

"Thank you, Auntie. Do I look as good in your hat as you do?" He was still staggering around.

"Better!" she laughed.

Diamond took it off and put it on Uncle Surf's head. "I think it looks better on Uncle Surf!"

Dora praised Lashes and Dutchey, *"Fluff-fluffs,* you both look gorgeous tonight! I'm so excited for you. Congratulations!"

Dutchey and Lashes exchanged a look, but held back their hisses. "Thank you. So do you! Your necklace is gorgeous!" They exchanged affectionate snuggles and kisses.

All misty, Dora told the fluff-fluffs, "I love you both. You are like my own *fluffettes."*

"We love you, too." She's another mom, too. Duke grabbed Dora and they danced away.

Dutchey whispered to Lashes, "*Those names!*"

Lashes squeaked, "Will we *ever* outgrow them?"

"It sure doesn't seem like it."

Next, the gang danced into Jett's family and they gathered around to inspect Jett's medallions.

Dad remarked, "You have made me very proud, Jett." He paused and asked, "Didn't you receive three medallions?"

"Cleo and Jade are wearing my other two." Dad nodded and smiled.

Ginger hugged her young tom and whispered in his ear, "I'm so happy for you."

"Thanks, Mom," he said as he twirled her in a circle.

Auntie Spicy and Uncle Clovis hugged their wonderful nephew and inspected his medallion. Next, Uncle Sanford and Auntie Frangelica did their inspection and exchanged hugs and kisses.

Uncle Sanford yelled to Jett, "You're going to be the next world famous tennis star, aren't you?"

Jett smiled and twitched his whiskers.

Auntie Frangelica slyly asked, "Will you play a high-spirited game with me? I want to see first paw what all this fuss is about."

"Auntie, I would love to play a high-spirited game of tennis with you!"

"Good. Then it's a date!" she replied with a gleam in her eye. "You better watch out though, tom. I'm quite good!" She winked at him.

"I look forward to the challenge, Auntie!"

Next, Frangelica inspected Jade's new *Key*. "You're pretty spectacular, Princess. Everyone loves you already!"

Jade smiled. "Thank you for bringing me along with you. I'm having a fantastic time."

"You're welcome, Jade." They exchanged warm hugs. "If only your parents could see you now. They would be very proud."

Ginger hugged her, "I'm so glad you're here, honey. I hope you're enjoying yourself."

"I am! I am!" She looked over and smiled at Jett who was wearing a goofy grin.

"Let me know if you need anything," added Jett's mom.

"I will, thank you. The guesthouse is gorgeous. I watched the sun come up this morning."

"I'm so glad you like it." Kool and Diamond bumped into Jett's mom. "Congratulations my magnificent toms."

Kool gave her a twirl around hug. "Thanks, Mrs. Stone."

Next, Diamond twirled her around the other way, so she could unwind. "Thank you, Mrs. Stone."

Ginger praised the Graduate fluffs with snuggly hugs. Yes, she's another mom, too.

Without warning, Diamond jumped up on stage and took the microphone in his paw.

"Aloha, Everyone!" He held the microphone out to the crowd.

"Aloha!" they yelled back.

"I say we should crank up the music! We have some serious partying to do! Let's rock this house down!" He started singing, "*Now put your paws in the air like you don't care!*" The crowd on the dance floor sang with him, putting their front paws up and waving back and forth. The music blasted out and everyone slam danced to *The Back Alley Toms* song, "I'm Gonna Catch Ya." Then, *TechnoCatz'* electrifying songs, "Spaced-Out" and "Shake Your Tail." There was a quick change to country western star, *Tabby Hunter,* and his #1 hit, "Fences." Auntie Belle got a tear in her eye. Bull challenged Diamond to a dance contest. Both cats used their best moves and were quite entertaining. The fluffs danced into their fur-dressers, Mickey Manx, Lorenzo, Tootie, and dates.

"You all look absolutely gorgeous tonight!" exclaimed Mickey.

"Fluffs, I am so excited for you!" gushed Lorenzo. "You are like movie-stars!"

"Congratulations, fluffs!" yelled Tootie.

"We couldn't have done it without you," chirped Lashes.

"How's the leg, Dutchess?" asked Mickey.

Her ears went back and she growled.

"That good, huh," replied Mickey.

Dutchey smiled a weak smile, "I'm having such a great time anyway, in spite of things."

"That's the spirit!" exclaimed Lorenzo.

A group of excited cats doing back flips on the dance floor pushed

Mickey, Lorenzo, Tootie, and their dates out of talking range. They threw paw kisses and joined the Conga line.

Next, the fluffs met up with their favorite cheerleading coach, Miss Dubois, who also taught their Poise and Balance class. She is a beautiful cat with soft brown fur and cream-colored swirl markings. They exchanged hugs and told her they will miss her next year.

"No. Don't be sad, fluffs. I just found out today that I am going to teach Advanced Poise and Balance at Heavenly Hills High starting in September! I'm also head coach for the Junior Varsity Cheerleading Squad, so you both better make it at tryouts!" She leaned in closer and excitedly screamed, "I'm one of the judges!" The fluffs screamed and jumped with happiness. They love Miss Dubois! "Then I will see you both this summer at practice. Congratulations and have a very fun evening…" She was swept off by her handsome escort. The fluffs were thrilled at this bit of great news!

Diamond's dad got his attention and gave him the claws up sign. The time has finally come to introduce the special guests. He nodded back to his dad and looked over at Dutchey and Lashes. "Ready to rock out, fluffs?"

"Yes! Yes!" They screamed and jumped up and down.

"Save my spot, I'll be right back." Diamond jumped onto the stage, again. The crowd was wild as they watched their class president stand behind the microphone. He howled into the microphone, then yelled out, "One… Two… One… Two… Can everyone hear me?" The crowd cheered and howled back. He stood there waiting and watching his out-of-control classmates chant, *"Kitty Maxx! Kitty Maxx! Kitty Maxx!"*

"Okay, Okay, Fellow Grads!" He caught Dutchey's eye and winked. She was screaming and jumping up and down, appearing to forget all about her leg. She landed in the splits position.

"I'm so excited!" squeaked Lashes, helping Dutchey up.

"This is the best night ever!" she exclaimed.

Finally, the crowd calmed down, just long enough for Diamond to begin his speech and introduce tonight's exciting entertainment. "As your Class President, for a few more hours anyway, I would like to congratulate all of us for making it this far!" Everyone laughed and held up their shiny medallions. "What a good lookin' bunch of cats! You're all so shiny, I need my shades!" He was extremely proud as he looked out over his classmates, who persistently howled and whistled. "You're a noisy bunch, too!" He looked over at Dutchey and shook his head. Bad leg or not, all the screaming and jumping—she is definitely out of control! Diamond continued, "I would like to introduce tonight's very special guest. This group has the #1 hit CD right now and is the hottest group around! Please put your paws together and help me welcome, *Kitty Maxx!*" The crowd was completely hysterical as the trio of nice looking toms came on stage, all wearing leis and tropical shirts. The cool drummer wore a hat with a pink flamingo feather sticking up. Diamond jumped off the stage and wedged himself between Dutchey and Lashes, who were screaming at the top of their lungs.

Hearing aid anyone?

51

Kitty Maxx began their performance with "Betchya Can't Dance." The Grads proved them wrong. Bull vibrated across the dance floor, Kool was tossin' it around and Diamond was doin' his version of the hustle. Jade and Jett were in their own little world. Lashes and Dutchey were still screaming.

"They are so cute!" Dutchey yelled to Lashes.

Lashes squeaked, "*I love them!* I hope they sing, "I'm Still Not Over You." I love that song!"

"I do, too! This is so awesome!" yelled Dutchey.

After *Kitty Maxx* finished their first song, the energized crowd howled and whistled ecstatically. A couple of fluffs were so excited they fainted. A couple of toms poured ice water on them and they quickly revived.

"Aloha, Grad Cats!" Jay, the enthusiastic lead singer said into the microphone. "We hear Congratulations are in order."

Loud cheering and Aloha's exploded from the boisterous crowd. The group up there on the Old Oak landing were howling and making a tremendous amount of noise.

Drummer Jazz added, "Work hard in high school and whatever you do, don't just dream it, *Be It!*"

More howling erupted from the dance floor as the music started. Neon strobe lights flashed through the crowd.

"I love "Jungle Kitty!" exclaimed Dutchey. "It's a great song!" Her fur was sticking out everywhere.

This song is a fast little number that took energy to a new level. Q was spinning on the dance floor. Ming and Siam Sam were dancing salsa style. Diamond II and Pearl were dancing the cha-cha. Sophia, Consuelo, Belle, Rose, and Savannah looked spectacular doing the shimmy-shimmy-shake. Jade let loose of all her royal inhibitions and Jett was seeing fireworks. Bull challenged Diamond to another shakedown competition. Now, that was definitely entertainment at its finest! Cleo and Fangy were prowling and laughing.

"Finally," Cleo exclaimed, "someone who knows the kitty meow!" Fangy laughed as they prowled and hissed at each other.

The dance floor was smokin'! *Kitty Maxx's* 12½-minute song ended with the crowd wild!

"Okay, Grads," said Shay, the guitar player, "we're going to take things down a notch and sing a love song for all you romantic cats out there. This song is called, "Falling for You." We hope you enjoy it."

The fur on Dutchey's back stood straight up. "I *love* this song!"

"I do too!" squeaked Lashes.

They both had purrfect mohawks as the band struck the first few chords of the song. Diamond moved a little closer to his Siamese friend. They locked eyes for a moment. Diamond's gaze can be so intense at times. Dutchey's tummy flip-flopped.

"Love your mohawk," he said to her.

"Shhh." Even her tail was fluffed out. They touched whisker-to-whisker and moved with the crowd to *Kitty Maxx's* #1 hit song.

As Jade and Jett swayed with the crowd, Jade commented, "I really like this band."

"I knew you would. They are definitely *hot!*"

Jade looked over at her friend, Cleo, and smiled. She was between Chip and Fangy, swaying with the crowd. Lashes and Kool were swaying side by side. Lashes with her big smile and Kool, well, he's just totally cool, even sporting a flowery lei. Mac II and Crystal swayed whisker to whisker. Even Siam Sam put a lid on his wild moves long enough to stare into Ming's eyes.

"You're just as crazy as these kittens," Ming whispered in her husband's ear.

"I love you, Mingypoo!" he whispered in her ear.

"I love you too, Sammypoo!" she whispered back.

After that romantic ballad, the band took the crowd into another dimension with, "Lovin' Life." The crowd loved them. The next song they sang was, "Blue Eyes."

Diamond looked into Dutchey's blue eyes and said, "I dedicate this song to you, blue eyes."

"You are so sweet," she whispered in his ear. Now his tummy took a flip.

Lashes looked at Kool face-to-face and declared, "I wish they would just get together or something! They look so cute!"

"Who?" he asked, looking around.

"Those two. Diamond and Dutch."

"Oh… those two. All in good time, blue eyes, all in good time," replied Kool, *the romantic*, staring into Lashes' blue eyes. "You know what?"

"What?" she asked, tilting her pretty little head.

"You have a cute face!"

"You have a cute face too, Kool Katt!" His ears fluttered.

Next, *Kitty Maxx* kicked up the energy with their cool song, "Blast."

Dutchey's leg cramped up and wickedly kicked outward. Everyone around her who saw Diamond get whacked by her kick thought she had just invented a new dance move. Within a few seconds, everyone was doing Dutchey's twitchy dance move. It was catching on like wild fire! Every cat was getting into the beat with the right leg jerk, laughing, twitching, and jerking.

After *Kitty Maxx* finished "Blast," Jay commented on this new dance move. "It's really fun to watch you cats get into the groove with a new move. What do you call it?"

Kool yelled out, "It's called *The Dutchess Twitch!*"

"I love it!" said Shay. The other toms in the band agreed.

Jazz added, "That move is cutting edge." He drummed out a drum roll and hit his cymbals.

"Are you ready for more, Grads?" Shay asked.

The crowd cheered and howled. "Now we're going to sing, "All I Want Is You."

This was another slow and romantic ballad. The crowd moved with the beat and fell in love. After a few more songs, *Kitty Maxx* said "goodnight" and left the stage. Diamond jumped on stage and got everyone going. The rowdy crowd would neither quiet down nor leave the dance floor.

Everyone yelled, "Encore. Encore."

After a few minutes of yelling and chanting that turned into one continuous roar, *Kitty Maxx* came back on stage and took their places. The crowd whistled and then hushed.

"You cats are great for our egos," said Jay. "Here's a song that is about every one of you in one way or another. It's called, "Eclipse." This song has a lively beat to dance to. The entire crowd—big and little cats were definitely enjoying the live entertainment. This was turning out to be truly *The Party of the Century*.

52

*T*he dance floor is stuffed to the *maxx!* The Heavenly Hills Country Club is filled to the brim with every kind of cat you could think of. Big cats, little cats, cats with long fur, cats with no fur, ultra deluxe cats, old and eccentric cats. It's pure enjoyment to just sit and watch!

After the third encore, that included Lashes' favorite, "I'm Still Not Over You," *Kitty Maxx* took a final bow and padded over to the Old Oak where a celebrity table was set up for autographs. Confetti covered the long table along with stacks of photographs. There was a long line of fluffs already waiting to meet the handsome trio of *Kitty Maxx* and receive an autographed photo.

Diamond jumped on stage. "*Is Kitty Maxx the best or what?*" he yelled at the howling crowd, who howled even louder. "*Kitty Maxx* is over by the Old Oak signing photographs. Meet ya there… " He jumped off the stage and landed next to Dutchey and Lashes. "Come on, fluffs, let's get some pictures of *Kitty Maxx!*"

"Yesss!" the fluffs screamed with excitement.

Dutchey instructed the fluffs, "Come on, Jade and Cleo. Come on, fluffs." Blanche, Jolene, Coco, and Clairese caught up and squeezed in line.

Blanche exclaimed, "Great dance move, Dutchey!" The squad laughed at her.

"You guys, it wasn't me. It was this dumb old leg," she complained and pointed at her back leg.

"I don't care what it was," teased Coco, "it's an awesome move!" She imitated poor Dutchey and her jerky dance move as her fluff-friends playfully joined in. Dutchey put her ears back and hissed at them, and then she laughed with them.

There was a gap in the line and Diamond urged, "Fluffs, let's get serious here. Catch up." They scrambled to close the gap. Finally, they were next in line.

As Dutchey limped to the table, Jay asked her name and wrote it on the photograph on the bottom right corner, wishing her love and luck. He looked at her curiously and asked, "Are you *the* Dutchess who invented *The Dutchess Twitch?*"

She smiled her biggest smile. "Yes! That's me!"

"Nice dance move!" he complimented and winked. Dutchey was so excited she almost passed out.

Jazz asked Lashes her name. She stood there, speechless, with a big smile and swollen chin. She was having a brain freeze.

"Her name is Lashes," piped up Cleo. "My name is Cleocatra and this is Jade."

"Hi, Cleocatra," said Jazz. "I love your name." He autographed a picture and gave one to her and one to Lashes. "Here ya go, curly whiskers." Lashes just stood there, frozen in time.

Shay looked at Jade. "Are you *the Princess Jade from Pintac?*" The Princess was having a brain freeze, too.

"Yes," Cleo answered for her.

"It is very nice to meet you, your Highness," said Shay, bowing his head. The toms of *Kitty Maxx* stood up and did a fancy twirl and bow for the special Princess.

"Thank you," she said, regaining composure. "You were all just magnificent tonight! You are all so talented! I will cherish tonight's memory and my picture forever!" She took her picture and kissed it. The group thanked her and asked her to sign one of their photographs for them. She was delighted to do so. The photographer took a picture.

"Thank you," squeaked Lashes, coming to as she and her fluff-friends were pushed out of the way by the excited cheerleading squad.

Kool, Jett, and Diamond were standing back by the tropical island cabana, waiting for the fluffs to come back. Diamond was keeping one eye on Dutch and one eye on all the happenings at the party.

Finally, here they come, each wearing a silly grin as they floated back to the grass. With scowls on their faces, the toms watched as the fluffs floated right passed them with photographs hanging from their teeth. The fluffs didn't even notice them.

"What's with them?" asked Kool. "Don't they see us? Did we suddenly become invisible?"

"Really!" scowled Diamond. "They appear to be in some kind of trance." The toms followed them to the grassy spot and jumped up on the rock overhead. They looked down at the fluffs, who were lying on their backs, gazing at the stars. They had swollen chins and big silly grins.

Jett shook his head. *"Dude!* I think they're still in *Kitty Maxx*-land."

"Hey down there, are you fluffs okay?" inquired Diamond. There was no reply. "Hey! You fluffs down there," repeated Diamond. There was still no reply.

"I think we lost èm," commented Kool, shaking his head.

"They are way gone," added Jett, staring at Miss Princess Velvet Fur.

"Hey," teased Diamond, "if you fluffs don't snap out of your *Kitty Maxx* trance, we're going to… uh… toss you in the pool!" Quickly the fluffs flipped over.

"No Way!" exclaimed Dutchess. "The pool is the last place I want to visit tonight!" Lashes and her big smile were in a daze. The bump on her chin was getting bigger by the minute. Jade and Cleo stared in awe at their new pictures.

Excited Cleo exclaimed, *"Wow!"*

"I know!" agreed excited Jade, outlining one of the cats with her French tipped claw.

They both screamed together, "This is so exciting!"

"Do we want group pictures?" asked Diamond.

"Yes!"

Kool said, "The line is over there." He pointed his big paw at the long line to the Big Pineapple.

Dutchey stood up, put her ears back, and then collapsed on the grass. "My leg hurts and it keeps jerking."

"How'd that happen, jumping bean?" teased Kool.

"I know, I know. I was a jumping maniac out there, wasn't I?"

Diamond laughed, "That's an understatement, but you did invent a new dance, all your own!"

She looked at him with a sad look on her face. "Did you like that, poor Diamond? You were the lucky one who got the high voltage kick that started this whole *Dutchess Twitch* thing."

Diamond head bumped her. "Awww, never mind, blue eyes. Let's get our pictures taken. Just lean on me."

Dutchey propped herself up between Diamond and Kool and the gang headed for the Big Pineapple.

53

" $\mathcal{T}$ here's Grandtom and Grandfluff," said Diamond. "Lashes, will you hold Dutchey up for a minute? I'll be right back." He strolled over to his Grandcats.

Diamond I and Diamond II are older versions of Diamond III, handsome gray and white toms. His mother, Pearl, is also Maine Coon with aquamarine colored eyes and long white fur with gray and brown designs. Grandfluff is more of a Castleberry than Grandtom, adding her stunning turquoise eyes to the Castleberry family tree. Purebred Maine Coons, each one with thick black eyeliner around strikingly intense eyes.

Grandfluff greeted Diamond with a nose kiss and a whisker pinch. "You are getting so handsome my celebrity Grandsontom. You make me so proud!"

"Thank you, Grandfluff. You look beautiful tonight, as always."

"Thank you, my dear." They exchanged more snuggles and whisker kisses and Grandfluff started purring.

Grandtom inspected his medallions and they did their traditional head bump and whisker pull.

"Very impressive, Grandsontom," said Grandtom. "Wear them with pride."

"I am, Grandtom. Thank you both for throwing this fantastic bash for all my friends and me."

"You are very welcome," replied Grandtom, nodding. "Your tropical paradise luau theme turned out purrfect. I couldn't have planned it any better myself. I like how it makes the club look."

"Thank you, Grandtom."

"We're just happy that you're happy," added proud Grandfluff.

"Can I get you both anything? A canary squeeze-freeze, a liver latté, or a crabby won-ton?" He tilted his cute head. "Snappy tom on the rocks, Grandtom?"

"Oh honey, no thank you," answered Grandfluff. "We just finished a piece of filet of sole, sushi and shrimp, *and* anchovy pudding." She licked her whiskers. "Besides, your Grandtom needs to watch his diet."

Grandtom put his ears back and growled. "This is a party, *dear.* I am supposed to be enjoying myself, aren't I, *dear?*"

"Of course, *dear!* We'll just watch your diet go by until tomorrow," she said, laughing at her old tom of forty-nine years. They have a very special wedding anniversary coming up soon. She gave him a big kiss and he started to purr.

Grandtom winked at Diamond and said, "Go to your friends, Diamond Thomas III, and get your picture taken so I can *hang* you in my office!"

"Okay." He rubbed whiskers with his Grandcats.

"Smile!" Diamond's mom, Pearl, said as she snapped a picture. "Beautiful!" She kissed her son and suggested, "How about a three generation picture?" She motioned the three Castleberry toms to squeeze together. Diamond took off two medallions and draped one around Dad's neck and one around Grandtom's neck. Pearl snapped candid shots and then she instructed Dad and Diamond to stand on either side of Grandtom. "Say fishy."

"Fishy."

Auntie Belle padded over with her *Kitty Maxx* photo.

"Get in the picture, Belle," said Pearl. "You too, Mona."

Belle held up her *Kitty Maxx* picture and smiled for the camera. Then she took the camera, "Pearl, you get in there. Sierra, come over for a picture." Everyone posed nicely except silly Diamond. He held his medallion over one eye like a pirate. Auntie Belle gave him a long hug and Pearl took back the camera to snap a picture.

Lily and Mac padded over and Mac took the camera. The mayor suggested, "How about a family picture. Let's get everyone in together now. Sophia, Beau, Brianna, Vienna, come over for pictures. Where's Crystal?" Mayor Mac snapped several more blinding pictures.

Diamond could hardly see now, but asked, "Can I get anyone anything? Mom? Dad? Sierra? Aunties? Uncle? Cousins?"

Mom replied for everyone, "No thank you, dear. Get back in the picture line and smile nice. And no goofing around."

"Yes, Mom."

Crystal ran over. "Wait! Wait! I want a picture with Diamond!" They exchanged a big hug and posed for the camera.

Auntie Rose ran over. "I want a picture with Diamond, too." They exchanged hugs and she put her pretty hat on him. They posed for a very snobby picture.

Mayor Mac said, "Just one more... got it!"

Diamond gave Rose her hat back and took off. "I love you all!" he yelled as he ran backwards to his friends and took his place in line.

Every cat that passed him, either coming or going, told him he throws the best parties in Heavenly Hills:

"This is a wonderful party, Diamond!"

"Can you throw me a party here on my birthday, Diamond?"

"You were so cute at the ceremony and tonight with Kitty Maxx!"

"You're great, Diamond!"

"Great bash, dude!"

"You're the bomb, handsome!"

"This party is tight, dude!"

With each compliment, he gave a proud smile and said, "Aloha, everyone! Remember this night forever!" He power purred to the *maxx*.

Finally, the gang reached the Big Pineapple, the festive background for the party photos.

"Cool pineapple, bud," commented Kool.

"I know! Don't you love it!" squeaked Lashes. She was so hoarse she could hardly talk.

Diamond suggested, "Let's take the group picture first, then individual pictures."

Jade and Cleo looked at each other. "Maybe we shouldn't be in your group picture," Jade said. "This is your big night and your big picture." She and Cleo turned to walk away, disappointed.

"You're wearing medallions, aren't you?" asked Jett. He tilted his handsome head to the side. Their frowns turned into big smiles and they excitedly got back in line.

Lashes chirped, "You're both in the picture. Now smile!" She looked over and squeaked, "Smile bigger!"

Everyone's smiles were worth a thousand meows.

"Hmmm… memories of last night," remembered Jett. He wore a handsome, yet goofy smile.

Next, they took individual pictures and everyone walked away seeing spots. They shuffled their way through the zillions of cats, back to the delicious spread of food, and then found a grassy spot to snack on cracked crab legs and lap up crabacinno. Jade enjoyed a liver latté.

The music was still playing top 40 hits for all those who still had enough energy to dance. The high-tech, triple x-treme stereo system was blaring out *Lone Cats,*' "Crazy for That Cat," the all fluff band, *The Cougars,* "Are You Gonna Be My Tom?" and "The Toms of Summer," *Shakatra's,* "Spin Out," and her number one hit from her new CD with the same name, "Kisses and Claws," *Tabby Hunter's,* "Hunka Hunka Burnin' Fur," and "Smitten Kitten," his first big hit that he wrote for Belle when they were dating, *Goldplay's* award winning hit, "Socks," *The Swiss Cats'* new song, "I Believe in Cheese…"

Q was out there spinning on his head while a circle of cats watched and cheered him on. Diamond and Kool scaled the Old Oak to take in the luau from up high on the landing. Everyone up there cleared a space for them.

A little fluffette looked adoringly at Diamond and said, "Hey, I like you. In fact, I think you're great."

Surprised Diamond said, "I like you, too. What's your name?"

"Violet."

"That's a purrty name for a purrty fluffette."

"Thank you, Diamond," she said in a shy voice.

"This is my bud, Kool. Kool, this is Violet."

"Hi, Kool. I like all the different colored heart-shaped designs in your fur. And Diamond, I like the diamond shape on the back of your head."

"Thank you, Violet. You're very purrty, too," said Kool.

"Thank you. You both have such big fur around your necks, like lions."

"Thanks for noticing," said Diamond.

Violet shyly said "bye" and clawed her way over to another branch where she whispered and giggled with her fluffette-friends.

Kool looked over at Diamond and laughed. "This party is the

bomb, dude! I've been to all your parties, but this one ranks as the best one yet!"

"Thanks, bud. I'm having a great time, too."

"What inspired you to think up a luau theme?"

"Well, actually, you!"

"Me?" Kool snarled and put his head to the side. *"Why me?"*

"I wanted to watch your reaction when you realized you had to wear flowers tonight." Diamond laughed obnoxiously as he held up what was left of Kool's lei. "This lei looks pathetic. Where did all the flowers go?"

Kool quickly responded with, "I dunno." There were only a few flowers left on his lei because he had been secretly pulling them off all night long. He curled his whiskers and remarked, "As if watching me wear that too-tight cape wasn't enough fun for you?"

Diamond laughed and laughed. "You are absolutely hysterical, bro."

Kool dryly replied, "I'm glad I made your night."

"You sure did!"

They both peered over the landing and enjoyed the view.

54

After a bit of patrolling from the landing, Diamond and Kool met up with their friends who were relaxing on the grass. Dutchey's leg was still doing the jerk, but she was happy anyway. She looked up at the star-lit sky and closed her eyes. After a few moments, she boldly stated, "I have eight more lives to live and I promise myself I am going to live each life to the fullest, no matter what! I have just decided that from now on, I *have* to make a new memory everyday!" Her friends cheered and howled for her.

Kool commented, "Positive thinking! Good job, Dutch."

"Thank you very much."

The snobby cats were kickin' back, listening to the music, and enjoying every second of their big celebration.

Diamond lay there swiping his tail back and forth. He looked over, grinning, "Hey Dutchey and Lashes, did you like all the little surprises I couldn't tell you about?"

Dutchey laughed at her forever-best-friend. "Yes, Sneaky Sneakerson!"

"I love it all!" squeaked Lashes. "This party is so awesome! Thanks, Diamond."

"Anything for my fluff-friends, *and* my best buds." Kool, Diamond, and Jett clicked claws.

"Your club is just superb!" exclaimed Jade.

"I love the theme," added Cleo. "Very trendy! And I absolutely love all the fish treats." She closed her eyes and licked her whiskers.

"You out-did yourself, bud," said Kool. "But I just can't believe you wouldn't clue me in."

"Hey, if I can't surprise my bud, who can I surprise? Let me tell you though, it was hard keeping so many secrets. I wanted to tell you every detail. *Dude,* it was rough keeping all the plans to myself. I could have used your help with the fountain show, too. All of you just don't know how I have suffered for the past six months. It's been pure torture for me!"

Dutchey piped up, *"For you?* It couldn't have been nearly as bad as how you tortured us by *not* telling! But… now I'm glad you didn't tell because I was delightfully surprised!"

Lashes crackled, "Me, too. I never imagined the club could look so tropical and beautiful!"

Dutchey agreed, "*I know.* Thank you for throwing us this spectacular party, Diamond."

"You're very welcome." He was one happy cat!

Jett and Jade were lying on their backs, counting stars. Jade exclaimed, "Look, Jett! There's a shooting star! Did you see it? Did you see it?"

"Yes. Make a wish."

"You make a wish, too. Close your eyes."

Jett closed his eyes and made a quick wish. Then he opened his eyes and looked at Jade. Her claws were crossed and she was whispering to herself. When she opened her eyes, he asked, "What did you wish for?"

"You know I can't tell, or it won't come true, and I definitely want this wish to come true!"

Jett's heart jumped to his throat while Cupid shot another arrow his way.

"Who's Fangy?" Cleo asked the gang. "Is he friends with all of you?"

"Fangy Bully… " laughed Kool, shaking his head, "is the third born triplet in the Bully family. They play on our soccer team."

"What about Bull and Chip?" she asked. "And why are you laughing?"

Lashes squeaked, "Well, Bull thinks he's the toughest because he's the first born, but he's really a softy… "

Kool relieved her, "Chip chipped his fang during a fight when he was a kitten, but Fangy's long fangs make up for it."

"Fangy's cute," replied Cleocatra. She licked her paw and smoothed her whiskers.

All of a sudden, Diamond III jumped up and ran so fast, you would think his tail were on fire. He jumped up on stage, stood behind the microphone, and howled again. "Okay, listen up all you toms out there." He took off his lei and twirled it over his head. "Now these are the most beautiful leis I have ever seen. I'd like to give a big thank you to Lily Holcomb for making all these leis and flower arrangements." The crowd whistled and howled for Mrs. Mayor. "But I sorta feel like a fluff-tom wearing them." All the toms out there agreed with major hissing. "So," he continued, "I think we should give our leis to that special someone we've been crushing on all year."

Every tom cheered, especially Kool as he took what was left of his lei and placed it around Lashes' neck. Lashes teased, "Now isn't hanging out with us better than hiding under that basket of daisies?" She playfully bumped heads with him and started purring.

Kool sighed, "Yeah, I suppose."

She poked him in his ribs and chirped, "You know you're having fun!"

"I can purr louder than you can," he teased.

"No way!" They laughed and out-power-purred each other.

Jade saw a thousand shooting stars when Jett took his lei off and placed it around her neck. His gold eyes made her dizzy.

When Diamond returned from the stage, he draped his lei around Dutchey's neck. "You're the best!" she said to him.

"So are you!" They purred and gazed at each other in the golden glow of the tiki torches.

Mac II took off his lei and put it around Crystal's neck. She smiled at him and he melted. Oh, those intense Castleberry turquoise eyes—a tom just doesn't stand a chance.

Felix and Oscar gladly put their leis around Savannah's neck.

"Toms, I can't see now!" complained Savannah.

Here comes Ming with her camera, medallion, jewels, and two leis. "Come, felines. Pose for me. Say *mice.*"

Ming was snapping pictures and Dutchey was snapping orders. "Take a picture of me and Diamond and me and Lashes and me and Cleo and me and Jade and Lashes and Kool and Jade and Jett and Cleo and Jett and Kool and Diamond and Jett and Jade and Me!"

Lashes laughed at her friend and squeaked, "Dutch, take a breath!"

"Okay, okay dear," laughed Ming, snapping away. "All fluffs and toms come over for pictures."

All the fluffs lined up in front of a big rock. What a pretty site! Then, all the toms lined up. What a handsome site! Everyone was officially blind now. Siam Sam grabbed Ming and they did the tango across the dance floor. They were very fun to watch!

"Oh! Oh! Oh!" gasped Dutchey. She watched in horror as her leg went into an overdrive muscle spasm, twitching all over the place. She lay down on the cool grass.

"Oh hun… " Lashes said to Dutchey's leg, "just a bit more fun, then you can rest."

Kool laughed, "Love the heart-to-heart you're having with Dutchey's leg."

Lashes paused for a moment. Her ears went back and she stared up at the sky. "That leg… trouble… I feel a cat's instinct."

"Don't say that!" Dutchey cried out. She knows that Lashes' instincts are always right on.

"Hang in there, little pal," reassured Kool, "you'll be fine. Ya know how I know that."

"How?" asked Dutch

"Because we're all here with you, and we'll keep ya out of trouble. What could possibly go wrong now?"

Dutchey looked back at her spastic leg and shuddered. She looked at Kool and mustered up a half smile for him. The other half of her smile quivered.

55

ℋere come the Bully brothers. Fangy put his lei around Cleo's neck and sat down beside her. Bull took off his lei and put it around Cleo too, then plopped down next to Jade. Chip just stood there not knowing what to do, so he put his lei around Cleo, too. She was wearing so many leis, she could barely see. "Umm, toms… you-who? A fluff does need to see, ya know!" Her mauve eyes peeked through the pile of flowers around her face. The gang laughed at her. She laughed, too. She's a good sport.

"Hey, Princess," said Bull, acting suave, which was completely out of his element, "I feel so special to have the Princess from Pintac at *my* party!"

Jett put his ears back, "Oh, now this is *your* party?"

"Well, yeah," Bull sarcastically replied, laughing, "I'm here, aren't I?" He looked around and quickly found that he was the only one laughing. "Okay, okay. *Our* party! Happy now?"

"I suppose," snarled Jett. He got up and deliberately wedged himself between Bull and Jade.

"Are you having a good time, Princess?" Bull asked as he got up and moved to her other side. He picked up her *Key* and inspected it, then sniffed it.

Jett growled.

Jade looked over at Jett, wide eyed, acknowledging his growl, then turned to Bull, "I'm having the *best* time! Thank you."

"Where's your B.G.?" asked relentless Bull.

Jett growled again.

"My *what?*" asked surprised Jade.

"Your bodyguard. Have you forgotten about him already?" Bull leaned in front of Jade and stuck his tongue out at Jett.

"Oh," she said, relieved, motioning to the dance floor. "He's dancing his paws off and spinning on his head, whatever... "

Cleo peeked through her flowers and was laughing so hard she could barely get the words out, "He'll probably have so many blisters tomorrow, he will need a paw pad soak!"

Everyone laughed and Jade mouthed to Cleo, "Good one."

Cleo couldn't stop laughing at big and bad Q. Fangy just stared at her in amazement. He curiously thought, *Who is this brand new fluff and what country is she from?*

Bull leaned in front of Jade and asked Jett, "Did you like how I set it up so you could smooch, smooch, kiss, kiss?"

"Was that *your* idea?" asked Jett, referring to the slam on the dance floor.

"Yep," boasted Bull, "I was just trying to help you out, bud."

Jett's eyes narrowed and he put his ears straight back. He snarled, *"Thanks for all your help bud! I'll make sure to remember you in my will!"* He rubbed his nose with his paw. Jade licked her nose and smiled. Bull acted extremely satisfied with himself and his matchmaking accomplishment. He started purring even though Jett hissed at him.

Fangy peeked through Cleo's flowery leis and looked into her eyes. He was acting very intense, as if this were his last chance to talk to her. "How long are you staying in Heavenly Hills?"

"Only one month," she sadly replied.

"I wish you could stay longer. I'd like to get to know you."

"Me, too. You seem really nice." She started purring.

"I am," Fangy said sweetly. He started purring.

"He's not," snarled Chip, at the same time.

"I am, too. Get outta here, Chiparoo."

Chip's ears went back. Fangy's ears were already back. Jump. Tackle. Brawl. They're such nice, mannerly toms.

"Guess our last name fits us," sighed Bull. He got up, and as if it were routine, broke up the fight. He licked his whiskers and said, "Come on, bro's, let's get some cake."

"Would you like some liver cake, Cleocatra?" Fangy asked in his most polite voice.

"I'd love some!" she replied, licking her whiskers.

As they padded away, one of her leis fell off. When she stopped to pick it up, she looked back and noticed the gang watching her, so she lifted up her other leis and grinned at them. The gang gave her the claws-up sign and she gave one back. Her fur fluffed out as she padded away.

Jade pondered to herself, "There goes my buddy, Cleo, wearing four leis, a corsage, a medallion, and hangin' with all three Bully brothers. It appears my little pal is making friends already."

56

$\mathcal{T}$he music lowered as Principal Fitt stepped up to the microphone on stage to make an announcement.

"Graduates, we will be taking the group picture now. Everyone pick a spot over by the pool where the photographer is setting up."

"Ugh," groaned Dutchey.

"Come on, fluff-friend," Lashes said to her best buddy. "We have just one more thing to do, then you can rest."

Dutchey stood up. Her leg was twitching and jerking more than it has all night. Diamond, Lashes, and Kool helped her to the pool area where they found Jett, Jade, Cleo, and the Bully brothers in the back row, at the pool's edge. They flopped down beside them. Dutchey cringed with pain and licked her swollen leg.

Cleo said, "This is your graduation class picture." She looked at Jade, then Jett. "Maybe we shouldn't be in it." The two fluffs got up to walk away.

"Get back over here, fluffs," demanded Diamond, pulling their tails. They got back in line and wore pretty smiles. Cleo sat beside Fangy who was wearing a happy and very content smile.

"I think Fangy likes Cleo," squeaked Lashes.

"I think Cleo likes Fangy," whispered Jade.

Twitch. Jerk. "Behave yourself leg," scolded chirpy Lashes to Dutchey's leg.

57

Someone in the crowd yelled, "The cheerleaders should make their pyramid!"

"Yeah! Yeah!" everyone agreed, cheering them on.

Dutchey and Lashes looked at each other with saucer eyes, in sheer panic.

"Oh, no!" cried Dutchey.

"Oh, no!" chirped Lashes. "Can you do it, Dutchey?"

"If you help me. You know we're always on top!"

"You can do it! I won't leave your side! I promise!"

The excited crowd was roaring and Dutchey had no choice. "I guess I have to try." They pinky clawed.

Principal Fitt announced, "Our award winning cheerleading squad is going to make their famous pyramid!"

Everyone whistled and cheered with anticipation. After all, the squad did make their pyramid *famous* at the Championships and *won* the coveted Pom-Pom trophy.

Bull started organizing. Diamond and Kool looked over at Dutchey. She looked back at them with a pitiful face. She knew there was nothing they could do to help her because Bull had already thrown the cheerleading squad on top of their backs. He continued organizing. All of a sudden, there went surprised Jade, thrown to the top of the pyramid with Lashes right behind her. They were trying their best to balance on the backs of Blanche, Clairese, Jolene, and Coco, who were awkwardly balancing on the backs of Diamond, Jett, Kool, Chip, and Fangy. Next, Bull tossed Dutchey and Cleo up the pyramid and they landed next to Lashes and Jade. Bull instructed Cleo to keep going up. He insistently threw his paws up in the air.

Cleo jumped on top of Dutchey, Lashes, and Jade to make the fourth tier. Dutchey's ears went back. She looked behind her at the water in the pool. She was feeling terribly unstable up there.

"I don't remember being up so high," squeaked Lashes, who was feeling quite unstable herself. She is usually on the second tier. She put her back leg in front of Dutchey's injured leg to brace her.

Wobbly Dutchey cried, "The toms are our bottom tier, Lashes! I don't know about this…" The pyramid was swaying back and forth. "We've never done this before."

Lashes chirped, "I know! Hold on, Dutchey!"

The photographer excitedly looked through the viewfinder of his camera. "Squeeze in everyone. S q u e e z e ! I need all of you in the picture. The pyramid *works!* Great idea! Okay, say mice!"

"Mice."

The photographer happily snapped away. Other cats took pictures, as well.

"Oscar, get in there! Felix, are we on?" asked Savannah.

"Yep."

58

"Grrrr."

"Dutch, are you okay?" chirpy Lashes asked, trying to get a steady paw-hold.

"Grrrrr."

"Say mousey mint pie," instructed the photographer. "I'm getting *great* pictures!"

"Mousey mint pie."

"Grrrrr."

The upper two tiers of the pyramid were extremely wobbly.

"Dutchey?" whispered Lashes. "Are you okay?" Dutchey's front leg slipped and fell between Jolene and Coco.

"Hey, what's going on down there?" asked Cleo, almost losing her balance.

All of a sudden, Dutchey cried out, *"My leg is having a cramp!"* Just then, Dutchey's leg let out a power kick that beat all other kicks of the night! Lashes got the full brunt of her kick and lost her balance. It was too late for Cleo; she was already on her way down the pyramid backwards, right into the pool, "*r e o w*" splash! But not before she clawed at Jade's corsage ribbon and pulled her in after her, "*r e o w*" splash! Completely losing her balance from the kick, Lashes clawed at anything she could. She managed to hook her claw into Dutchey's corsage ribbon, "*r e o w*" splash! Dutchey was gagging and clawing at anything available. She hooked onto Coco's ribbon and practically strangled her. They both fell in, "*r e o w*" splash! But not before Coco grabbed Jolene around her tummy and pulled her in, "*r e o w*" splash! Jolene clawed for Clairese's ribbon and hooked it, "*r e o w*" splash! Clairese pulled Blanche's fluffy tail and there went Blanche, "*r e o w*" big splash!

… gurgle … gurgle … gurgle…

The photographer grabbed his camera off the tripod and rushed to the edge of the pool, snapping picture after picture. "I've got it all on film," he announced. "What a fun group! Fluffs in the pool. It's purrfect! I love it!"

The fluffs landed at the bottom of the deep end in a circle facing each other. A few seconds passed. Everyone was waiting for them to surface. Another bit of time passed, but the fluffs were still at the bottom of the pool. Everyone was anxiously waiting for them to surface, but all they saw were air bubbles popping on the surface of the water. Another few seconds passed.

Realizing their dilemma, wide-eyed Diamond held up his medallion and realized just how heavy it really is and yelled, "They can't surface! The heavy gold medallions are holding them down! Come on, toms! We have to rescue them!"

Diamond dove in.

59

$\mathcal{H}$ere come the toms to the rescue! Kool, Jett, Bull, Chip, Fangy, Mac II, Bobby, and Q followed Diamond into the pool. When they got down to the bottom, the fluffs' eyes were bulging and bubbles were coming out of their noses. The toms began clawing at the medallion ribbons. In desperation, the fluffs began clawing, too. It was turning into a clawing frenzy down there. Crystal ran to the edge of the pool and watched intently. She was just about ready to dive in, too.

"Throw in the life preservers," someone in the crowd yelled. Everyone gathered around the pool and watched. The music stopped. The club was completely quiet, except for the sound of cameras snapping away. Felix got in there and taped the whole dilemma. Savannah took matters into her own paws, grabbed the extra camera, and began snapping pictures.

"I think we have a situation here!" said worried and flustered Grandtom as he rushed to the pool. "Excuse me. Excuse me," he said, anxiously pawing his way through the crowd. "Mona, call 911."

Principal Fitt, Dr. Fitt, and the Hissy sisters rushed over to watch the underwater commotion.

Crystal dove in.

60

The underwater frenzy continued! The crowd of cats were pushing, shoving, and standing on top of each other at the edge of the pool to get a good look.

Savannah put the camera down and whispered into her microphone, "The cheerleading squad was up on their pyramid when, one after another, each one fell into the deep end of the heart shaped pool. I don't exactly know what happened, but several brave toms have gone in after them. It looks like they're all clawing at the heavy medallions to get them off the fluffs' necks. There are so many cats down there, I can't tell what's happening." She leaned in closer to look and almost fell in herself.

Another few moments passed and the clawing frenzy continued.

Savannah said, "I don't know about anyone else, but I'm getting nervous. They have to be running out of air… "

More bubbles popped on the surface of the water.

Another precious moment passed.

Grandfluff Mona informed everyone, "I've just called 911 and they are on the way."

Savannah yelled into her microphone, "It's just a wavy blur down there. Come on, toms. The clock is ticking."

Another heart-pounding moment passed.

Then, finally, plop… plop… plop… all the fluffs surfaced. They were gasping for air and clawing for life preservers. Then… plop… plop… plop… up came the toms. Bull surfaced first, sporting a white lily pad on his head. Next, Chip, Fangy, Bobby, and Mac II surfaced. Then Jett, then Kool. Finally, Diamond surfaced, sporting a bright pink lily pad and a paw full of medallions. Crystal helped Q to the surface and got him his own preserver. He clung on for dear life, huffing and puffing. Crystal loosened his collar a few notches and assured him he would live.

The anxious crowd cheered with relief and chanted, "Heroes! Heroes! Heroes!"

Diamond threw the medallions on the grass and gasped for air. The fluffs were all in the middle of the heart shaped pool gasping for air, choking, and spitting.

Savannah shouted into the microphone, "I think everyone has surfaced!" She started counting cats. "They all seem to be out of breath, but okay. I'll check it out." She went off camera and said, "Oscar, take a picture of all those shiny medallions at the bottom of the pool. And get one of Diamond and his pink lily pad hat."

"Felix, do you have enough tape?"

"Yep."

"Great! Can you get an aerial shot?"

"Yep." They took off running. They climbed the big rocks surrounding the pool and went to work, filming and snapping pictures.

61

"*Did I do that?*" gasped Dutchey, spitting water and sneezing. The fluffs looked at each other and burst out laughing. They were clinging to a life preserver, cat paddling, and gasping for air. "I'm so sorry, fluff-friends," laughed Dutchey, "Lashes, I'm sorry I kicked you so hard."

"I just knew that leg of yours was going to get us into trouble," chirped Lashes, "I had a cats' instinct, ya know." Her curly whiskers drooped. Double sneeze.

"We're so beautiful!" exclaimed Blanche.

"Oh yes, dahlings," replied Jade.

"We've never looked so good!" agreed Coco.

"Look at your chin, Jolene!" said Clairese.

"Look at yours!" replied Jolene, pointing her claw. Triple sneeze.

Diamond and all the heroic toms swam over to the fluffs. Q appeared to have recovered and squeezed in between Cleo and Jade, keeping an eye on things and forever shaking his white paw. Everyone was choking and laughing.

Out of breath, Diamond asked, "Is everyone okay?"

"I think so," said Dutchey. "Cleo and Jade, are you okay?"

"Yes!" they laughed and sneezed.

"My poor squad. Are you okay, fluffs?"

"Yes." Sneeze. Sneeze. Sneeze.

Dutchey declared, "Our heroic toms! Thank you for rescuing us!"

All the fluffs sang together, "Thank you, toms! Thank you!" The heroes nodded, huffing and puffing.

"Thank you, Crystal," added the fluffs.

Crystal shook her head and laughed, "The toms are your heroes! They deserve *all* the credit!" Sneeze.

"You fluffs, it's always something!" exclaimed Bull, shaking his head.

"Oh, look at my rose corsage. It's all wilted," squeaked Lashes.

"Oh, mine, too," said Jade, looking down at hers.

"I can't believe it," replied Diamond, looking quite cute with the pink lily pad on his head. "They almost drowned and they're worried about their flowers!" He shook his head and the lily pad fell off.

The relieved crowd laughed and yelled, "Bravo! Bravo!" The fluffs' leis were floating on top of the water.

The mom-fluffs: Ming, Lily, Dora, Ginger, Frangelica, Pearl, Belle, and Miss Fancy pushed and shoved their way to the edge of the pool. Frantic Ming yelled, "Are all cats accounted for?"

Kool yelled out, "Yes! Everyone's okay! Right, cats?" Everyone in the pool cheered.

Ming and Lily frantically looked at each other, then they both looked at Pearl, who started laughing.

Pearl remarked, "We know, we know…"

"Fluffs will be fluffs!" the lady-fluffs all said together. They shook their heads and laughed, knowing exactly what that meant. They were young once, too.

62

"My leg feels better!" Dutchey announced. "Look, everyone! It's not twitching anymore! I'm staying in this cool water for the rest for the night!" The crowd laughed and cheered for her.

Bull said, "Come on in, everyone! The water feels great! Is that okay, big Diamond?"

He didn't even get a chance to answer. Splash… splash… splash. The Graduates and guests jumped into the pool to cool off. Q jumped off the diving board and made a huge cannon ball splash. Other cats took off their medallions, climbed the huge rocks, and jumped into the deep end of the pool. Some swam behind the waterfall. The water felt so refreshing after all that dancing and sweating. A group of little kittens woke up and crept out from under a bush, yawning and stretching. With renewed energy, they jumped in the pool, too. The power music started up again.

Diamond and Lashes helped Dutchey to the pool steps.

"Does your leg really feel better?" squeaked Lashes.

"Yes! Look! It stopped jerking! So much for my new dance move!" They laughed and sneezed.

Diamond said, "I'm going down to get the rest of the medallions. Dutch, will you be okay here for a minute?"

Lashes squeaked, "I'll take care of her."

Dutchey assured him, "I'll be okay, Diamond. I have my friend here to watch me so I don't get into any more trouble."

"Okay, I'll be right back. Come on, buds," he said to Jett and Kool, "let's get some medallions."

They dripped out of the pool, climbed the big rock, and dove into the deep end. Jade and Cleo cat paddled over to the steps. The rest of the lovely cheerleading squad paddled over and busted up laughing as they surveyed each other.

"Do you have your necklace, Dutchey?" squeaked Lashes, who grabbed at her neck and found that her necklace was still on. Dutchey grabbed at her neck, but her necklace was gone.

"Oh, no!" exclaimed Dutchey. "It's probably down at the deep end of the pool. I hope it isn't caught in the drain."

Jade felt for her anklet. "My anklet isn't here or my *Key*."

Nurse Hissy, Dr. Fitt, Miss Hissy, and Principal Fitt rushed over to the steps where Dutchey and her friends were.

"Is everyone okay?" asked concerned Dr. Fitt.

"Yes," everyone nodded. They all had swollen chins and slicked back fur. You couldn't help but laugh.

Principal Fitt exclaimed, "You fluffs almost gave me a heart attack! Can't we even take a class picture without a disaster?"

Nurse Hissy laughed, "Dutchess, I just knew that leg couldn't be trusted!"

"I had a cat's instinct… " squeaked Lashes.

"I bet you did," agreed Nurse Hissy.

"But it feels so much better in the cool water," explained Dutchey.

Dr. Fitt replied, "Maybe this is the best place for you to stay for a while."

Relieved, Diamond's Grandcats were standing close by and listening. Grandtom was nervously swinging the heavy medallion he was wearing back and forth with his big paw. He said to Mona, "*Now I need a snappy tom!*" He glanced over at her and teased, "These young cats remind me of you when we were young."

Grandfluff smiled at him and winked. "You stirred up your share of mischievous antics too, Snappy Tom!"

"We did have a lot of fun, didn't we?" added Grandtom with a wink. "*You* and all *your* ideas!" They exchanged a playful look. Even an old tom doesn't stand a chance looking into those stunning turquoise eyes!

The toms surfaced with more medallions and threw them on the grass.

"Diamond, come here. Hurry," yelled Dutchey, "I lost my necklace."

"I lost my anklet, too!" exclaimed Jade. "And my *Key!*"

"Okay. Don't worry. We'll find them."

The toms made another dive. Meanwhile, all the guests and graduates were jumping off the high rock, aiming for the leis. Q and Bull kept doing cannon balls from the diving board and the *Biggest Splash* competition was established. Everyone had to do his or her own version of a cannon ball. Other cats were doing the matrix (spinning like a screw through the water) across the pool.

Diamond's Grandcats were over at the Big Pineapple speaking to their hired photographer. They were discussing which pictures were to be viewed by the public and which pictures were to stay on the cutting room floor. He motioned to Savannah to come over and talk to him, "Would you be an angel and let me preview your video and still pictures before they go public?"

"Of course, Sir. You know I wouldn't have it any other way! I'll have them ready by tomorrow."

Grandtom winked at her. "I know I can always trust you, my dear. Of all the pepperazzi, you are my favorite!"

"Thank you, Mr. Castleberry. I love covering your events here! One can always count on that certain element of surprise!"

Grandfluff Mona agreed, "You know Savannah, you make an excellent point."

"The club looks sensational tonight. So tropical," commented Savannah.

"Thank you," said Grandtom. "Feel free to take as many pictures as you like, dear."

"Thank you. Oscar, Felix, reload and follow me." She pawed her way through the crowd and headed straight over to the lovely fluffs in the pool.

Mickey, Lorenzo, Tootie, and their dates stopped by to check up on the wet fluffs. They all had horror on their faces.

"Oh, fluffs!" exclaimed Lorenzo, shaking his head in disbelief. "All that fluffing and misting this afternoon and look at you! Just look at you! All wilted with flat fur! I cannot believe it!" The fluffs looked at them with pitiful faces.

Mickey reassured, "Don't worry, fluffs. You are all so beautiful anyway. No matter what you've been up to!"

"Or into!" added Tootie. The fluffs perked up and laughed. So did Lorenzo.

Miss Dubois padded over and exclaimed, "Oh my! What happened to my award winning cheerleading squad?! We will need a bit more practice with our pyramid, fluffs!"

"Just a bit," laughed Dutchey.

Miss Hissy and her sister picked up all the medallions on the grass and put them on the lei table for the Graduates to pick up as they leave the party.

"My goodness, what a night!" exclaimed Nurse Hissy.

Miss Hissy agreed. "Paw Valley Middle School just won't be the same without them." A tear fell from the corner of her eye. Her sister dabbed her whiskers with a wet medallion ribbon and tried to comfort her.

The older teenage fluffs padded over to the pool.

"Your pyramid looked great!" laughed Jasmine. "For a minute, anyway!"

"Are you fluffs okay?" asked Toffee.

"I think so," replied Dutchey. "There went our fur-do's!"

Auntie Rose to the rescue. "Don't worry, fluffs! I brought my blow dryer!"

Savannah asked Rose, "This never happened to our squad, did it?"

"Not that I recall. You fluffs just have all the fun!"

Ming, Lily, and Miss Fancy padded over, waded down the steps, and sat down in the water with the fluffs.

Ming asked, "What happened up there?"

Savannah held out her microphone and Felix pointed his video camera.

"Well," squeaked Lashes, "we were up there so high, and we were so unstable, so I put my leg in front of Dutchey's to brace her, but it didn't work, obviously."

"I am so sorry, fluff-friend," laughed Dutchey.

"It's okay, Dutch," chirped Lashes. "It was kinda fun!"

They laughed and sneezed. The lady-fluffs shook their heads in disbelief.

Savannah asked Cleocatra, "Was it scary down there?"

Cleo replied, "It was so scary! We were trapped at the bottom and we were running out of air! I thought we were all goners! I was never so happy to see the toms in my life!"

"I bet," replied Savannah. She shook her head and turned to Jade. "So, Princess Jade, how's your vacation going so far?"

Jade laughed, "I really am having a great time!"

Savannah laughed, "I'm so glad. Now, about that new dance move called *The Dutchess Twitch?* Does that have anything to do with your falling pyramid?"

Lashes squeaked into Savannah's microphone, "I guess you could say that. Dutchess had an accident yesterday and now she has a power twitch in her leg, like this." She kicked her leg out, imitating Dutchey.

Dutchey laughed and complimented, "You do that quite well."

"Thank you very much!" chirped Lashes.

"Are you feeling better now, Dutchess?" asked Savannah.

"I think so. The cool water seems to be helping."

"I must say, I was getting a little worried. You fluffs were down there for a long time."

All the fluffs nodded in agreement. "We know, we know."

"Will you all smile for my camera?" The wet cheerleading squad squeezed together and smiled purrty.

"Thank you, fluffs. I hope you feel better Dutchess. Lashes, I hope you get your voice back soon. And fluffs, I'm so glad you are all okay!"

"Thank you, Savannah."

Finally, Diamond and Jett surfaced with the necklace, the anklet, and the *Key*.

Oscar was still snapping pictures and Felix kept his camera rolling.

Dutchey's necklace was dangling from Diamond's fang and Jett was wearing the *Key* around his neck and Jade's anklet around his ear.

Savannah spoke into her microphone, "Diamond, were you the first one to realize their awful dilemma and the first to dive in?" She held the microphone out to Diamond and the dangling necklace.

"Yes, this is what happened. I was part of the bottom tier of their pyramid when something happened up on the third and fourth tiers, and one after another, the fluffs fell in the pool. It was like watching dominos go down. Then they landed in a circle at the bottom of the deep end. Now, of course, it's never good to land anywhere in the bottom of a pool, but anyway, when they didn't come back up, and so much time was passing, I thought about how heavy my medallion is, so I knew right then I had to get down there and free the fluffs so they could come up for air." The necklace around his fang swung back and forth as he talked.

Kool added, "It was crazy down there!"

Dutchey declared, "You saved our lives!" The toms nodded their heads and were quite proud of themselves.

Savannah asked, "Will you heroic toms pose for a picture?"

The brave toms dripped out of the pool, hulked up, and posed wet macho poses, dangling necklace, ear anklet, *Key,* and slicked back fur.

"Great macho picture, toms. You are all very brave!"

"Thank you, Savannah." replied the dripping wet toms.

Diamond looked over at Dutchey and Jade. "We found your necklace, your anklet, and the *Key.*"

"Whew," said relieved Dutchey. "I thought it was lost forever. Thanks, Diamond, and thanks for saving me in the pool, and yesterday. Again, my hero. It never ends, does it?"

"I'm just glad you're all okay," replied Diamond. He got back in the pool and put the necklace with the jagged square that said *Best* around Dutchey's neck. "There, good as new!"

Jett delivered Jade's anklet to her. She laughed as she took it off his ear, "Thank you, my hero." He draped her *Key* around her neck and their eyes locked.

Mac II shook his head and said, "I'm telling you. I don't think Heavenly Hills High is ready for you fluffs!"

Crystal laughed and agreed, "He may be right!"

The fluffs looked at each other and laughed.

"Thanks for saving us, big bro," squeaked Lashes.

"Thanks, Mac," said Dutchey. They both gave him big wet hugs.

Bobby received sopping wet hugs, too. "Good thing you'll have us around next year to keep you out of trouble."

The rest of the fluffs smiled, shivered, laughed, and sneezed.

Dutchey whispered to Lashes, "They may be right you know…"

Lashes tilted her head, smiled, and sighed.

63

$\mathcal{S}$irens were blaring as the ambulance sped to the club. The paparazzi from the local television station, *WCAT,* and *The Morning Chew,* weren't far behind.

The emergency team checked out the fluffs and saw that all was well, except for a few swollen chins and one split one, Kool's bump on his head from yesterday, Diamond had three scratches across his nose from the clawing frenzy, and of course, Dutchey's power leg.

For their trouble, Grandtom offered the Emergency Medical Team some drinks and good eatins' on the house. The crew from *The Morning Chew* ran into the club and started snapping pictures as fast as they could. They have a story to write by morning—only a few hours away. The crew from WCAT was quickly setting up their equipment, too. They have an exciting story to tell *now.*

Class President Diamond III held them at bay with Q's expert assistance. Big and bad Q was standing under the floral archway as the press ran in. He tried to hold them back, flashing his rusty old badge and shouting, *"Special Forces Here,"* but it was as if he were invisible. They ran right over him and left him in a heap under the lei table.

Diamond III graciously gave them an interview of what happened. The press had to know every detail of the luau, *Kitty Maxx,* the pool dilemma, and last, but certainly not least, Princess Jade. Their cameras were busy capturing it all.

Grandtom gathered the reporters and photographers together and offered them some fancy food, too. Diamond III asked for one of their cameras and took pictures of them with the *Hula Fluffs.*

A reporter from *The Morning Chew* offered Grandtom a great

deal of money for the rare picture of the fluffs at the bottom of the pool. Grandtom told the reporter he would have to see what pictures his photographer comes up with and then invited him to enjoy some tasty food. He does like the publicity for his club. "It's good for business," he always says about the 'pepperazzi,' except for photos of stranded fluffs at the bottom of the pool.

64

Fangy padded down the sandy beach part of the pool and sat down beside Cleo.

"Thank you for saving us," Cleo said, piercing him with her mauve eyes. "You are so brave."

Fangy tilted his head in embarrassment, "You're welcome. Umm, what happened to your chin?"

"I guess the medallion was bouncing off of it when I was jumping and being crazy during *Kitty Maxx*. Does it look bad?" She put her wet chin up in the air for inspection.

"It looks swollen, that's for sure. Put it down in the water." All the fluffs put their chins in the water. All you could see were their eyes, noses, ears, and whisker tips. What a hilarious site!

"Ahhh. This does feel better," the fluffs agreed.

…splash… splash… splash…

The elite felines of Heavenly Hills were having a splashtastic time partying in the pool. Over on the grass, there was a hula contest, which was entertaining to try and to watch. There seemed to be more Grandfluffs over there trying out their moves than anyone else.

Super reporter Savannah asked her crew, "Are you getting all of this Felix and Oscar?"

"Yep. You'll be scratching our backs," said Oscar.

"We want a raise," demanded Felix, laughing.

"After covering this event, we all should get a raise!" replied Savannah.

Although this last part in the pool was not in Diamond Thomas Castleberry III's big plan for the evening, it was still turning out to be splashtacular! Dutchey's little surprises were not part of his master plan either, but oh well, she always has been unpredictable. There's no telling what will happen when Dutchey and her sidekick, Lashes, are around.

65

After a bit in the pool, Dutchey's leg finally calmed down. The lady-fluffs found a grassy spot to relax with their bowls of liver latté. They each wore two leis now. Q gave his lei to Belle.

Ming announced, "I have a crock-pot of delicious creamed fish stew cooking at home. Is everyone still coming over to our place to finish out this party?"

"That sounds great," said Pearl, licking her whiskers, "I haven't had creamed fish stew since, well forever. Did Miss Fancy get everything done?"

"Yes, we can always count on Miss Fancy to get everything done. She just left for home to put on the finishing touches."

"She is an absolute jewel," Pearl commented.

"I agree. I don't know what I would do without her."

The lady-fluffs licked their whiskers in anticipation because they know all about Ming's fabulous parties. They lay on the grass and gazed at the starlit sky.

"What a beautiful night!" declared Frangelica. "The weather is lovely here."

"Welcome back to eventful Heavenly Hills, Frangelica," laughed Pearl.

"Thank you, Pearl."

"Where there's never a dull moment!" added Lily.

Ginger shook her pretty head and commented, "Oh Lily, look at all the beautiful leis you made floating in the pool!"

Lily laughed, "Oh well. They look beautiful in the pool, too." She looked up at the sky. "Look at that formation of stars over there. Isn't that Cateous the Fighter?"

Auntie Rose screamed, "Where? Where?" Lily pointed her paw at the sky. "I see him! I see him! I bet he would be so handsome if he were a real twenty-four-year-old cat!"

The lady-fluffs sighed and gazed at the stars.

After a few moments, Ming stood up and stretched. She padded over to the pool and sat down next to Dutchey. She was sitting on the steps all by herself, stretching out her leg. Her fluff-friends were swimming around with the toms in the middle of the pool, splashing, dunking, and pulling each other's tails.

Mom said, "I've invited our friends to come over tonight for creamed fish stew beside the bonfire. Remember we started making plans for Diamond's party?"

"Oh, Mom. With all the excitement, I forgot all about our surprise." Her whiskers drooped even more. Sneeze. Sneeze.

"Gesundheit!"

"Thank you!" Triple sneeze.

Mom waited until Dutchey was through with her sneezing marathon. "Don't worry about a thing, Dutchey. The party is still on. Miss Fancy and I have taken care of all the details. Would you like to invite your friends over? You can have a slumber party and stay in the pool all night if it makes you feel better!"

"That's sounds great, Mom! I'll see if they can come!" She excitedly splashed over to her fellow award winning squad.

Kool, Jett, and Diamond were hangin' out at the edge of the pool, watching everything. They noticed Dutchey paddling and broke into song, "Here she comes to save the day!"

"Ha-ha," gagged Dutchey as she took in an unexpected gulp of water. Lashes pulled her over to the preserver. "Hey fluffs," she spit, "my mom is having an impromptu bonfire party afterwards, and I want all of you to come over for a pool/slumber party. Can you? Can you?" She sneezed.

"Yesss!" The fluffs screamed with excitement.

"Let's camp out by the pool. My leg feels so good in here! I might stay in the pool all night!" Her friends laughed. "And, my mom has creamed fish stew simmering right now. There's oyster snick-snacks, too!" The fluffs licked their whiskers and screamed again.

Meanwhile, the toms slipped underwater and swam over to a bunch of tails dangling in the water. It was just too hard to resist.

First Dutchey disappeared underwater, then Lashes disappeared, and then Princess Jade. After a few seconds, the fluffs popped up to the surface.

Dutchey looked around and spit, "Where are those toms? They pulled our tails and dunked us!"

Cleo was laughing, "We wondered where you went!"

Lashes squeaked, "I'm gonna get those toms! Where are they?"

Jade just laughed, then double sneezed.

"Guzundheit!"

"Thank you!"

The toms surfaced by the side of the pool, then swam back over to the fluffs. What happened to those thick, fluffy ruffs?

Dutchey spit, "Very funny, toms."

"What? What?" asked the toms, acting all innocent.

Diamond planted himself between Dutchey and Lashes. "So, what are you fluffs cooking up over here? We saw you all lickin' your whiskers."

Dutchey replied, "We're having a… no… I'm not telling. It's a surprise. See… I can be tight whiskered, too!" She put her swollen chin in the air.

Diamond hung his head to the side. He knew he'd been had. "Okay, what do I have to do?"

Dutchey thought for a moment. "Well, when the time comes, you will have to close your eyes. No, better yet, you will have to wear a blindfold," she schemed.

Kool and Jett smirked. "Guess it's your turn, bud," Kool said with very little sympathy. Diamond sighed.

Dutchey head bumped him. "Poor Diamond. You have had such a rough time these past few months, keeping all your secrets to yourself. Well, we want to give you a break from all your secrets and surprises and surprise *you*." She pierced him with her blue eyes.

Diamond wondered, "I don't know what she's up to, but she sure is cute, soaking wet, swollen chin and all." He said with a smile, "Okay! I'm ready for a surprise! Surprise me! Surprise me big time!"

"Okay, we will!" Dutchey said to her friends, who were nodding, enjoying the conversation.

Lashes squeaked, "I wish they would just… "

Kool interrupted, "I know, get together. You, my dear, are a hopeless romantic!" Lashes twirled her wilty whiskers with her claw and smiled. She's very pretty, even with a split chin.

Everyone in the pool was having a splashing good time, jumping and dunking each other.

The night was purrfect!

66

$\mathscr{I}$t looks like the Tropical Luau Celebration is soon to be history. All the cats in the pool were laughing and happy as they waded past the fluffs sitting on the pool steps and climbed out of the pool to shake.

"Nice dance move, Dutchey!"

"Great pyramid, fluffs!"

"Let's do it again sometime, Dutchey!"

Everyone had fun teasing Dutchey. She smiled and thanked them all as they made their little comments. "It was my pleasure, as always."

As the soaking wet cats passed by Princess Jade, they all had something to say:

"Wonderful speech this morning and tonight, Princess!"

"We're so glad you came to party with us, Princess Jade!"

"Welcome to Heavenly Hills!"

"The Key to the City? What an honor!"

Jade graciously congratulated everyone, even if they weren't graduates.

Kool ran over to her and Jett and whispered, "Jade, would you mind signing the CD's we're passing out to everyone as they leave?"

"I'd love to," she replied. Her and Jett stepped out of the pool and shook out their fur. Jade looked magnificent, even wet. The three cats rushed over to Diamond to join him in saying good-bye to their classmates as Jade signed autographs on the *Kitty Maxx* CD jewel cases. Jett ran to get her a green and white striped towel—which he placed around her as she signed: *With love, Princess Jade from Pintac.* Diamond stood under the floral archway and draped medallions, then the wet grads stood in another line, on the other side of the floral archway inside the foyer, waiting for Jade to sign the jewel cases. She seemed to be taking her sweet time, making the *J* just purrfect.

Jett noticed the long line forming and urged her, "Diamond can only drape the grads so many times, so try to hurry."

"Okay, okay. I'm hurrying."

Everyone complimented Diamond as they waited in line:

"Great party, dude!"

"Wonderful club! You are so cute!"

"Terrific party, Diamond!"

"You're awesome, Diamond!"

"Rad party, dude!"

"Have a great summer!"

"See you in September!"

There were long hugs and long looks of admiration from the fluffs for Diamond! His head wasn't swelling at all! Oh, no. He thought, "I love being the Master of Ceremonies!" He draped medallions and power purred.

Dutchey was still sitting on the pool steps. She casually looked over at Diamond and noticed all the fluffs flirting with him. She stuck out her snaggle claw and counted six, no seven fluffs in a circle around him. She felt a twinge of jealousy and heaved a heavy sigh.

Lashes rushed to her side, and a splash of water landed in her mouth. "Whatchya thinkin' about, fluff-friend?"

"Oh, that tom over there," spit Dutchey. She pointed at Diamond Thomas Castleberry III.

"Hmmm, he looks like he's enjoying himself," squeaked Lashes. She sneezed.

"Gesundheit!"

"Thank you!"

"Oh, look!" Dutchey sat up, straining to see. "Look at Sabrina! She's giving him a hug!"

"No Way!" squeaked Lashes, straining to see.

"A really long one! Just look at her with her wet, stringy fur!" spit Dutchey. "She's disgusting!"

"Okay... Sabrina!" chirped Lashes. "You can let go now!"

"Oh ... my ... gosh... !" exclaimed Dutchey. "Hours are passing!" She growled and hissed.

Sabrina finally peeled herself off Diamond and left.

"Gosh! Finally!" squeaked Lashes.

Dutchey spit, "The audacity of some fluffs! Unbelievable!" A moment passed and Dutchey sighed, "Wow. I'm speechless." She shook her head, looked down, and stirred the water with her paw.

Lashes shook her head, too. "I am so disgusted with her."

Dutchey put her ears back and hissed, "I am so done with her. I'm never talking to her again. I don't care how many classes we have together." The fluffs continued watching *Mr. Master of Ceremonies* do his host-with-the-most thing. They watched as other fluffs were caught up in his intense turquoise eyes and lingered far too long. "I think I'm going to be sick," said Dutchey. She stuck her claw in her mouth as if she were gagging.

"I know! They're all over him," chirped Lashes. "We sound like we're jealous! Are we jealous, Dutchey?"

Miss Siamese looked over at her friend with a blank stare.

"Well, are we jealous?" Lashes squeaked again. They both looked at each other, then stared out into the distance. A few moments passed as the fluffs thought about this.

Finally, Dutchey said, "I guess he does deserve the attention. He did put on quite a party, didn't he?"

Lashes cleared her throat, "He sure did! He was awesome at the ceremony and just purrfect on stage!"

"And he didn't even fumble!" added Dutchey, feeling an overwhelming sense of pride for her long-time friend.

"Not once!" squeaked Lashes.

"No wonder everyone loves him."

"But, ya know Dutch, all those relentless fluffs didn't have to hang on him for so long. That was just a bit much!"

"*I know,*" agreed Dutchey.

A few moments of silence passed when Lashes commented, "Dutchey, you didn't answer my question, fluff-friend. Are we jealous?"

67

As the wet crowd was leaving, Kool and Diamond passed out the last of the medallions, but came up two short. Now this was a major *cat*astrophe! Diamond ran over to the pool and spotted the two medallions in the deep end. He reassured the two sad fluffs that were missing theirs, "I see them right down there, wait one minute." He climbed the big rock and dove straight down to the bottom as Lashes and Dutchey watched and shook their heads.

Dutchey sighed, "Hero again… *doesn't he ever get tired?*"

Diamond surfaced with the two medallions and tossed them on the grass. Marie and Joyce were sad, but now are the very happy recipients of their precious medallions.

"Isn't he the greatest?" they giggled as they passed by Dutchey and Lashes.

"Oh, gag," spit Dutch.

"I know," squeaked Lashes.

Diamond swam over. "Whatchya doin' fluffs?"

"Talkin' about you," replied Dutch.

"Me? What about me?"

"We're just talking about how charming you are with everyone. Huh, Lashes?"

"Yep," chirped Lashes.

Diamond said, "I think everyone kicked up their paws and had a good time tonight! Don't you? Did you fluffs have a good time?"

"We had and are still having the best night ever!" replied Dutchey. Then her smile deflated. "I'm sorry I ruined everything—falling into the pool and ruining the class picture."

Diamond head bumped her, "Everything turned out *great*,

Dutchey! I think everyone had a fantastic time! I know I'm having fun."

Lashes nodded in agreement and squeaked, "This is the purrfect ending to three purrfect years together at Paw Valley Middle School."

Dutchey perked up and agreed, "It sure is! Thanks for making our special night so special, Diamond." She gave him a long wet hug of her own. Lashes gave him a hug too, at the same time.

Kool jumped in the pool and joined the gang by bumping Lashes into Diamond. This pushed Diamond into Dutchey, who got another unexpected gulp of water. She coughed and spit and gagged. "Sorry, Dutch. So, what's next on the agenda?"

Dutchey looked at Kool and her eyes twinkled. "We may be getting close to the blindfold part." She sneezed.

They all looked at Diamond, who was wading around in the shallow end. "Bring it on. I'm ready!"

The mom fluffs padded over and Ming asked, "When is everyone ready to go? It looks like the crowd is thinning out."

"We can go now," answered Dutchey. She looked at Lily and asked, "May I borrow your scarf? I won't get it wet, I promise."

"Sure, darling." She untied it from around her fluffy neck.

"Will you please tie it around Diamond's eyes so he won't be able to see anything. Get close, Diamond."

Diamond waded over to the edge of the pool and Lily tied her Belgian lace scarf around his wet head.

Dutchey instructed, "Don't get it wet now, Diamond."

"Well, what am I supposed to do? I'm still in the pool! *And,* I'm still all wet!"

"We'll help you," answered Dutch. "Kool, will you please help Diamond out of the pool?" Kool escorted Diamond and all his long wet fur out of the pool. He shook and the lacy scarf went flying into the pool and sank to the bottom.

Dutchey dove under water and retrieved the scarf, and as graceful as she had wanted to be at the ceremony, she stepped out of the pool. Dripping wet with the scarf hanging from her fang, Dutchey asked, "Kool, will you please put Diamond's blindfold back on him?" Kool took the wet scarf and did as he was asked. Diamond stood there limp and cooperative.

The rest of the fluffs stepped out of the pool and it was their turn to shake out.

"Ahhh. I feel so much better, now. Look everyone!" exclaimed Dutch. "My leg even looks smaller!"

Everyone looked over at her leg and cheered. Everyone except blindfolded Diamond, that is.

68

$\mathcal{C}$leo and the Bully brothers were cat picking over at the banquet tables when Fangy took her tail with his and led her to a grassy area where they could hear each other talk over the music. Fangy shyly asked, "Can I talk to you tomorrow or sometime?"

"Sure. I'm staying with Jett." She started purring.

"I have his number," he replied with a hopeful grin.

"Psssst. Psssst." Dutchey waved at her. The gang was guiding blindfolded Diamond out of the club.

"Wait right here. I'll be right back," she promised Fangy. She ran over to Dutchey and asked, "What's going on? Are we leaving now?"

"We're all going to my house for Diamond's surprise party." Dutchey looked over at Fangy who appeared to be waiting for Cleo to come back. "Umm, ask the Bully brothers if they can come over to my house. I know it's a last minute invite, but maybe they can come. Tell them it's an all night pool party."

"Okay." Cleo ran over to the toms and they talked to their parents.

After a moment, she ran back screaming hysterically, "They're coming! They're coming!" Her fur was sticking out everywhere!

"Okay. Let's catch up. Tell them to come as soon as they can because we're leaving right now."

"Okay!" Cleo ran back and forth. She was so excited!

69

$\mathcal{D}$utchey and Cleo caught up as Diamond was being guided into the limo. Dutchey looked at Diamond and smiled. She and her mom talked about his surprise party, but they never got around to finalizing the arrangements because of everything that happened yesterday with the tree accident. Her mom and Miss Fancy, they always take care of everything.

Miss Pansy Fancy has been with the Woo family ever since Dutchey was born. She is a beautiful Silver Spotted Cattish short furred feline and she talks with a cute Cattish accent.

Ms. Savannah Sizzleton spoke into her microphone, "This truly has been *The Party of the Century*. Congratulations to all 333 Paw Valley Graduates for accomplishing goals and finishing their middle school years with this spectacular luau celebration. It has been a very eventful evening! The amazingly limber *Hula Fluffs* led the hula lessons and contest that followed. That was very entertaining. And the lower the limbo bar went, the more impossible it was for cats with big bellies to keep from knocking it down. What fun! We have just watched Diamond III being led away wearing a blindfold. There may be a few surprises waiting for him this time. For the class photograph, everyone wanted their award-winning cheerleaders to make their famous pyramid. One of the cheerleaders, Dutchess, who incidentally invented a new dance called *The Dutchess Twitch*, apparently had a leg cramp that caused a chain reaction, and the entire cheerleading squad fell backwards into the pool. They had a bit of a problem coming up for air because of the heavy gold medallions they were wearing. Fortunately, several heroic toms dove in and saved them, and the cheerleading squad is just fine! Even Princess Jade from Pintac was part of the falling pyramid, and she's fine, too. Then everyone jumped into the heart shaped pool to cool off. I have never seen so many wet cats in all my nine lives! It looks like the crowd is thinning out now. By the smiles on everyone's faces and all the laughter, I think a good time was had by all! The music from *Kitty Maxx* was fantastic and the cuisine was an absolute culinary delight! I'm so stuffed I won't be able to eat for a week! Well," she continued, "I had a fantastic time. I got to see a few old friends I haven't seen in years. Rose and Monique, come over here for a minute." The two twenty-four-year-old beauties padded over. Savannah suggested, "I think we should do an alumni prowler howl. It'll be fun!"

Monique agreed, "On three, fluffs. One… two… three… "

Felix pointed his camera at the lovely fluffs, who howled louder than ever prowler howls. Everyone who was still at the luau looked over and howled with them.

Rose exclaimed, "That was fun! Sometimes, don't you wish we were all back in high school again?"

Savannah sighed, "Yes, I miss the good old days."

Monique said, "Well I still am in High School. I'm teaching at Heavenly Hills High in September."

"Really?" asked Savannah. "You always wanted to teach high school!"

"I know! And I'm head junior varsity cheerleading coach, too. It's a dream come true!"

Savannah said, "That's exciting news! Let's do a cheer!"

Rose agreed, "Okay. Which one?"

Monique suggested, "Let's do the Power Machine Cheer! Here Maurice, wear Rose's hat for a minute, please." He looked ridiculous. The retired cheerleaders got into position. Monique started, "Fluffs, ready? Let's go!"

"We're not vicious. We're not mean. We're just kick tail power machines! Yea!" They howled another loud prowler howl. After they finished their cheer and howl, they jumped and screamed and hugged.

Savannah exclaimed, "That was so fun!"

Rose hugged Monique. "Congratulations, Monique. You will make a dynamite cheerleading coach at our old alumnus!"

Ecstatic Monique replied, "Thanks, Rose! Congratulations to

you, too! It seems I can't pick up a magazine these days without seeing your curly whiskers on the cover. And Savannah, I just adore your column and your show!" They all exchanged hugs and made a date for a reunion.

Monique suggested, "Let's go to Moskitos. I love sitting on the upper deck and watching all the boats slip into the harbor while I enjoy a liver smoothie!"

"I'd love to!" said Savannah. "Call me! We'll talk out the details!"

Rose added, "Let's make a night of it, fluffs!"

Savannah agreed, "It's a date! I can't wait!"

The three beauties hugged and screamed, "*Who knew?!*"

Rose took back her fancy purple hat from Maurice and they padded over to the food to graze a bit more.

Savannah continued, "What a fun night! But, most of all, congratulations to Paw Valley's Graduates! This is Ms. Savannah Sizzleton; signing off, *Live* from The Heavenly Hills Country Club Party of the Century. Aloha, everyone. This is a wrap." She shut off the microphone, unbelted her tummy pack, and sat down. "Felix and Oscar, you both did a terrific job tonight! Thanks, toms."

Felix joked, "Anything for you, Ms. Savannah Sizzleton—celebrity at large!"

"Oh, will you stop teasing me, Felix. Let's get packed up and split so we can see what we've got. Don't let me forget, I have to find my scarf." She gave the club one final perusal and pondered, "I wonder if Mr. Castleberry would let me have that big pineapple… "

70

*D*renched cats were everywhere! The happy graduates were riding in the limo, all smiles, still pumped from an evening filled with excitement! Q was totally exhausted and needed to lie down. Kool popped in his *Kitty Maxx* CD. Jade found a camera under the seat and was snapping pictures of everyone.

"This is the best night of my life!" gushed Cleo, smiling for Jade's camera.

"*Kitty Maxx* rocks!" exclaimed Jett. He smiled for the camera.

Lashes stood up and tried to talk, but it just wasn't happenin.' Kool sat her down and talked for her, "I've been friends with Lashes for a really long time now, so I think I can say what she wishes she could say for herself: *She is so excited!*"

Everyone laughed, even Lashes. She swiped him with her soggy tail as he sat down on the seat next to her.

Proud Diamond sat in the back seat with his lacy blindfold on and his chin in the air.

"How's Diamond?" teased Kool.

"I'm just fine. Ya know why?"

"Why?"

"Because *I Am Mr. Snobby Cat.*"

Everyone laughed at him and before they knew it, they pulled up in the driveway.

71

"*D*oes *Mr. Snobby Cat* know where we are?" asked Kool.

"Are we at Dutchey's house?" asked Diamond.

"Maybe... maybe not!" everyone said at the same time, teasing him.

"We're at Dutchey's house. I know the way and I know every turn the limo made. So ha-ha."

Jett opened the door and hopped out. He paused to smell the air. "Something sure smells good. Come on, *Mr. Snobby Cat.*"

Dutchey took Diamond's medallion ribbon with her tail and led him out of the limo, up the front steps, and into the mansion. Kool was on one side of him and Lashes was on the other. Jade, Cleo, and Jett were close behind and Q followed. They slowly padded through the house, carefully guiding Diamond so he wouldn't knock over anything.

However, then there's Q. He bumped into an end table with a fragile glass statuette of *Mrs. Felinestein* on it. Jett jumped to rescue the statuette as it wobbled off the table and was about to crash on the marble floor. She was so slippery, she slipped right through his paws. Q got in there and the statuette landed in his paws and was about to slip through. He tossed it back to Jett. They kept tossing *Mrs. Felinestein* back and forth, as if she were a hot potato. Jade stepped in front of Q and caught *Mrs. Felinestein.* She carefully placed her back on the end table and scowled at Q—more so than Jett. "Toms! Behave yourselves!" she scolded. Cleo was laughing hysterically.

Dutchey led Diamond through the kitchen and outside to the patio. His nose twitched and he uncontrollably licked his whiskers.

"It sure does smell good out here! Mmm. I smell red snapper, and is that creamed fish stew, I hope?" Everyone was silent.

Jade looked at the pool and gasped, "Another beautiful pool!"

The soggy grads felt the warmth of the bonfire and led Diamond over to it. He was literally drooling now. Ming snapped several pictures. Everyone still kept silent.

Salivating Diamond asked, "Dutchey, when can I take the blindfold off?"

She laughed and hooked the blindfold with her snaggle claw. "Well, I guess… *now!*"

72

"*Surprise!*"

Diamond opened his eyes and there, standing before him, were Mom and Dad, Grandtom and Grandfluff, Auntie Belle, Miss Fancy and the rest of his family and all his best friends' families. Red snapper and red herring kabobs were sizzling away on the bar-be-que. Creamed fish stew was heated to purrfection along with several large bowls of oyster snick-snacks. On the center of the table was a deluxe seven layer salmon cake. Diamond looked around and was totally elated as he noticed all the different colored balloons tied to the patio roof, floating in the breeze. Some said, "Congratulations!" There were sparkly streamers and "Happy Graduation" signs hanging everywhere.

He spotted the elaborate seven layer salmon cake on the center table. There was a plastic cat with a tiny royal blue cape on, standing behind a little microphone. The writing on the cake said:

Congratulations Diamond Thomas III!
Great Job!

"Wow! What is all this?" he asked.

Ming gave him a hug and said, "You did such a wonderful job tonight, so we decided that *you* deserve a party, too."

Diamond's mom padded over to him and kissed his whiskers. He stood before his family and friends, grinning from ear to ear. "Everyone, this is great! Thank you!" He made the rounds and gave whisker kisses to everyone.

Leg twitch. "I don't know about you cats," announced Dutchey, "but I'm getting back in the pool!" She took off her necklace, medallion, and her corsage and put them behind a planter. She hobbled over to the diving board, dragging her poor leg behind her, and dove in. One by one, her friends took off their medallions, the *Key*, corsages, and anklet and jumped off the diving board into the deep end. Lashes and Kool decided to go down the spiral slide. Jett and Jade challenged each other to see who could stay at the bottom of the pool the longest. Diamond got in the pool by running full speed from the edge of the yard and jumping off the diving board, making an incredibly huge splash. Dutchey, unexpectedly, received another gulp of water. They cat-paddled through the waterfall and sat on the bench so Dutchey could finish coughing and spitting.

Diamond lightly tapped Dutchey on her back as she coughed and gagged. "We've come this far tonight, Dutch. You can't croak on me now." She sneezed five times in a row. After she stopped, they laughed uncontrollably. They relaxed on the underwater bench and enjoyed the lights on the bridge twinkling through the waterfall.

Dutchey commented, "You were amazing tonight, my friend!"

"Really?"

"Yes. So cool under pressure, so calm during crisis."

"Thanks, Dutch, but I don't think any of us were very *calm during crisis* when we were in the pool clawing at each other."

They laughed as Dutchey leaned closer to inspect the scratches on his nose. "Ooh, poor Diamond." Their noses were about a half-inch away. Diamond's gaze caught her up and carried her away. They silently enjoyed each other's company while their tummies did somersaults. After a while Dutchey said, "By the way, thanks again for saving me yesterday and again tonight. I don't know what it is about me lately. I just can't seem to stay out of trouble."

"Awww, Dutchey. It wasn't your fault, but I gotta tell ya, you scared me yesterday. And before I forget, I do appreciate you not passing out on me tonight!" He playfully head bumped her.

"I don't know what happened up there in the tree. I heard the branch snap and I felt myself falling, but I just couldn't catch hold of another branch. I don't remember anything after that."

"I heard you screaming and saw you falling through the branches. I knew you were in trouble because you usually don't scream like *that*. I didn't know what else to do except try to break your fall."

"I am so glad you did. Otherwise I would have hit my head on the ground."

"I know and that would have hurt."

She cringed. "Meowch. Thanks for always lookin' out for me. You are the best!" They head bumped again and sat a little closer.

"Well, I'm just glad you were able to come tonight for our celebration. It wouldn't have been as exciting without you."

"Really?" she asked and started to purr.

"Really!"

Lashes and Kool cat-paddled around the side of the pool, talking and laughing. They met their best friends behind the waterfall and the four snobby cats talked about their dreams, their accomplishments, and their life-long friendship.

"This is really fun!" said Diamond. "I could use some relaxin.' I was under a lot of pressure tonight!" He yawned.

Kool replied, "But you pulled it off, bud!"

"Right down to the last detail," added Dutchey.

Lashes nodded in agreement. *"Kitty Maxx* was great!" she squeaked. "I hope my picture didn't get wet."

Diamond sneezed.

"Gesundheit!" said Kool.

"Thank you!"

After a few minutes, Jade and Jett surfaced behind the waterfall, out of breath and laughing. Everyone sat close together on the underwater bench, talking, laughing, and calling for Cleo.

73

"Cleo, oh, Cleo," they sang.

Cleo swam through the waterfall with a group of fluff-fluffs, tom-toms, and the little fluffettes and tommy-toms. There was plenty of room for everyone to sit behind the waterfall. And here comes Q, floating on his back and spraying water from his mouth like a fountain. It's finally time for Q to relax. He has had an exhausting two days. Jet lagged and all that dancing. Whew! It will take him days to recuperate, maybe even weeks. Being a bodyguard sure is hard work!

Jade declared, "What an outstanding celebration this turned out to be!"

"I can't wait to see all the pictures," laughed Cleo. Everyone laughed and snickered at Dutchey.

"You guys," explained Dutch, "I went there tonight just to create a few memories. That's all!"

"Not to create a new dance or fall in the pool?" teased Kool.

"I just knew that leg was going to create a saga," squeaked Lashes.

"It feels like the swelling is going down," reassured Dutchey, "I won't be kicking anyone for the rest of the night, I promise!"

... splash ... splash ... splash ... splash ...

"Fluff-friends!" Lashes squeaked.

The toms sang, "Here comes the squad. Here comes the squad."

"We stopped to get crab cakes for the morning," said excited Clairese.

"What do you mean *the morning?*" inquired Diamond, waiting for another surprise.

Dutchey announced, "We're having a slumber party and we're sunning by the pool all day tomorrow to recover from tonight! *And* all of you toms are invited to stay! We are camping out here by the pool. Please stay, toms! It won't be the same without you! Please! Please! Please!"

Kool looked around and slowly said, "I feel kinda out numbered, us toms to how many of you fluffs?" He put his claws out and started counting.

"Please stay!" begged the fluffs.

The toms looked at each other, then they looked at eight cute, wet faces. Jett already knew his answer. Diamond smiled and purred.

"Okay, okay," said Kool. "Who can say no to those purrty faces?"

"Hooray!" cheered Dutchey and her squad.

Auntie Rose and the older teen-cats jumped in and paddled over. It was getting crowded behind the waterfall.

Diamond said, "Hey, ya know what I read in *The Morning Chew* a couple of days ago?"

"What?"

"There was an article in the entertainment section about Sven Steelbird bringing his crew here to Heavenly Hills to shoot a movie."

"Really?" everyone's attention turned to Diamond.

"Yeah. The name of the movie is *The Ultimate Revenge of Catzilla.*"

"*Really?*"

"Yeah. And it said something about needing extras to run frantically screaming through the streets of Heavenly Hills."

"*R e a l l y ?*"

"Who's starring in it?" asked Dutchey.

Diamond replied, "It said something about Lance Lot, Foxx Deezel and Tad Fitt." (Principal and Dr. Fitt's twenty-four-year old little brother).

Auntie Rose piped up, "And *me!*" Everyone looked over at Auntie Rose with eyes as big as saucers.

"*What?*" everyone asked.

"That was one of my big surprises! I'm going to be in a movie!"

Lashes squeaked, "Oh my gosh, Auntie, that is so fantastic! Can you get us parts as extras?"

"Of course I can, dahlings. I know Mr. Steelbird personally. We're having lunch next week."

The fluffs screamed and the toms nodded a "that's cool" nod.

Jade and Jett were sitting at one end of the bench watching the water flow down in front of them. Jett commented, "That would be so cool to be an extra in a movie!"

"It sounds very exciting!" Jade replied. "How would we audition?"

"I guess we would have to run fast and have frantic looks on our faces."

"I can do that." Jade made a frantic face and they both laughed.

"You look very frantic! You're hired!"

"You try," she said.

He opened his gold eyes very wide and curled up one side of his whiskers. "How's this?" he asked.

"I'm convinced. You've got the part!"

"Thank you," he said in a snobby voice. *"Tell Mr. Steelbird I'll be in at 11:30 ~ a.m. that is."* They both laughed at each other and sat a little closer.

Jade commented, "This pool is marvelous!"

"I know," agreed Jett, "I've grown up in this pool. We watched it being built. We helped dig."

"I love the bridge and the waterfall! And I love all the wisteria vines and purple flowers blooming along the bridge. It's just lovely. You and all your friends seem really close."

"We are. We've hung out ever since we were kittens."

"Do you go anywhere together? Like on vacation?"

Diamond cut in, "As a matter of fact, we're going to Whisker Pines in a few weeks for our annual summer vacation."

Dutchey explained, "His family has a rustic cabin up in the Calpine Mountains, only a few hours from here."

"We go twice a year," added Kool, "once during the summer and once at Christmas time. It snows and everything!"

"We have adventure after adventure," said Diamond. "We always have a great time!"

"We have tons of stories to tell!" added Kool.

"What else do you have planned for the summer?" asked Cleo.

"Soccer practice and tryouts," said Diamond.

"Cheerleading practice and tryouts," squeaked Lashes.

Dutchey added, "We've had such a blast cheering you toms on for these past three years, haven't we fluffs?"

"Yep!" The wet squad nodded in agreement.

Dutchey exclaimed, "Guess what? We saw Miss Dubois on the dance floor and she told us she is teaching at Heavenly Hills High in September. And she's going to be head coach for cheerleading!" The squad screamed with excitement!

Lashes chirped in, "She's also going to be one of the judges at tryouts, too!" The fluffs screamed even louder.

Dutchey looked over at Cleo and Jade and commented, "You two should try out for cheerleading with us."

"You have to!" agreed Jolene.

Blanche added, "You're two of us now! As of tonight, you are both honorary members of our cheer squad. We'll help you practice before tryouts."

The fluffs looked at each other with big eyes and nodded their heads. They always seem to know what each other is thinking.

"That would be so fun!" agreed Jade.

"Big fun!" said Cleo.

"But, what would my parent's say?" asked Jade.

"Mine, too," said Cleo. "Come on, fluff. It's just try-outs. We would have fun practicing! We're already experienced with the pyramid part!"

"I know!" Jade smiled that mischievous smile of hers and sneezed.

"Gesundheit!"

"Thank you!"

Dutchey said, "Now don't let tonight's falling pyramid in the pool change your opinion of us. We each have gold Pom-Pom trophies to prove just how talented we really are, don't we, fluffs?"

"We sure do," agreed Coco.

"I'll show you when we go up to my room," added proud Dutchey.

"We weren't exactly planning to have you toms as our bottom tier," stated Clairese.

"You fluffs were up there so high!" exclaimed Coco.

Jade added, "It was unexpected... fun!"

"Poor Cleo didn't stand a chance!" laughed Dutchey, looking over at Cleo.

Cleo laughed, "While I was up there trying to be all cool and poised, you two were twitching around down there, and before I knew it, I was falling backwards into the pool! Reow!"

Crystal added, "Actually, you fluffs fell quite elegantly! The toms should always be your bottom tier."

The toms smirked, "Yeah, right."

"Whose crazy idea was that anyway?!" asked Clairese.

74

Splash… splash… splash. The Bully brothers have arrived!

"Hey cats!" yelled Bull. He took his time placing a floating pad in just the right spot in the water under the slide. Then he climbed the ladder, slid down headfirst, and landed on top of it. With all that beefy weight, the floating pad sunk and got away from him. So much for all that careful planning.

Fangy paddled over to Cleo. Not only was she wearing a big chin, but now she was also wearing a big smile.

Chip was still in matrix zone, spinning through the pool in slow motion, and then complaining about water in his ears.

Kool declared, "Toms, am I glad to see you!"

"Feeling a little out numbered?" asked Fangy. He looked around and started counting all the fluffs.

"Just a little," laughed Kool.

"Where's your lily pad, Bull," asked Diamond.

"Ha-ha. Where's yours? And where's your lei, Kool?"

Diamond and Kool looked at each other and started singing, "We're too macho for our leis… too macho for our leis… too macho, yeah!" Everyone laughed and splashed the macho toms. Cleo and Fangy sat side-by-side, laughing.

"It's been a fine evening," bellowed Q, floating by on his back. He kept floating through the waterfall, back and forth, back and forth.

"Did you have fun tonight, Q?" asked Jade.

"I did and I still am."

"We couldn't tell!" she replied. Everyone laughed at Q.

Kool asked, "What's the Q short for? That's not your real name, is it?"

Jade and Cleo said together, "You don't want to know!" and started laughing.

Q shot them both dirty looks and continued his conversation. "You sure know how to throw a party, big Diamond."

"I'm glad you're enjoying yourself, Q. You'll have to come down to the gym at the club and work out with us!"

"The gym at the club is called The Tail Curl," said Dutchey. "I love the name. That's fun."

"What's fun?" asked Jade.

"Floating through the waterfall. You just have to keep your mouth shut or you'll get a big gulp of water." She would know all about that! She got on her back, took a deep breath, closed her mouth, and floated behind Q through the waterfall. Diamond rolled over on his back and followed Dutchey. Everyone rolled on their backs and floated through the waterfall.

75

$\mathcal{D}$iamond's dad yelled out, "Calling all Grads! Calling all Grads!" As each cat floated through the waterfall, they heard, "Calling all Grads." The Grads swam over to the table that is built right into the pool with an underwater circular bench to sit on. The table was loaded with bowls of creamed fish stew, oyster snick-snacks and plates of red herring and snapper for everyone to gnaw on. The tasty food smelled delightful! The cats squeezed onto the bench, munched down, and purred. Mayor Mac snapped more pictures.

"We're going to cut the Salmon cake soon," Pearl announced.

"I love the cake, Mom. It's very original!" Diamond yelled.

"I'm glad you like it, dear. Make sure you thank Miss Fancy."

"You really looked good up there tonight, Diamond," commented Dad.

"Thanks, Dad. I think I like being behind the microphone!"

"Well, you performed fabulously!"

Grandtom Diamond I announced, "Congratulations, everyone! The time you have all been waiting for has finally come! You have all earned the right of passage from *tom-toms* and *fluff-fluffs* to full-on *Toms* and *Fluffs!*"

"Hip hip hooray!" the cats howled. "Bravo for us!"

"Congratulations to all of you," added Grandfluff Mona. "We know you have worked very hard for this honor!"

"Thank you, Grandfluff," everyone sang.

Lashes and Dutchey exchanged a happy look. So did the toms.

Lily took off her leis and tossed them in the pool around the table. The other lady-fluffs took theirs off and tossed them in the pool, too, but one landed in the stew.

"Eeewww!" snarled all the fluffs.

Dutchey clawed it out of her bowl of stew and tossed it into Lashes' bowl. She tossed it in Kool's bowl. It was tossed around the table and landed in the stew several times.

Bull had food all over his face and was losing his patience. "Can't I just enjoy my food, please?"

Diamond tossed the sloppy lei in Bull's bowl of stew. Bull snarled and hurled it across the water at the waterfall. "Can I *please* just enjoy my food?!" His mouth was full of oyster snick-snacks and there was a piece of stew hanging off his whiskers. He played, "look!"

"Eeewww! Bull's gross!" exclaimed Dutchess.

Spontaneous Diamond sprung out of the pool, ran over to Miss Fancy, and gave her a long wet hug and a kiss. "Thank you for doing all this for me. I love you."

Miss Fancy adores him. "You're welcome, honey. You sure are growing up to be a fabulous tom. Just look at you... I am so proud of you and what a great leader you have become. Diamond Thomas, I love you like you're my own!" They gave each other another long hug.

After the hug, Pearl called over, "Diamond, come and cut your cake."

"I want to make a toast first," announced Diamond. "Everyone raise their bowl. To all of us: The Fabulous Snobby Cats of Heavenly Hills!" He raised his bowl, too.

"Here, here." Everyone clinked their bowls and drank. Soaking wet Diamond ran over to the cake, extended his claw, and cut straight through all seven layers.

"Good job!" complimented Mom. The cats in the pool cheered and the adult felines licked their whiskers.

"We'll get some later," said Diamond, "go for it, but save us some, please." He ran and jumped in the pool, splashing everyone and getting the food all wet. The grads booed and hissed at him. Oh well. He licked the salmon off his paw, but some of it floated away in the water.

Siam Sam was snapping more pictures for Dutchey's photo album.

"Hey," said Dutchey, "I can think of another thing we can do this summer."

"What?" everyone asked.

"Put together this humongous photo album of tonight's celebration."

Everyone laughed, gnawed on their food, and purred.

76

$\mathcal{A}$fter the grads finished eating, they slowly waded around the pool and cat paddled with the floating pads. There were leis and salmon floating in the water everywhere. They all swam back behind the waterfall and talked about everything cats talk about. They talked about memories of the past and hopes for the future, old friendships, and new ones. They talked about their teachers and about how much they will miss Principal Fitt and Miss Hissy. They talked about how much fun they will have this summer, and how much time they will have for all the beauty rest they need.

"Umm, Dutchey, Kool, and Lashes," announced Diamond. "I have one more fantastic surprise for you." They looked at Diamond with happy faces. "I've gotten us all jobs at the club this summer!" They looked at Diamond with blank faces. "Aren't you excited?" Jett and Kool looked at each other, then at Dutchey and Lashes. They swam over to Diamond and encircled him. "You guys, just part time. Nothing hard. No big deal. I promise." The circle was closing in. "No, really. You cats won't have to do anything but show the guests how to take naps in the sun. It will be easy. I promise!" They looked at each other, then at Diamond Thomas Castleberry III. Without saying a word, they did a paw stack on his head and dunked him.

Gurgle…

Gurgle…

Gurgle…

77

$\mathcal{D}$iamond went down, down, down, but, don't worry, he escaped under the waterfall to the other side of the pool. "Over here cats. I'm over here," he teased and then went underwater again. He came up by the table and grabbed a piece of red snapper. All the cats were chasing him while he was leisurely eating at the table. "Over here, over here," he teased and dove again. Just when they thought they were on his tail, *wrong*. "Over here, slow cats," he said as he surfaced at the steps. There was a lei around his tail. He tossed the lei at Bull, but he slipped underwater and it landed on Chip's head. The fastest toms on the team and no one could keep up. They never did catch him. He got out of the pool and shook his fur. He had water in his ear so he shook his back leg and tilted his cute head to the side so the water could run out. Everyone laughed at him and told him he looked hilarious. He sneezed four times in a row.

"Gesundheit four times!" said Dutchey.

"Thank you four times! Hey it worked. I can hear again. I'm getting some salmon cake. Come on, all you wilted lilies. Let's warm up by the bonfire."

The grads climbed out of the pool and shook while Diamond flipped the switches that turn off the waterfall, the bridge, and the pool lights. The only light was the flickering flames and the glowing embers in the bonfire. As they shook out their wet fur, they heard talking and laughing coming from inside. The adult fluffs and toms were playing *Pick Your Fish* at the grand dining table in the great room. Miss Fancy brought in another pitcher of black cat espresso with crème. All bowls were empty, so she refilled them and sat down to play. Those *Fish* games can last all night. The little cats were upstairs in Blossom's room, tucked in and sound asleep. Mac II, Crystal, Bobby, Heather, Jasmine, Toffee, Taffee, and Auntie Rose were resting in the gazebo, listening to the waves come in and reminiscing about their years at Paw Valley Middle School. The grads sat on the bricks around the bonfire and ate their salmon cake. Diamond and Dutchey shared a plate. Kool and Lashes shared theirs. Jett and Jade shared a slice. Cleo and Fangy sat side-by-side and happily munched down. Blanche sat between Bull and Q, who raced to see who could eat theirs the fastest. Chip enjoyed his cake with Jolene, Clairese, and Coco. Wow! He's never been so popular!

What a day! What a night!

78

"I have absolutely wonderful memories of tonight," whispered Lashes. Maybe she will get her voice back tomorrow.

"Me too," yawned Dutchey, "I'm so tired I could pass out right here." She sneezed.

"Gesundheit!"

"Thank you!"

With a toothy grin, Diamond stood up and declared, "I just want all my best friends to know how happy I am that we all graduated… *and* that all of you had a blast tonight."

Everyone said together, "Thank you, big Diamond."

"And, are we going to kick some tail at Heavenly Hills High School in September?!"

"Yes!" The cats cheered.

Diamond continued, "Good-bye Paw Valley Panthers! Hello Heavenly Hills Prowlers!" The grads tried out their prowler howls and the cats in the gazebo laughed.

Crystal yelled, "We think you need more practice." Everyone tried again. Even Q.

Diamond made the final toast of the evening to his friends, who all sat at attention. "Here's to us—The Fabulous Snobby Cats of Heavenly Hills!"

The cats cheered and yawned, then collapsed on the bricks. With full bellies, a warm fire, great company, and the sound of waves breaking in the distance, the snobby cats power purred themselves to sleep under the starry sky and the sliver moon.

Until tomorrow...

Any similarity between cats and events is all in fun!

About the author

$\mathcal{A}$uthor Lynne Westwood lives with her teenage daughter and two cats, Dutchess and Diamond. She was inspired to write this book by her Siamese cat, Dutchess. One hot August day, the big Maine Coon, Diamond, was lying on the tiled floor, trying to get cool and minding his own business. The smart and bold Dutchess crept over to him while he was looking the other way, and for no reason, she smacked him with a quick right and then ran away. Lynne and her daughter laughed and came up with the idea: what if cats really could talk and live long lives and went to school, and much more! From then on, their imaginations took off and a story was born.

Lashes

Diamond

Jett

Dutchess

Kool Katt

Princess Jade

Cleocatra

www.ingramcontent.com/pod-product-compliance
Lightning Source LLC
Chambersburg PA
CBHW020404120726
47904CB00002B/692